Charles E. Ryan

With an Ambulance During the Franco-German War

Personal Experiences and Adventures with both Armies, 1870-1871

Charles E. Ryan

With an Ambulance During the Franco-German War
Personal Experiences and Adventures with both Armies, 1870-1871

ISBN/EAN: 9783337178666

Printed in Europe, USA, Canada, Australia, Japan

Cover: Foto ©Andreas Hilbeck / pixelio.de

More available books at **www.hansebooks.com**

WITH AN AMBULANCE

DURING THE

FRANCO-GERMAN WAR

PERSONAL EXPERIENCES AND ADVENTURES
WITH BOTH ARMIES

1870-1871

By CHARLES E. RYAN, F.R.C.S.I., M.R.C.P.I.

KNIGHT OF THE ORDER OF LOUIS II. OF BAVARIA

WITH PORTRAIT AND MAPS

LONDON

JOHN MURRAY, ALBEMARLE STREET

1896

ABERDEEN UNIVERSITY PRESS.

TO

JAMES TALBOT POWER,

MY OLD FRIEND AND SCHOOLFELLOW,

I DEDICATE

THE FOLLOWING PAGES.

PREFACE.

ERE I attempt to set before the public this slight record of my experiences during the Franco-German War, I must first disclaim all pretence to literary merit.

It was written in 1873, and is simply an embodiment of a series of notes or jottings, taken during the war in my spare moments, together with the contents of a number of descriptive letters to my friends. They were written solely for them, and nothing was farther from my mind at the time than the idea of publication.

Thus, they remained in a recess of my study for nearly a quarter of a century, until a new generation had grown up around me ; and doubtless, but for their friendly importunity, there they would have lain until the memory of their author, like the ink in which they were written, had faded to a blank.

I would ask my readers to bear in their kindly recollection that the scope of such a work as the following must of necessity be limited.

As a medical man, I had at all times and in

all places my duties to perform ; hence I have been unable to be as elaborate as other circumstances might warrant.

I would also remind them (and every one who has been through a campaign will know) how vague and uncertain is the information which subordinates possess of the general movements of the army with which they are serving.

It happens occasionally that they are wholly ignorant of events occurring around them, the news of which may have already reached the other side of the world.

Again, I am greatly impressed with the difficulty of representing, in anything like adequate language, those scenes—some of which have already been delineated by the marvellous pen of M. Zola in *La Débâcle*—which the general public could never have fancied, still less have realised, except by the aid of a masterly exposition of facts such as that stirring chronicle of the war has given. In it the writer has dealt rather with history as it occurred, than invented an imaginary tale ; and those who were eye-witnesses of Sedan can add little to his description.

For many reasons, therefore, I am filled with the sense of my own incompetence to do justice to my subject. But I console myself with the reflection that my theme is full of interest to the present generation. Nor does it appear a vain undertaking if one who was permitted to see much of both sides should give his impressions as they occurred, and in the language he would have used at the time. My feeling throughout has been that of a witness under examination. I have endeavoured to narrate the incidents which I saw, certainly with as close an approach to the reality as I could command, and, if in a somewhat unvarnished tale, yet, as I trust, have set down nought in malice. I have added no colour which the original sketch did not contain; and have been careful not to darken the shading.

CHARLES E. RYAN.

GLENLARA, TIPPERARY,
January, 1896.

CHAPTER I.

FROM DUBLIN TO PARIS VIA BRUSSELS.—THE WAR FEVER.—LEVIES TO THE FRONT.

THE first question friends will naturally ask is, how I came to think of going abroad to take part in the struggle between France and Germany, what prompted me to do so, and by what combination of circumstances my hastily arranged plans were realised.

These points I will endeavour to explain. From the outset of the war I took a deep interest in the destinies of France, and warmly sympathised with her in her affliction. I longed earnestly to be of some service to her ; indeed, my enthusiasm was so great at the time that I would even have fought for her could I have done so. I was then studying medicine in Dublin, and was in my twenty-first year. Just about the time of the battles of Weissenburg and Wörth nearly every one in Dublin was collecting old linen to make *charpie* for the French wounded ; and, as I could do nothing else, I exerted myself in getting together from my friends all the material I could procure for the purpose. Day by day news poured in of French defeats following one another in close succession, with long lists of killed and wounded; while among other details I learnt that the French were very short of medical men and skilled dressers, and that the sufferings of the wounded were, in consequence, beyond description. I thought to myself, "Now is my opportunity. If I could but get out to those poor fellows I might render them some substantial assistance; and what an amount of suffering might one not alleviate did one but give them a draught of cold water to appease their agonising thirst!"

For a few days these thoughts occupied my mind almost to the exclusion of every other. It happened one evening, when I was returning by train from Kingstown, that I met Dr. Walshe, surgeon to Jervis Street Hospital. During the course of our conversation, which was upon the then universal topic of the Franco-German War, he remarked that if he were unmarried and as young and active as I was, he would at once go over to France, and seek a place either in a military field hospital or in an ambulance, or endeavour to get into the Foreign Legion, which was then being enrolled, adding, that he greatly wondered no one as yet had left Dublin with this object. I replied, "I shall be the first, then, to lead the way"; and there and then made up my mind to set out.

It was the 12th of August, 1870.

I endeavoured to discover some kindred spirit who would come out with me and share my adventures, but not one could I find. Those who had not very plausible reasons at hand, to disguise those which perhaps they had, laughed at my proposal, and appeared to look upon me as little better than a mad fellow. How could I dream of going out alone to a foreign country, where the fiercest war of the century was raging? Even some of my professors joined in the laugh, and good-humouredly wished me God-speed and a pleasant trip, adding that they were sure I should be back again in a few days. Two of them had, in fact, just returned from Paris, where they could find nothing to do; and they reported that it was dangerous to remain longer, as the populace were marching up and down the streets in the most disorderly fashion, and strangers ran no small risk of being treated as Prussian spies.

All this was unpleasant to hear; but I was determined not to be thwarted; and so, portmanteau in hand, I stepped on board the Kingstown boat. It was the 15th August, a most glorious autumn evening, and the sea was beautifully calm. I now felt that my enterprise had begun, and as I stood on deck watching the beautiful scenery of Dublin Bay receding from my view, the natural reflection occurred that this might be the last time I should see my native land. I was leaving the

cherished inmates of that bright little spot, which
I now more than ever felt was my home. It
would be my first real experience of the world,
and I was about to enter upon the battle of life
alone.

Arriving in London on the morning of the
16th, and having spent the day with some of my
school friends, in the evening I went on board
the Ostend boat at St. Katharine's wharf. We
were to start at four o'clock next morning. I
slept until I was awakened by the rolling of the
vessel out at sea. The boat was a villainous little
tub, and appeared to me to go round like a tee-
totum. We had an unusually long and rough
passage of sixteen hours, and I was fearfully ill
the whole time. When we arrived at Ostend, so
bad was I that I could not leave my cabin until
long after everybody else. Hence a friend of
mine, Monsieur le Chevalier de Sauvage
Vercourt, who had come up from Liège to meet
me, made certain when he failed to perceive me
among the passengers that I had missed the boat.
On inquiring, however, of the steward if any one
had remained below he discovered me.

My friend gave me two letters of introduction,
one to M. le Vicomte de Melun, which subsequently got me admitted into " La Société
Française pour le secours aux blessés de terre et
de mer "; the other to the Mayor, M. Lévy, asking
him whether he could find a way for me into the

Army as an assistant. When I had pulled myself together a bit, Vercourt and I dined together in the open air, at a Café on the Grande Promenade.

It was the fashionable hour, and every one seemed to be in gala dress. Half, at least, of those we saw were English, the remainder French and Belgians. It is a curious sensation, that of being for the first time in a foreign country, where one's whole surroundings differ from all one has been accustomed to see and hear in one's native land. My boyish experience made everything, however trivial, a subject of interest. As I walked through the town with Vercourt, I was greatly struck by the civility of the people, their cleanliness and the neatness of their persons and dress, and above all by the absence of any visible wretchedness even among the poor.

These points occupied our attention and conversation until we found ourselves on our way to Brussels. The country through which we passed, though really most unattractive, had for me many points of interest, and gave me an agreeable picture of what was meant by "foreign climes".

The bright clean cottages and farmsteads, with their gardens and flowers, contrasted lamentably to my mind with the tumble-down dilapidated hovels of mud, surrounded by slush and water, which I had been accustomed to see from my childhood. Everything bespoke the comfort, happiness, and prosperity of these people. The neatly trimmed hedges with which every field is fenced, the lines of poplars skirting the road-ways and canals give a surprisingly smart and cultivated aspect to the whole face of the country. I was greatly struck by the blue smocks and wooden sabots of the men and women. Even the children in the rural parts of Belgium wear these wooden shoes. During our stoppages at the different stations the Flemish jargon, as in my untravelled ignorance I called it, of the rustics amused me. I noticed in one part of the country that all the pumps had their handles at the top, and that these moved up and down like the ramrod of a gun. It was novel to see the people on stools working them. At ten o'clock that night we arrived in Brussels, and put up at the Hôtel de Suède.

My friend and I rose early next morning, and went sight-seeing. He was an *habitué* of the place, so our time was spent to the best advantage. That Brussels is a most charming town was my first impression; and I think so still. My delight at seeing the Rue de la Reine and the Boulevards leading from it I shall not easily forget. A city beautifully timbered and abound-ing in fountains, grass, and flowers, was indeed a novelty to one whose experience of cities had been gained in smoky London and dear dirty Dublin. In the Rue de la Reine I remarked the two carriage-ways, divided by a grove of trees. This plantation consisted of full-grown limes, elms, sycamores, arbutus, and acacias. There was yet another row on the footpath, next the houses. The breadth of this long Boulevard may be about that of Sackville Street. It was a beautiful sunny day, and as I sauntered along beneath the trees something new met my eye at every turn. I was struck by such a simple matter as seeing the carriages dash into the courtyards through the open gates, instead of stopping in the street, whilst the occupants were making a morning call. Then the high-stepping horses and the gaudy equipages were enough, as I thought, to dazzle the youthful mind. One could live here a lifetime and never know that such a thing as dirt existed,—at all events, in the sense with which we were only too conversant in some parts of my native land twenty-five years ago.

These simple observations of the boy at his first start in life make me smile as I read them over. Yet I do not think that I ought to suppress them ; for who is there that has not felt the indescribable charm of those early days, when the commonest things in our journeying fill the mind as if they were a wonder in themselves? And what is there in the grown man's travels to equal that opening glimpse of a world we have so often heard talked about, yet never have seen with our eyes until now ?

But to return. It was in the Rue du Pont that I first saw the tramways. I went in one of the cars to the superb Park, which is as fine as any in Europe, and of which Brussels is so justly proud. It amused me beyond measure to see the butchers', bakers', and grocers' boys driving about their carts drawn by teams of huge dogs, varying in number from one to four. While the drivers were delivering their goods the poor animals would lie down in their harness with their tongues out, until a short chirp brought them on their feet again, ready to start This seemed for them the most difficult part, since once set going, they went at a great rate, apparently without much trouble, and rather enjoying their task than otherwise. I have seen teams of dogs so fresh that they were all barking whilst they tore along the street at full speed. In the evening the cafés were beautifully illuminated; and seated beneath the trees hundreds of people enjoyed their cigarettes and *café noir*, while they discussed, with many and vigorous gesticulations, the affairs of Europe. In the afternoon of the 18th I bade good-bye to my kind friend Vercourt, who had been so admirable a cicerone to me, and took my seat in the train for Paris.

During our journey I was rudely awakened from a sound sleep at one station by every one suddenly jumping on their legs and crying out, "*La douane!*" while they seized their luggage, and rushed out of the train as if it were on fire. If you did not do the same you were unceremoniously bundled out by the officials. To every inquiry I got the same answer, "*C'est la douane*". Now this word was not in my vocabulary. I may observe that at my school French was taught on the good old plan, out of Racine and "Télémaque," in which commercial terms are not abundant, and hence I did not know in the least the meaning of "*la douane*"; it might have signified fire, blood or murder; and I was for a long time sorely puzzled. I thought in my drowsy confusion that some part of the train had broken down, and that all the passengers and luggage had to be removed with as much haste as possible. But when I, a passenger to Paris, saw a fellow seize my portmanteau and disappear with it through one of the doors, it was too much for me; I went after my effects, collared him, and asked him, in the best French I could muster, where he was going with my property. A big gendarme explained the situation, and pointed to a large room, where the rattling of keys and opening of boxes soon made his interpretation unnecessary.

On returning to my carriage I found myself next a middle-aged gentleman, who, though he spoke French fluently to his neighbours, was evidently an Englishman. We joined in conversation, and he seemed to know more about

Ireland and Irish affairs than I did myself, which, in truth, might easily have been. He had such a frank, genial manner, and appeared to feel so genuine a sympathy, not only with my own countrymen, but with poor suffering France, that I confided to him my story and mission, which evidently pleased him; and he told me that he would get me a cheap billet from his landlady in the Hôtel de l'Opéra, a comfortable hotel centrally situated opposite the new Opera House. He had told me his name was Steel, but vouchsafed no further information about himself. When we arrived in Paris he was accosted by several of the officials as Monsieur le Général; and he bade me stay with him, and said that he would accompany me to my hotel. Having, after much tiresome waiting, got possession of our luggage, we passed out of the station between two lines of soldiers, and were carefully and closely inspected before being allowed to proceed. A whisper from my new friend the General appeared to be a magic pass, for every one seemed to know him. A stalwart gendarme demanded my passport, took down my name and address, where I last came from, and what was my business in Paris, and then let me go. When we arrived at the Hôtel de l'Opéra, again the concierge greeted my mysterious friend with the title of M. le Général, when he hurried upstairs, bidding me wait until he came down, and he would go out with me to dine at a restaurant.

As I stepped outside the door and looked up and down the Boulevards, I knew at once that what I had heard and read of the beauties of Paris as seen by night was no fiction, but a bright reality. What added to the novelty of the scene was that the whole populace seemed to be in a fever of excitement. I asked my friend what was it all about. He told me that they were rejoicing because a proclamation had just been made from the Mairie of three glorious victories won by their arms. This accounted for the bands of civilians, thousands in each, composed of labourers and artisans, who were marching boisterously up and down the streets, cheering and singing the " Marseillaise," with flags and banners flying of every colour and description. The sight was at first appalling, as that momentary glance recalled to my mind so vividly what I had read about the scenes enacted in the streets of Paris during the first Revolution, by a similar communistic and ungovernable mob. Yet I thought the whole thing good fun ; but my friend warned me not to speak, and told me to keep out of the streets at night. It was dangerous for a stranger to go out after dark, since the populace were apt to take him for a spy, or as being there in the interest of the enemy, and this might mean instantaneous death. Such

things had occurred lately. We now turned
into the Café Anglais, and dined very well, after
which my mysterious friend took leave of me
and disappeared. I only saw him again for five
minutes a few days subsequently, and have never
set eyes on him since, nor could I get any satisfactory information at the hotel, although they
informed me that he was a resident in Paris, and
was often at the Hôtel de l'Opéra. Perhaps
some reader of these pages may know more concerning M. le Général Steel than I ever did.
Who and what was he? But conjecture is idle
work, and I must get on with my story.

Having seen Brussels before Paris, the latter
did not make that impression which it generally
does on one who views it for the first time, before
he has visited any other of the capital cities on
the Continent,—for Brussels is a miniature Paris.
I walked up and down the Boulevards, observing everything and everybody, until, feeling
somewhat tired, I looked at my watch, and found
to my astonishment that it was nearly one o'clock,
so I returned to my hotel and went to bed, and
dreamed of the glories of the city of pleasure.

Next morning, the 19th, I sallied out in
quest of the Mansion House to which I had
been directed. For some time I walked up
and down the Boulevards in order to make
observations as to my whereabouts, and to note
my surroundings. My first great landmark was

the beautiful new Opera House, which is one of the sights of Paris. Its massive pillars and wonderful display of allegorical figures, all in white marble, delighted me—as also did the wooded Boulevards with their gorgeous shops and all the pleasing sights which met my gaze at every turn.

Having been only a few days in the country, I naturally felt a little shy at venturing into anything like a long conversation with the natives. Soon, however, I mustered up sufficient courage (to be wanting in which was to fail in my errand) to ask my way of one of those gaily dressed officers of the peace, who, from their gorgeous uniform and the dignity of their manners, I had made up my mind could be nothing less than majors-general of the reserve out for a stroll.

My bad French elicited from this worthy only the most courteous civility, and he took the greatest pains to explain to me my route. As I went on I felt elated at this first experience of the proverbial civility of Frenchmen, and was sure that I should find it easy to get on with them.

After some two miles of pleasant rambling, I arrived at the Mairie in the Place du Prince Eugéne ; but found that M. le Maire was out, so returned and dined at the Café Royale, opposite the Madeleine and afterwards visited the church, and walked outside it several times. It was from all sides alike massive and beautiful, nor was I disappointed at its interior, though I confess it did not impress me so much as the façade. Having spent an hour inspecting its details I took a cabriolet to the Mansion House, where, having sent in Vercourt's letter, I was ushered into the presence of M. le Maire, after about ten minutes waiting.

This polished gentleman received me with the greatest kindness and civility, but explained that he could not procure me a place in the Army Medical Department. He referred me to l'Intendance Militaire, Rue St. Dominique, which was the Foreign Legion Office. I at once started afresh, and, having found out the officials to whom I was directed, they informed me that they had not the power of giving appointments, but that M. Michel Lévy, Medicine Inspecteur, Val de Grace, was the person to whom I should apply, at the same time assuring me that there was not the least use in my doing so, as the Foreign Legion was fully equipped and all the vacancies filled up. Believing this information to be correct, I set this last proposition aside and kept it in my sleeve as a *dernier ressort*. Although defeated in my object I was not in the least discouraged, for I had determined to make every effort before confessing myself beaten.

As I was much fatigued, and it was too late to prosecute my plans any further that day, I went out for a stroll on the Boulevards. Presently I heard the trampling of horses coming down the street, mingled with the loud cheering of the populace. It was a troop of Cuirassiers, and in another minute I was in the midst of a seething crowd, and could perceive nothing around me but a sea of hands, hats, and heads in commotion. The civilians, who were in a wild state of excitement, cheered the troops, "Vive les Cuirassiers!" while the dragoons in return shouted "A Berlin!" and "Vive la France!"—not "Vive l'Empereur!" When they had passed, the excitement continued in another form, for a desperate-looking mob marched up and down in detachments as they had done upon the previous night, with flags flying, and banners waving, singing all the while "La Marseillaise" and the "Champs de la Patrie," with intervening shouts of "A Berlin". All this was of great interest to me, especially the singing. When the crowd joined in the chorus of their National Anthem the effect was something never to be forgotten.

I now went to bed, feeling sleepy and done up from sheer excitement. Next day, the 20th August, a lovely morning, I found my way to the Palais de l'Industrie, where, after waiting three hours in a crowded ante-room, I presented my letter to M. le Vicomte de Melun, who came out to see me. This kind old gentleman spoke graciously, and desired me to come next day, when he would give me a place in an Ambulance. Fully satisfied this time with the result of my efforts I returned with a light heart, and having dined in the Rue Royale went out sight-seeing. A few hundred paces brought me into the Place de la Concorde, and, oh, what an incredibly magnificent sight presented itself from the centre of that beautiful square! I passed the rest of the evening in the Bois de Boulogne, and rising early next morning, full of hope, hastened to the Palais de l'Industrie, where, without much delay, I saw M. de Melun. He informed me with regret that every place in the Ambulances about to start had been filled up previous to my application. However, if I left my letters and certificates and came again on Tuesday morning, he would let me know, should there be a vacancy for me in any of those which were starting at the end of the week.

This second disappointment greatly annoyed me, but I did not give in. As it was Sunday I hastened back to High Mass at the Madeleine, a grand choral and musical display. The constant clink of the money and the click of the beadle's staff as he strode along bespangled with gold lace and gaudy trappings, made prayer and recollection well nigh an impossibility. Coming out of church, I met an old schoolfellow of mine, a Parisian, with whom I had a long chat and pleasant walk in the Tuileries. He pointed out to me the Empress leaving the Palace by a private way, accompanied by some of her ladies-in-waiting. I may remark that she wore a dress of grey silk, trimmed with black crape.

During the whole of this day troops continued to march through the city, some mere regiments of beardless boys, awkward and un-soldierlike, but with a true martial spirit, if one might judge by the hearty way in which they sang as they went along, and joined in the choruses.

These were the latest levies, and were going to the front. Next day, Monday the 22nd, after many circuitous wanderings, I made my way to the Irish College ; and left my letter of introduction to Father M——, who was not at home, but was expected the following day. When I got back I found that the Boulevards and Champs Elysées were thronged with noisy workmen singing the " Marseillaise " on their way home from the fortifi-cations, where they had been employed in great numbers on the extensive works which were being now pushed forward night and day. To avoid being jostled by the mob I took a place on the top of an omnibus. It was dusk, and as we came down the Champs Elysées, the beautifully illuminated gardens, with their cafés chantants, merry-go-rounds and bowers,—surrounded by the most fanciful and pretty devices imaginable, and lighted up with miniature lamps,—together with the lively din of music and singing followed by rounds of applause, made me feel transported for the moment to fairyland. But it was a short-lived delusion; and who would imagine, with all this folly, at once so frivolous and so French, that the great tragedy of war was being enacted around us? However, that such was the case even here was abundantly evident, for it was the sole topic of conversation. Soldiers were everywhere in the streets; the public vehicles and omnibuses were crammed with them; their officers seemed to monopolise half the private carriages; they crowded the public buildings, and soldiers' heads appeared out of half the street windows. I had always heard that Frenchmen were a highly excitable people, and the truth of that saying was never so clearly demonstrated. Here they were in their thousands, moving about in a state of restless, purposeless commotion, singing songs from noon to midnight, and, as it appeared to me, most of them quite out of their senses.

Tuesday, the 23rd August, I went once more to try my luck at the Palais de l'Industrie; and M. le Vicomte de Melun again told me that there was no vacancy, but my name had been placed on the Society's books for an appointment, and when the vacancy occurred he would communicate with me at the Hôtel de l'Opéra. I felt disappointed that every effort up to this had been a failure, but consoled myself at having gained one point, *viz.*, that of having

been registered as a member of the Red Cross
Society.

I now determined to try some of the working
staff, who, though perhaps less influential than the
Vicomte, might be able to help me quite as well.
Not to be daunted, I went to another part of the
Palais, where I informed a gentleman, who, I
perceived, was a superintendent and active
manager, that my name had been placed on the
Society's books by M. de Melun. This made him
all attention. He spoke English well, and was
very civil to me. His name was M. Labouchère,
77 Rue Malesherbes. In few words I told him
the object of my mission, how I wanted to work,
and was willing to accept a place in any capacity
whatever, in the service of the wounded. He
now informed me that there was one vacancy as
aide in a Belgian Ambulance, and as I was most
anxious to fill it he had my name put down. He
gave me the casquet and badge of the Society,
and told me to come to-morrow for my outfit and
all necessaries.

In the meantime I was sent out with eight
or ten others of the Swiss Ambulance, to collect
money in the streets through which we passed.
We went in a body, and had each a little net bag
at the end of a long pole, very like a landing
net, but with a longer handle and a smaller
net. As we passed along we cried out, " Pour
les blessés," and as the omnibuses and carriages

drew up while we were passing, we availed ourselves of this opportunity by putting our bags up to and sometimes through the windows, and landing them in the laps of those within. By this means we got heaps of silver pieces, and even gold from some of the best dressed personages. We also put our nets up to the windows, wherever we saw them occupied, and into the shops. Large crowds gathered along the route, and everybody gave something,—a great many two and five franc pieces. It was several hours before we reached the railway station, as we went very slowly. All knew by my accent that I was a foreigner, and perhaps British; and they seemed to like the idea, for they pressed forward to throw their coins to me, when there were other nets nearer them. When the time of reckoning came I found that I had collected more than my comrades. I saw ladies in the carriages that passed us crying bitterly, and the weeping and evident grief of the ambulance men on parting with their friends at the railway terminus were very touching. Having placed my money in the van I returned to the Palais de l'Industrie, where I was introduced to M. le Verdière, second in command in the Belgian Ambulance. He desired me to come at nine o'clock next day to get into my uniform and prepare for starting.

Highly pleased at what I considered at last a success, I went, as I had previously arranged, to see Dr. M—— at the Irish College. He received me very warmly, and introduced me to a Chinese bishop with a pigtail, whom I found a most intelligent and agreeable man.

That evening I saw troops going to the front in heavy marching order; and although they were four abreast, they reached from the Arc de Triomphe to within some little distance of the Place de la Concorde. On my way home I met a man who told me sorrowfully that before the war he had been a successful teacher with a large class, but that all his pupils were drawn in the conscription, and his occupation was gone.

Next morning, the 24th, I was all excitement, as I fully expected that this day might see me on my way to the front. I hastened to the Palais de l'Industrie, where M. Labouchère informed me of the nature of my appointment in the Belgian Ambulance. What was my astonishment when I found that I should have ten *infirmiers* under me, for whom I was to be responsible, and to whom I must issue orders ! Much as I desired to accept this most tempting offer, common sense got the better of my ambition ; and I declined, feeling conscious that my imperfect knowledge of French would prevent my being able to discharge my duties with efficiency.

All this was a disappointment and a humiliation, but I had now become used to reverses.

My friends, of whom I had already quite a number, comforted me by saying that I should be most likely sent to Metz, which was full of wounded with but few attendants, numbers of the latter having been carried off by typhus fever, which was making great havoc in the town. I stated that I had not the least objection to going if the Society wished me to do so; but I felt that I should prefer some other mission. Later on in the day, as I was searching for M. Labouchère in the Palais de l'Industrie, I was astonished to perceive that one of the large open spaces of the Palais, which was used but yesterday for drilling the recruits, now contained rows of mounted cannon placed close beside each other, while the unmounted guns were piled in lines one above another; great heaps of cannon balls were also stacked in the centre, like ricks of turf. This change, wrought since the evening before, will give an idea of the rapidity and energy with which the Government plans were being executed. Emerging by one of the upper doors of the building, I was startled at seeing the whole Champs Elysées occupied by masses of soldiers, flanked at each side by double rows of cavalry. They were being inspected before going to the front. It was a splendid sight. I went out afterwards to the Bois de Boulogne, where the timber next the ramparts was already being cut down. There were crowds of men at work on the fortifications as I passed through, making ready for the siege.

As it was growing dusk I moved towards home, and met on my way a stream of soldiers dressed in a most elaborate uniform, differing in every way from that of the Line. From the enthusiastic reception they met with on all sides, and the familiar smiles and nods which they exchanged with the admiring citizens, I knew that they were the Garde Nationale, the pride of the Parisians.

CHAPTER II.

AUGUST 25th I went to my official quarters full of hope, but found that nothing further had been decided. M. Labouchère told me that I was certain of a place in a French Ambulance, and presented my testimonials and papers to the chief of the 8th Ambulance, who disappeared with them into the committee room, promising to send me an answer at once. This he never did, though I waited his reply for some hours, until hunger compelled me to go in search of dinner, which I found in the Boulevard St. Michel, No. 43, Café-Brasserie du Bas Rhin, where I had as much beef as I could wish for. (I was afterwards told that nothing but horse flesh was sold at this restaurant.)

I then returned to the Palais de l'Industrie, where I was offered a post in the Medical Staff in charge of a train between Paris and Metz. I declined, upon the ground of my expecting to hear every minute of my having been appointed to an Ambulance. Hours passed without a syllable from the Chief of the 8th Ambulance ; and now for the first time I felt discouraged, but pulled myself together, and again threw myself with energy into the struggle.

I still had forces in reserve ; for my friend, Madame A——, lady-in-waiting to the Empress, had promised me letters of introduction, which I daily expected, but which had not yet arrived. As I was whiling away the time conversing with one of the understrappers of the Palais, he told me that the siege of Paris by the Prussians was confidently expected by most Parisians ; they talked of cutting down all the trees around Paris, and demolishing the farmsteads and farm produce in the vicinity, and my informant observed, " Dejà on cherche la démolition du Bois de Boulogne ".

I walked out to the fortifications and saw batches of men throwing up mounds, whilst others were making excavations beneath the mason-work of the permanent bridges, to facilitate their being blown up on the approach of the enemy. Upon my return the garçon at the Hotel showed me with much pride his uniform and accoutrements, with which he had been presented that day on being made a member of the National Guard.

The loud beating of drums and the clatter and din of horses and men as they passed along the Boulevards before dawn, made it easy to be up at an early hour next morning, the 26th of August.

I set out for the Palais de l'Industrie, where

an order was handed me to hold myself in readiness to start that night for the front, so I returned quickly to my hotel, paid my bill and packed up my traps.   I found two letters awaiting me : one from Madame A——, with an introduction to Professor Ricord, the Emperor's surgeon ; and another from the Princess Poniatowsky, enclosing a note to the Count de Flavigny, President of the Society.   They were now of no use, as I had been appointed to an Ambulance ; but had I got them at first I should have been saved many days of anxious waiting.   As it afterwards turned out, it was my good luck that they did not arrive sooner.   An order was now issued that all strangers should quit Paris ; and a heavy gloom seemed to be settling down rapidly over every one and everything.   The conviction was daily growing that the Prussians were approaching Paris ; but no one really knew, as every day's intelligence contradicted that of the day before. There seemed to be a great national competition in lying, in which every one manfully struggled for the prize.

At this juncture I was introduced to Dr. Frank, second in command of an Ambulance which had lately been organised in Paris by a number of English and American surgeons, and which was known as the Anglo-American.   Dr. Frank received me courteously, and appointed me one of his *sous-aides* or dressers.   Having given me directions as to my outfit, he sent me off with another young member of the Ambulance, John Scott of Belfast, to procure all necessary supplies. The pleasure I experienced at finding myself in harness at last was beyond expression ; and it was not lessened by discovering in my new mate a bright, jovial, and witty companion and a fellow-countryman to boot. We hurried off to the Palais Royal, where we ordered our uniforms, knapsacks and kits, and then went out and had a chat and a stroll.

Saturday morning, the 27th, Dr. Frank introduced me to Dr. Marion Sims, now chef or surgeon-in-chief, and also to his staff, which was composed of Drs. MacCormac, Webb, Blewitt, May, Tilghman, Nicholl, Hayden, and Hewitt, and Drs. Wyman and Pratt, as also to Mr. Fred Wallace and Harry Sims. Hewitt and I worked away for some hours getting the stores ready. Having finished this task we went to be photographed at Nader's, in full marching kit. I now packed up everything I did not want and sent them to M. de B——'s house (where they remained until after the war was over), and made my final preparations for starting. I received a month's pay in advance from Dr. Frank, so there was but little chance of my being hard up for money, as we were to be found in everything. Colonel Loyd Lindsay's English branch of the " Societé pour le Secours aux Blessés " furnished the English contingent of the ambulance with the sinews of war; and of this Dr. Frank was the representative.

On the 28th August I went in full uniform to the Madeleine, after which I took all my traps to the Palais de l'Industrie, where I met Marion Sims and had a chat with him. He addressed me kindly as "my dear boy"; and from the gentleness of his manner and his sympathetic nature, I felt that I should like him very much; and so it afterwards came to pass. We all now worked with a will, getting together our stores, provisions, horses and waggons, and making all ready for the procession, which, after a scene of confusion, noise, and excitement, left the Palais de l'Industrie about three o'clock, in the following order:—In front, carried by Dr. Sims' three charming daughters, the flags of England, France, and America; then the surgeons and the assistant surgeons; after these the dressers or *sous-aides*, of which I was one; then the *infirmiers*, all fully equipped, with the waggons for stores and wounded bringing up the rear.

While we were standing in our places, in the Champs Elysées, waiting for the final start, a young girl, pretty, and elegantly dressed in deep mourning, stepped up and tried to address me, but she sobbed so much that I could with difficulty understand what she said. After a little time she made her wish intelligible. Should her husband ever come across my path in a wounded condition, she charged me to be kind to him, and to bestow upon him particular care for her sake. The earnestness with which she confided her sorrow to me, a stranger who had nothing to recommend him but his youth, well nigh overcame me, so that the poor thing very nearly had a companion in tears. She gave me her card, which I still possess. The girl could not have been more than twenty. I tried to say something to her that was kind ; but so confused and upset was I that I could hardly utter a word. Presently the Count de Flavigny came forward and addressed us in a long and eloquent speech, flattering alike to our nationalities and to our cause.

A death-like silence reigned throughout the crowd as he reminded us of the scenes upon which we were about to enter ; the cause we were to vindicate ; the hardships we were likely to undergo ; the good that each of us was bound in duty to perform ; the sacrifice of every personal consideration, and even of our lives if necessary, in the grand and holy cause of the service of the wounded.

There were tears in many eyes, for not a few of the bystanders had at that moment friends near and dear, in dread suffering and perhaps in the agony of death. These few minutes made a deep impression upon me.

I now realised that I was entering upon a hazardous campaign, and felt the weight of the task that I had undertaken; and as the word "*Marchez*" was given I stepped out strong in mind and body, proud of the privilege which it had pleased Providence to bestow upon me, and yearning to fulfil that mission of charity which we had that day inaugurated.

As we passed through the streets in the order I have already given, the dense crowds cheered us along the way to the railway station (de l'Est), crying, "Vive les Americains!" "Vive l'Angleterre!" while the handkerchiefs of the ladies waved from all windows. Tears flowed abundantly on every side, as they readily do in France for less reason than the present one. All were delighted at the practical sympathy of the foreigners, on behalf of their wounded and suffering fellow-countrymen.

The crowds were so great that we found it difficult to make anything like rapid progress, and were several hours reaching the station.

Having arrived at our destination, we took our seats in the waiting-room, not knowing in the least where we were going, as no one did but the chief and Dr. Frank. After waiting a couple of hours we got into a train in which we started off into the darkness, for it was ten o'clock. We travelled all night, and as morning dawned arrived at Soissons. Here we learned that we were under orders to join MacMahon's army at once. As from information received, Dr. Sims supposed him to be somewhere in the vicinity of Sedan, it was his intention to make for Mézières, a small town in that neighbourhood, which we reached on Monday night, 29th August, arriving at Sedan the following morning, Tuesday, 30th, and remaining there to await further orders.

As we entered the town I was astonished to perceive that not a single soldier was visible, and that the sentinels on duty at the gates were peasants dressed in blue blouses, bearing guns upon their shoulders, a military képi being the only attempt at uniform.

All was still as we hastened through the streets to our quarters, at the Croix d'Or in the Rue Napoléon.

CHAPTER III.

ON the 30th of August we got orders through the *Courrier des Ambulances*, the Vicomte de Chizelles, to proceed at once to Carignan, where hard fighting had been going on, and where, we were told, the field had been won by the French. Accordingly at noon the whole ambulance moved out of the town, by the Torcy gate to the railway station, a few hundred yards outside the ramparts, whence a special train was to have carried us on to the field of our labours. Through some mismanagement on the part of the French authorities, and through a combination of adverse circumstances, our transport was delayed so long that we were unable to leave that evening. The railway officials contended that the cause of the delay was neglect, on the part of our *comptable*, to specify the exact amount of accommodation required for the transport of our waggons, stores, and horses, without which we could not work efficiently on the field of battle ; but the real cause of the delay,

we subsequently discovered, was the capturing
and blocking of the line by the Prussians, which
fact was, in French fashion, studiously concealed
from us.   All this was very annoying to our chiefs,
who were most anxious to get to the front.   In
order, therefore, that we might be able to start at
daybreak next morning, we took up our quarters
for that night in the station house.   Being much
fatigued after the excitement of the day we went
to the bureau, where all our luggage was, and,
after much ado, got hold of our wraps.   There
was one large waiting-room through which every
one was obliged to pass in order to enter or leave
the station, and here I and a number of my comrades stretched ourselves upon the bare boards,
covered up in our rugs and overcoats.

Shortly after eleven o'clock, the arrival of a
train caused us to start to our feet.   The Germans, we knew, were in the neighbourhood, and
the thought of a surprise flashed simultaneously
through the mind of each one, when, to our intense astonishment, the door opened, and Napoleon,
with his entire état major, marshals, and generals,
walked into the room.

The Emperor wore a long dark blue cloak and
a scarlet gold-braided képi.   At first he seemed
rather surprised at our presence, and for a moment
or two delayed returning our salute, which he
eventually acknowledged by a slight inclination of
the head.   He had a tired, scared, and haggard

appearance, and, besides looking thoroughly ill, seemed anxious and impatient.   After a few moments' delay he hurried off on foot, in the midst of his *entourage*, through the station house, and along the road leading to the town of Sedan.

I and two of my comrades followed until we saw the Emperor and his attendants arrive at the gate, through which, after some parley with a blue-bloused sentry (for there was not a regular soldier in the town), they gained admittance.   As we were about returning to our temporary quarters, speculating on the probable future as suggested by the scene I have described, we met a party of soldiers straggling along, composed of men of different regiments, both line and cavalry.   We addressed one of them, who seemed more tired and worn out than the rest.   He told us they belonged to the 5th and 12th Army Corps, and that they had escaped from the affair at Beaumont, where, having been several days short of provisions and exhausted with hunger and fatigue, the French were thoroughly routed.   He said that they numbered about eighty, and were accompanied by an officer whom I afterwards heard give the name of De Failly, when challenged by the sentry.   This was no other than the General de Failly who, on that very day at Beaumont, was deprived of his command for bad leadership, and superseded by De Wimpffen.   In the rear of this party of fugitives was a cartload of women and children.   One of the women told most pitifully how the Prussian shells had that morning devastated their homes in the vicinity of Beaumont and Raucourt, and how several parts of those villages were then in flames.   These poor creatures, numbed with cold and fright, gladly partook of the contents of some of our flasks ; and we were all pleased when, after half an hour's parley with the peasant sentry, the drawbridge was let down and they were admitted into the town.

I now returned to my quarters in the station, where I slept soundly until I was awakened at break of day by Dr. Frank, who enjoined us to get ready at once, so as to push on to the front. This was the morning of the 31st August.   At early dawn there was a thick fog, which, however, soon cleared away, revealing to us the fact that we were not far from the Prussian lines, and that they had actually during the night got full possession of the range of hills commanding the station and the whole town of Sedan.   At times we could see distinctly numbers of Prussian Uhlans appearing now and then, from behind woods and plantations, on the heights of Marfée opposite us, and again disappearing, leaving us fully convinced that there were more where those came from.   A little later, when the fog cleared off, we perceived in the opposite direction, at the north-east side of the town, numbers of troops moving about.   These we found to be MacMahon's forces.   Now we became conscious of how we really stood. Our chief called us together, and with the stern manner and firm voice of an old veteran said, " Gentlemen, by a combination of unforeseen circumstances over which I had no control, we are now in the awkward position of finding ourselves placed between the line of fire of two armies. If they commence hostilities we are lost. It is therefore my intention as promptly as possible to retreat behind the French lines." Having said so much, he gave the order to move on. This we did across some fields, which we traversed with ease ; but presently we came upon some heavy potato and turnip plots. Here our progress was necessarily very slow, heavily-laden as we were, with our three waggons ploughing through the soft furrows ; and as we were not quite sure of the country that lay between us and the army, our position was most unenviable.

Two of our party, Drs. May and Tilghman, went ahead upon horseback, one of them carrying an ambulance flag. These two galloped along rather too impetuously as it appeared, for they came unexpectedly upon the French outposts, who, not knowing them to be friends, quickly fired a volley at them. Having discovered who they were they did not repeat this salute. It was just as our waggon horses had come to a standstill, being completely exhausted from pulling and floundering in the soft ground, that

Drs. May and Tilghman returned at a gallop to inform us that the Meuse lay between us and the main body of the army, and that there was no bridge, or other means of crossing, without going round through the town.

Just at this moment a courier came up in hot haste to say that, as the Prussians had just been seen in the immediate vicinity, the gate of the town would be immediately closed, and that the Military Commandant required us at once to make good our retreat, and get in the rear of the French army. We now saw that there was no alternative but to leave our baggage, stores, and waggons just where they were, and to fly into the town, which we did with all possible expedition, as from the position of the enemy we expected every minute that an engagement would take place. When we got inside the gates, two civilians volunteered, for a reward, to recover the baggage and waggons, with May and Tilghman as their leaders. These two gentlemen were veteran campaigners of the American Confederate Army, as were also all the other Americans of our ambulance, save Frank Hayden, who hailed from the North.

These not only brought back all our effects, but also a quantity of potatoes which were found in the field where the waggons had been left, and upon which we largely subsisted during the week following.

We now reported ourselves to the Intendant Militaire, who told us that he had the night before received an order to have in readiness 1800 beds for the use of the wounded. There was not a military surgeon in the town, nor any medical stores or appliances save our own ; and of civilian doctors we never heard, nor were they *en évidence*.

The Intendant Militaire put all the beds which he had provided at our disposal, and gave us full control over their disposition and management.

Accordingly we took possession of the Caserne D'Asfeld, and made ready for receiving the wounded. We also had our stores arranged so that everything might be at hand when required.

It was while thus busily engaged, transporting our stores, and putting things in their place ready for use, that I saw the Emperor Napoleon slowly pacing up and down in front of the Sous-Préfecture, cigar in mouth, with his hands behind his back and head bent, gazing vacantly at the ground.

All that morning we had heard the distant booming of cannon, in the southward direction of Carignan and Mouzon. As the day advanced the cannonading came nearer, and grew more distinct, until it seemed to be in the immediate neighbourhood of the town. At nightfall the firing ceased, and we could perceive the glare of a distant village, in the direction of Douzy, lighting up the darkness.

A brief sketch of the defences of Sedan, as well as an explanation of the position in which our hospital stood with regard to the fortifications, will not be out of place. The river Meuse, on the right bank of which Sedan is situated, communicates by sluice-gates with two deep trenches about thirty feet wide, separated from one another by a high embankment. On opening these gates, the trenches and a vast expanse of meadow land, extending nearly to Bazeilles and along the river beyond it, had been flooded, and the city was thus defended by a double wet ditch for about three-fourths of its circumference. All this lay external to the stone-faced ramparts, upon which stood heavy siege-guns, ostensibly to protect the town. They were, in fact, obsolete dummies. Outside these, again, were high earthworks, faced by strong palisades of spiked timber. At the summit of the north-east corner of the fortifications, towering above the plateau of Floing, rose the Citadel,—a huge, dark mass of masonwork and grassy slopes, which seemed to frown over a series of steep cliffs upon the town beneath. Above this stood our hospital of the Caserne D'Asfeld, called after a French Marshal of Louis XIV.'s time. The Prussians afterwards knew it as the "Kronwerk D'Asfeld". It was a fortress which had a drawbridge and defences of its own. From these details we may judge what a stronghold Sedan would prove, were it not for the range of hills opposite, called the Heights of Marfée. But these command the town ; and the Prussians had been permitted to occupy them.

Now, as to the Caserne itself. Standing on the highest point of the fortifications, about 100 feet above the Meuse, it might have seemed the very position for a hospital. It was a two-storied bomb-proof building, with a flat roof, 240 feet long, and contained nine large wards, fifty-three feet by seventeen, and ten feet high, as well as four small ones with twenty beds in each. There were two spacious windows in every ward. The floors were concrete. On the fortifications outside were rows of magnificent trees, which gave the grounds a picturesque appearance. But in front, facing the town, there were no trees ; and from this point we had an unbroken view of Sedan and the valley of the Meuse, with the hills opposite. The villages of Donchery, Frénois, and Wadel-incourt were all visible.

Six cannon commanded the outer breastworks, behind the buildings, and two sallyports led out beneath the fortifications, on to the plains of Floing. We heard from the wounded, as well as from other sources, that the French were retreating on Sedan, and that the Prussians held the left bank of the Meuse, and the valley and hills about it. The French, on their side, occupied the Illy heights to the north of the town above the plateau of Floing, the Bois de Garenne, and the east and south-east plains, from Daigny and the valley of Givonne to Bazeilles. Hence, it was evident, even at so early a date, that the French army had only the strip of small country to the north and east of Sedan, between the right bank of the Meuse and the Ardennes, by which to make good their retreat on Mézières. And of this narrow space, the defile of St. Albert alone was available for the passage of large bodies of soldiers.

The Prussian outposts were already in Vendresse and Donchery. Could they succeed in moving further north before the French started, they might cut off the retreat of the whole army.

The movements of the French in these straits had been extremely perplexing to us. They must have known their situation, if not on the 29th, certainly on the 30th and 31st. Why, then, did they not keep to the left bank of the Meuse, and seize the only available strong position visible on that side—the Heights of Marfée, which they could have held, and the possession of which would have covered their retreat along the defile of St. Albert? Instead of doing so, they chose to fall back on Sedan; a trap out of which no sane man, military or civilian, could, under the circumstances, expect an army to free itself. These positions were occupied by the Prussians at the earliest possible moment. But even if the French could not have come up by the left bank of the Meuse, they might, as late as the night of the 31st, have retreated by Moncelle, the plain of Floing, and the right bank of the river. Thus, at all events, they would have got clear of the enemy's heavy guns, which assailed them from the hills in front; and would have had some chance of meeting their foes on more equal terms. But they went to their destruction like men in a dream.

Late that evening, several large batches of wounded came into the Caserne. These kept us employed till after midnight, when we slipped out and ascended the fortifications, that we might look once more at the still blazing village, the name of which we had not then heard. Of course it was Douzy. And now we perceived, by the innumerable camp-fires gleaming around us on all sides, that we were close to the ill-fated army, of which Marshal MacMahon held the command. To-morrow it would cease to exist, and with it the Napoleonic Empire would come to an end.

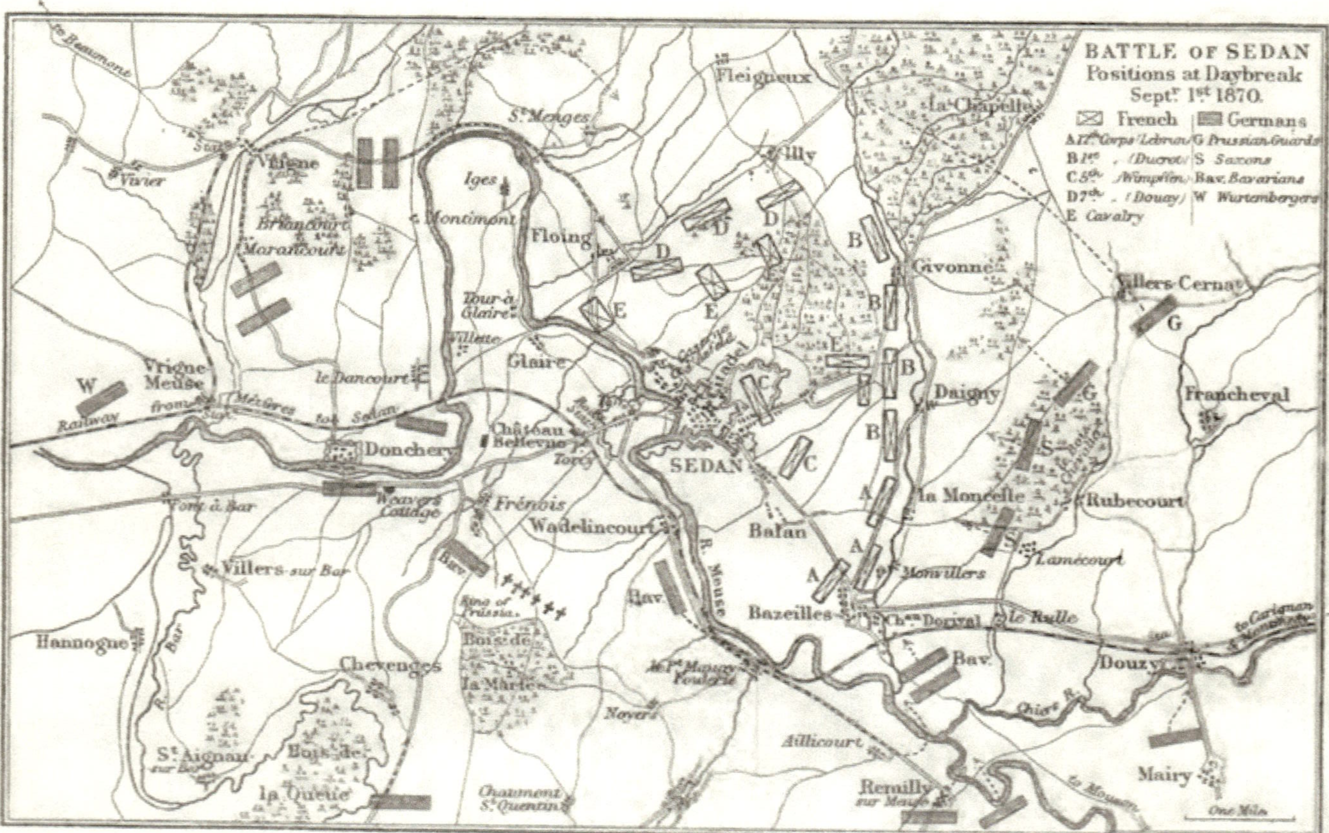

BATTLE OF SEDAN
Positions at Daybreak
Sept. 1st 1870.
French
Germans
A 12th Corps (Lebrun)
B 1st , (Ducrot)
C 5th , (Wimpffen)
D 7th , (Douay)
E Cavalry
G Prussian Guards
S Saxons
Bav. Bavarians
W Wurtembergers
One Mile
to Beaumont
Fleigneux
La Chapelle
St Menges
Illy
Villene
Vivier
Iges
Briancourt
Moraucourt
Montimont
Floing
D
D
B
Givonne
Villers Cernat
G
Tour à Glaire
D
E
E
E
B
Villette
Glaire
B
Daigny
Francheval
Vrigne Meuse
W
le Dancourt
C
B
G
Railway
from Mézières to Sedan
Château Bellevue
Torcy
Donchery
SEDAN
C
A
la Moncelle
Rubecourt
Pont à Bar
Weaver's Cottage
Frénois
Wadelincourt
Balan
A
Monvillers
Lamécourt
Villers sur Bar
Bav.
A
Bazeilles
Ch.au Dorival
Le Rulle
Hannogne
King of Prussia.
Bav.
Mt Mougy Fond Pré
Bav.
Douzy
Chevenges
Bois de
la Marfée
Noyers
Chiers
St Aignan sur Bar
Bois de la Quelle
Aillicourt
Chaumont St Quentin
Remilly sur Meuse
Mairy
R. Meuse
R. Bar
to Carignan
One Mile
London, John Murray, Albemarle Street.
E. Weller

CHAPTER IV.

FULL of strange forebodings, I retired to the guard-room at the end of the building which overlooked the town, where Père Bayonne, our Dominican chaplain, Hewitt, and myself had our stretchers. Tired out, I slept as soundly as if nothing had happened, or was to happen. But about a quarter to five on the following morning, —that historic Thursday, the 1st of September,— Père Bayonne and I were aroused by the strange and terrible sound of roaring cannon. We heard the shells whizzing continually, and by-and-by the prolonged peals of the mitrailleuse. On looking out, we saw a thick mist lying along the valley, and clinging about the slopes of the hills in front of us. Presently it cleared away; the morning became beautifully fine, and the sun shone forth with genial warmth.

Immediately beneath us lay the town, with its double fortifications, and its trenches filled by the

Meuse, which seemed a silver thread winding through a charmingly wooded and delightful country. The whole range of hills which commanded the town was occupied by the Prussians ; and we could see their artillery and battalions in dark blue, with their spiked helmets and their bayonets flashing in the sunlight.

Neither had we long to wait before 150 guns were, each in its turn, belching out fire and smoke. For the first couple of hours the heaviest part of the fighting was kept up from the left and further extremity of this range of hills. But as the morning wore on, the guns immediately opposite us opened fire, although the main body of the Prussians had not yet come up the valley into view. The plains and hills to the north and north-east of the town and immediately behind us were covered with French troops, the nearest being a regiment of the Line, a Zouave regiment, and a force of cuirassiers. It was magnificent to see the bright helmets and breast-plates of the latter gleaming in the sun, as they swept along from time to time, and took up fresh positions. I watched them suddenly wheel and gallop at a headlong pace for some hundred yards, then stop as they were making a second wheel, and tear up to the edge of a wood on a piece of high ground, where they remained motionless. A regiment of the Line then advanced, and opened fire across them, down into the valley beneath the wood ; while for twenty minutes a hot counter-fire was kept up by a force of advancing Prussians, the French still moving forward, and leaving plenty of work for us in their rear. As the firing ceased, the cuirassiers, who had been up till then motionless spectators of the scene, suddenly began to move, first at a walk, then breaking into a trot, and, finally, having cleared the corner of the wood, into full gallop. They dashed down the valley of Floing and were quickly lost to our view. This was the beginning, as I afterwards learned, of one of the most brilliant feats of the French arms during that day. It has been graphically described by Dr. Russell, the war correspondent of the *Times*. Beyond doubt, until noon, when all chance of success vanished, the French fought bravely. I shall here instance one out of many personal feats of valour, which came under our notice.

While I was assisting in dressing a wounded soldier, he told me the following story, which was subsequently corroborated by one of his officers who came to see him. This soldier was St. Aubin, of the Third Chasseurs d'Afrique, concerning whom I shall have more to say by-and-by. He was only twenty-three, and a tall, fair, handsome fellow. He had been in action for seven hours, and had received a bayonet thrust through the cheek. His horse was shot under him during the flight of the French towards Sedan. Still undismayed, he provided himself with one of the chassepots lying about, and falling in with a body of Marines, the best men in the French army, he, in company with this gallant band, faced the enemy again. Numbers of his companions fell ; he himself got a bullet through the right elbow. Promptly tearing his pocket handkerchief into strips with his teeth, he tied up his wounds, and securing his wrist to his belt, seized his sword, determined to fight on. Unfortunately, the fragment of a shell struck him again, shattering the right shoulder. In this plight he mounted a stray horse, and, as he told me, holding his sword in his teeth, put spurs to his steed, and joined his companions at Sedan, where he sank out of the saddle through sheer exhaustion and loss of blood.

Early in the day vigorous fighting was going on outside the town, about Balan and Bazeilles, and between us and the Belgian frontier. As early as ten o'clock, it was evident that the Prussians were extending their line of fire on both sides, with the ultimate object of hemming in the French army, now being slowly forced back upon the town. By eleven o'clock, the plains to the north and east between us and the Belgian frontier were occupied by dense masses of the French ; and at noon, the Prussian artillery on the hills in front turned their fire over our heads, on the French troops behind us. From this moment, we found ourselves in the thick of the fight. Around us on every side raged a fierce and bloody conflict. The Prussian guns in front, which had kept up an intermittent fire since early morning, now seemed to act in concert, and the roaring of cannon and whizzing of shells became continuous. It was an appalling medley of sounds; and we could scarcely hear one another speak.

During this murderous fire, we received into our hospital twenty-eight officers of all grades (among them two colonels), and nearly 400 men of all arms. Occasionally, one of the shells which were passing over us in quick succession would fall short, striking, at one time, the roof of our Hospital or the stone battlements in front, at another the earthworks or a tree within the fort. One of these shells burst at the main entrance, close to where I was at work, killing two *infirmiers* and wounding a third,—the first two were, indeed, reduced to a mass of charred flesh, a sight of unspeakable horror. A second shell burst close to the window of the ward, in which Drs. MacCormac, Nicholl, Tilghman, and May were operating, chipping off a fragment of the corner stone; a third struck the coping wall of the fortification overhanging the town, about twenty feet from our mess-room window; and a fragment entered, and made a hole in the ceiling. The bomb-proof over our heads came in for a shower of French mitrailleuse bullets, which so frightened our cook that he upset a can of savoury horseflesh soup, which he had prepared for us. But, to add to the danger, about half-past two a detachment of artillery, bringing with them three brass nine-pounders, came into our enclosure (for, as I have said, the guns supposed to be guarding our fort were absolute dummies), and opened a hot fire on the enemy, in the vain attempt to enable Ducrot's contingent to join De Wimpffen at Balan. It was a brave and determined effort, but as futile as it was rash, for it brought the Prussian fire down upon us ; and in less than half an hour, the French had to abandon their guns, which were soon dismantled, while the trenches about them were filled with dead and wounded. At one time, Dr. May and I counted on the plain a rank of eighty-five dead horses, exclusive of the maimed. The sufferings of these poor brutes, which were as a rule frightfully mutilated, seemed to call for pity almost as much as those of the men themselves. For the men, if wounded very badly, lay still, and their wants were quickly attended to ; but the horses, sometimes disembowelled, their limbs shattered, kept wildly struggling and snorting beneath dismounted gun-carriages and upturned ammunition waggons, until either a friendly revolver or death from exhaustion put an end to their torment.

Everywhere on this plain, to the north of the

town, there was now the most hopeless confusion. The soldiers, utterly demoralised—more than half of them without arms—were hugging the ramparts in dense masses, seeking thus to escape the deadly fire directed on them by the advancing Prussians. It was clear that the fortunes of the day were going against the French; and if we ask the reason, some reply may be found in the testimony of a Colonel, who told us, with sobs and tears, that for six hours he had been under fire, and had received no orders from his General. A little later on, about half-past three, an officer, carrying the colours of his regiment, rushed into our Hospital in a state of the wildest excitement, crying out that the French had lost, and entreating Dr. May to hide his flag in one of our beds,—a request with which the latter indignantly refused to comply.

About a quarter to four, although the din of battle was still raging, we could see the white flag flying, and rumours of a truce were current. The space round the Caserne D'Asfeld was at this time crowded with troops; and a knot of them were wrangling for water about our well, which, being worked only by a windlass and bucket, gave but a scanty supply. The events that now followed have been described by the French as an attempt on the part of Ducrot to get his forces through the town, and out by the Balan gate, there to re-inforce General Wimpffen, and sustain his final attempt to break through the German lines. But what really happened was this: The French, aware that the battle was lost, had become panic-stricken, and getting completely out of the control of their officers, their retreat on Sedan was, in plain truth, the stampede of a thoroughly dis-organised and routed army. It was a strange sight, and by no means easy to picture. A huge and miscellaneous collection of men, horses, and materials were jammed into a comparatively small space, all in the utmost disorder and confusion. Soldiers of every branch—cavalry, infantry, artillery—flung away their arms, or left them at different places, in stacks four or five feet high. Heedless of command, they made for the town by every available entrance. And I saw French officers shedding tears at a spectacle, which no one who was not in arms against them could witness without grief and shame.

A Colonel, who had carried his eagles with honour through the battles of Wörth and Weissen-burg, related how he had buried the standard of his regiment, together with his own decorations, and burned his colours, to save them from falling into the hands of the enemy. All these officers had but one cry: "*Nous sommes trahis!*" openly declaring that the loss of their country, and the dishonour of its arms, were due to the perfidy and incompetence of their statesmen and generals. That some of these allegations of treason were well founded is beyond question : the universal incompetency we saw with our own eyes.

I observed one remarkable incident during this state of general disorder. A regiment of Turcos came into our enclosure with their officers, in perfect order, fully armed and accoutred. These gaunt-looking fellows, fierce, bronzed, and of splendid physique, stood stolid and silent, with their cloaks, hoods, and gaiters still beautifully white. Watching for some minutes, I noticed a movement among them, and they commenced a passionate discussion in their own tongue, evidently on a subject of interest to them all. In another minute the conclusion was manifest. Approaching the parapet in small parties, and clubbing their rifles, they smashed off the stocks against the stonework, and flung the pieces into the ditch beneath. In like manner they disposed of their heavy pistols and side-arms. Then, having lighted their cigarettes, they relapsed into a state of silent and dreamy inactivity, in which not a word was spoken.

Along the roads leading to the gates of the town, more particularly along the one beneath us, streamed a dense mass of soldiers belonging to various regiments, with numbers of horses ridden chiefly by officers, and some waggons, all bearing headlong down on the gates. As they passed over the narrow bridges, literally in tens of thousands, packed close together, some horses and a few men were pushed over the low parapet into the river, and many of the fugitives were trodden under foot. At length, between four and five P.M., the firing gradually slackened. For some time it was still kept up, but in a desultory manner, towards Balan. At half-past five it ceased altogether; and the sensation of relief was indescribable.

The grounds about the Caserne D'Asfeld had, in the meanwhile, become packed with runaway soldiers, whose first exploit was forcibly to enter our kitchen and store-rooms, and plunder all they could lay hands on. Of course, they were driven to these acts by the exigencies of the situation. The blame for such excesses cannot but attach to that centre of all corruption, the French Commissariat, which broke down that day as it had done at every turn during the whole campaign. We had some wounded men in the theatre, Place de Turenne, down in Sedan; but the streets and squares were so densely crowded that it was with difficulty some of our staff could make their way to them. All were now burning with anxiety to know whether the French would surrender, or hostilities be resumed on the morrow. A continuance of the struggle, as we felt, would mean that some hundred and twenty thousand soldiers, and ourselves along with them, were to be buried in the ruins of Sedan.

Our fears, however, were soon allayed. Before nightfall we heard that the Emperor had opened negotiations with the German King, and that the capitulation was certain.

At last darkness set in. The stillness of the night was unbroken, save for a musical humming sound as if from a mighty hive of bees ;—it was the murmur of voices resounding from the hundred thousand men caged within the beleaguered city. As we stood for a moment on the battlements, sniffing the cool air, with which was still inter-mingled the gruesome odour of the battlefield, how impressive a sight met our gaze! Bazeilles was burning ; its flames lit up the sky brilliantly, and brought out into clear relief the hills and valleys for miles around ; they even threw a red glare over Sedan itself ; while above the site of the burning village there seemed to dance one great pillar of fire, from which tongues shot out quivering and rocketing into the atmosphere, as house after house burst into flames.

The number of Frenchmen wounded during those few hours of which I write, is said to have been 12,500. Probably a third of that figure would represent the number of Prussian casualties. As for our own ambulance, during that day it afforded surgical aid to 100 officers and 524 men. The number of those killed will never be known ; all I can state is, that in places the French were mown down before our eyes like grass. There is a thicket on a lonely hill side, skirting the Bois de Garenne, within rifleshot of the Caserne D'Asfeld, where six and thirty men fell close together. There they were buried in one common grave; and few besides myself remain to tell the tale.

Such is the story of Sedan as I beheld it, and as faithful a record as I can give from my own experience, of that never-to-be-forgotten 1st of September, 1870.

CHAPTER V.

To our labours in the Hospitals I shall presently return. On the 31st, Drs. Frank and Blewitt had established a branch hospital at Balan, and during that day and 1st September, had rendered assistance, both there and at Bazeilles, to those who were wounded in the street-fighting or injured by the flames. Dr. Blewitt informed me that at one time, the house in which they were treating a large number of wounded had its windows and doors so riddled with bullets, that, in order to escape with their lives, they had to lie down on the floor, and remain there until the leaden shower was over. The French inhabitants also, he said, had fired upon the Bavarians; they had set their bedding and furniture alight, and thrown them out on the heads of the Germans, who were packed close in the streets; and after the first repulse of the invaders, several wounded Prussians had been barbarously butchered, some even (horrible to relate) had had their throats cut with razors. This, it was reported, had been the work of French women. On the other hand, several of the native soldiers had been found propped up against the walls in a sitting posture, with pipes and flowers in their mouths. Upon retaking the village, when the Germans discovered what had been done, they retaliated by shooting down and bayoneting all before them, nor in some instances did the women and children escape this cruel fate. So exasperated, indeed, were the Germans by the events of those two dreadful hours on the 1st, that not a life did they spare, nor a house did they leave intact, in that miserable town.

Such, in brief, was the history of Bazeilles. It is not a subject which one can dwell upon. When, within a day or two later, I had occasion to pass through it, and saw the still burning ruins which bore witness to the awful deeds done on both sides, my heart sank. All that fire and sword could wreak upon any town and its inhabitants was visible here; and it is not too much to affirm that, so long as the name of Bazeilles is remembered, a stain will rest on the memory of French and Germans, both of whom contributed to its ruin.

On the 5th September Dr. Frank took possession of the Château Mouville, which belonged to the Count de Fienne. It is situated between Balan and Bazeilles, and was quickly filled with wounded from both places. But for some time our ambulance was unable to get its waggons through the streets, so impeded were they with the charred remains of the dead and dying.

I have now described what I can vouch for, on the testimony of some of my companions, as having occurred at these two places ; and I will leave my own account of what I saw myself in Bazeilles until a later occasion.

To go back to Sedan. As night drew near, the refugees outside the Caserne lighted their fires, and put up their tents. Those who had no tents rolled themselves in their cloaks, and lay down just where they happened to be. All were overcome by fatigue, long marches, and want of food and sleep ; they seemed only too glad to rest anywhere, and to enjoy a respite from the sufferings and hardships which during so many days had weighed upon them.

The true story of these unhappy soldiers will never become known in detail ; and if it did, the public would hardly believe it. Many of them started, as I heard from their own lips, with only two-thirds of the kit they were booked as having received. In some instances their second pair of boots were wanting ; or, if not, the pair supplied had thick brown paper soles covered with leather, and were often a misfit. The men, as we read with perfect accuracy in *La Débâcle*, were marched and countermarched to no purpose ; they received contradictory orders ; and I learned from their statements, that neither general officers nor subalterns knew whither they were going ; and that one corps was constantly getting foul of the other, simply from not being acquainted with the map of the district in which they found themselves. More than one declared to me that their officers were *officiers de salon ;* they were *canaille*, said the men, who when under fire were the first to seek shelter, and from their position of security to cry "*En avant, mes braves !*" In fact, the common soldiers felt and expressed the heartiest contempt for them.   Of this I had abundant evidence.   It was enough to see how the rank and file came into the cafés and sat down beside the officers of their own regiment, as I have seen them do, taking hardly any notice of them, or deigning them only the lamest of salutes.   On the other hand, when officers came into a café (which they did upon every possible occasion), the men would pretend not to see them.   I have observed, not once, but scores of times, captains of the Line, wearing decorations, seated in taverns drinking beer and absinthe with the common soldiers. They were as despicable in their familiarities as in their want of courage ; and who can be surprised if their men did not respect them, or wonder that such leaders had no control over the privates when in action ?

As I mentioned before, we treated a number

of officers of high grade who were wounded on
the 1st.   They, in their turn, did not hesitate to
show how **small was** the confidence which they
reposed in the grades above them, **by** insisting
that they had been sold and betrayed.   They had
received no orders; and the generals of division
had failed to make their different marches in the
appointed time, and to bring up their commissariat,
because their movements were hampered by the
Emperor and his staff, with their infinite baggage
and useless attendants.   Statements such as these,
together with what I witnessed myself, convinced
me **in a very** short time that it was not the soldiers
of France who **were** wanting in courage and endurance, but their officers who were thoroughly
incompetent, **and** their commissariat and whole
military organisation, which **was** rotten to the
core.

But to my Hospital.   **As** I walked around the
building **the sight was** picturesque **and** very
human,—the camp **fires** showing all the ground
strewn beneath the great trees with jaded sleepers.
Entering by one of the doors, I stumbled against
something, which turned **out to be** a slumbering
Turco.   **The** fellow yelled out words quite unin-
telligible to me, **and** rolled over, without giving
himself any more trouble, **out of my way.**   The
medical staff now retired, and attacked what bread,
meat, and soup had been saved from the depre-
dators of our larder that morning; after which we

resumed work once more. We were kept at it the whole of that night, the following day, and some hours of the night after that, without intermission. During the whole of the next day we were engaged in receiving and conveying wounded men from the cottages and farmsteads scattered over the plains at Illy and Floing, all of which were crammed with disabled combatants. My duty in the Caserne was to dress the lightly wounded, and assist at the operation table until the afternoon, when I was desired by our kind and considerate chief to take four hours off duty, and get some sleep.

Instead, however, of taking this rest, which no doubt one required, I sallied forth with F. Hayden on an expedition into the town, to the Croix d'Or, where I had left something on the 31st, which I thought I might recover. We found it hard to get out of our own enclosure ; and even on the steep path leading to the town, men were lying asleep, while others roamed about in search of food. But when we got into Sedan, the streets were thronged with soldiers. At several corners we stopped to see men who were hacking and hewing the carcases of horses, which they had just killed. Hungry crowds surrounded them, many of whom were munching the lumps of raw meat, which they had secured, without waiting to have it cooked ; and in the Place de Turenne lay the bloody skeletons of two horses, from which

every particle of flesh had been cut away.   Here,
as our cook, " nigger Charlie," assured me, was the
source of my morning's meal, which I had washed
down with brandy, and thoroughly relished.   I
may be pardoned for turning quickly from the
revolting scene.

Finding that it was impossible to proceed, we
retraced our steps to the Caserne, and, making
our exit this time through one of the sallyports,
went over the scene, at least in part, of yesterday's
battle.

It was a beautiful autumn evening, and the
sun shone bright.   Butterflies flitted to and fro,
and myriads of insects danced in the light as if
for a wager.   Just as we were walking along the
entrenchments outside, we very nearly met with
an inglorious end from a shower, not of bullets,
but of *pistols*, which came over the battlements, and continued falling at intervals.   On
looking up, I perceived, standing on a projecting
angle, a stalwart Turco, who made signs that I
should keep in close to the parapet, which I
did.   This friendly fellow persuaded his comrades
to desist for a little, and thus enabled us to
retreat.

On getting clear of the ramparts, we found
ourselves north of the town, with the Bois
de Garenne crowning the heights in front, and
the valley of Floing sloping away to our left.
But the plateau which yesterday swarmed with

a surging mass of soldiers in conflict with the enemy, and upon which we had seen the Cuirassiers and Chasseurs d'Afrique, at the sound of the trumpet, tear headlong in their mad career to death,—was now hushed, and presented a field of such horrors as are not to be described.

The burying parties had been hard at work for hours, but still the dead lay scattered about on every side :—here singly, there in twos and threes,—and again, in groups huddled together, which had been mown down where they stood, by the same missile. Their features in some instances were contorted and dreadful to behold,—some with portions of their skulls and faces blown away, whilst what was left of their features remained unchanged ; others with their chests torn open and bowels protruding ; others, again, mangled and dismembered. The larger number lay either on their backs or faces, without any apparent indication of the nature of their death-wound. And some there were who had received the first aid of surgical treatment, and died in the positions in which they had been placed.

Lower down the valley the corpses in red and blue, and the ranks of dead horses, the broken spears and sabres, and the bent scabbards, spoke silently but forcibly of the fury of that historic encounter. When one looked along the plain for about half a mile on each side, one saw that now deserted battlefield strewn as far as the eye could reach with guns, and ammunition, and upturned waggons. There were carriages, and dead horses by the side of them ; firearms of every kind, in places stacked several feet high, and knapsacks innumerable ; caps, helmets, belts, plumes, shakos, spurs, and boots, and every description imaginable of military accoutrements. We remarked, besides, all manner of articles—sponges, brushes, letters, pocket-books, soldiers' regimental books, band-music, tin boxes various in size, and showing the most diverse contents, others empty and their former contents scattered about ; as also nets for hay, saddles, saddle-trappings, whips, bridles, bits, drums, portions of band instruments, and, in fact, as many descriptions of objects great and small as would furnish an immense bazaar.

In one place I found a chassepot inverted together with a bayonet, set at the head of a French soldier's grave, and a cavalry sword which lay unsheathed beside its owner, who, still unburied, gazed vacantly in front of him with a glassy stare, whilst the flies swarmed about his half-opened mouth. The only indication of how he met his death was a small patch of blood-stained earth beside him—not red, but tarry-black. Near at hand, also, lay, covered with blood, a bit and bridle, without anything to betoken how it came there.

The dismal monotony of the scene was relieved only by those little mounds of fresh earth scattered here and there, which marked where the bodies of the slain, varying from one to ten in each place of sepulture, had been consigned. Burials were still going on before our eyes.

Over many of the graves were set up rustic crosses, made with two pieces of wood tied together, or more frequently devices in arms.

Silent as the prospect lay in front of us, its mournful stillness was occasionally broken by the neighing and scampering of bands of horses, still uncaptured, which were wandering in a fruitless search for food and water. As they looked wildly round with their nostrils distended,—some with just sufficient trappings left to indicate the military status of their former masters,—one could almost think that, still unconquered, they sought their comrades and the fray.

In my ramble I passed through several gardens and orchards skirting the Bois de Garenne. It was pitiful to see their condition. The trees were utterly ruined, and their branches all broken ; the flower beds were ploughed up by the bursting of shells, and the houses had become mere wrecks. Through some of them these missiles had made a clean breach. Further on to the right, there had been a pretty little cemetery, planted with yew trees, evergreens, and flowers, which had many small monuments in marble and cut stone ; but these, for the most part, were broken or disfigured, and the iron railings and the shrubs around them had been torn down.

As I walked through, I paused for a moment to look upon the two graveyards,—the one with a history of centuries, judging from its many ancient tombs,—the other of yesterday's making —its only monuments the little mounds of fresh earth, over which, a few months hence, the green corn of spring would be waving, to obliterate the record of to-day's ghastly scene.

Hastening from this melancholy spot, I passed several burying parties. The ceremonies which they used were rude and scant enough ; for all they did was to heave the body into the newly-made grave, and heap the earth over it in silence.

Next we ascended the tree-crested height above the plateau of Floing, where we had seen the cavalry massed on the morning before. We first entered the wood. It was intersected by walks which led to an observatory and a Château in the centre. Here, as everywhere else, disorder reigned. One might easily have conceived that an army had been annihilated in the act of preparing their toilet : for all things belonging to a soldier, from his full-dress uniform to his linen and boots, were scattered about in all directions. Rifles and arms of all sorts were cast away in hundreds. The brushwood in many parts was very thick ; but even in the midst of almost impenetrable scrub we found arms and accoutrements in abundance. More than once we came upon the corpses of French soldiers, who lay as if asleep. They had probably dragged themselves from the scene of carnage to this lonely spot, and there expired, unmolested.

At one place in particular the underwood was so thick, that I had to crouch down in order to get through it. My attention was drawn thither by the signs of a path having been forced in that direction. A little further in, I found an open space of a few yards square, which was now occupied by a grave. It had no device upon it, except a cross scratched in the red clay. Lying beside it, I found a piece of shell, a religious picture, a prayer-book, and fragments of a uniform, which I still have by me. I fancy some kind comrade had paid his friend a last tribute, by giving him, as it were, a special burial in a place to himself.

In order to reach the building in the centre of the wood, I had to pass through a little garden, whose only flowers seemed to be rows of dahlias, of every colour and description. Among these the shells had made havoc. In one bed, I remarked a deep hole where a shell had fallen, and some of the plants had been lifted several feet away. In other places, furrows of some yards in length were made by shot and shell, as if a plough had worked intermittently here and there. Some were deep, others just skimmed the surface and

ran a zigzag course, as if a gigantic animal had
been turning up the ground with his muzzle.   The
building, into which I made my way, seemed to
be an observatory or pavilion, belonging to the
Château, which stood some distance behind.   Its
doors and wood-work were riddled with bullets,
and the roof was blown away.   There, curiously
enough, a large quantity of music was strewn
about.   Under cover of this wood, the Bois de
Garenne, we had seen the French massing their
troops ; and they had evidently been lying here
in ambush when the Prussians detected and
shelled them, before the final rout, during which
they abandoned their arms and ammunition.
Down the slope of the hill, and in the bottom of
the valley facing the Meuse, dead men and horses,
with groups of hastily-dug graves,—many of them
German,—and broken spears, and numbers of
unsheathed cavalry swords, told the same tale
of a death struggle in which hundreds must have
perished.

Further along the valley, beside a lonely
thicket, was a large mound with a stake driven
into it, and an inscription in German characters,
made with some material which looked like black-
ing, " Here lie thirty-six men of the 5th corps".
Who shall reckon the number of French dead in
the many graves adjacent?

As my time was up, I now hastened back to
my post, feeling like one who had awakened

from a terrible nightmare. Yet I was much invigorated by this expedition, so mournful in its circumstances, and went to work with renewed energy.

On the evening of the 3rd, word was brought us that some of the wounded lay in a bad way in a cottage outside Balan. Dr. MacCormac, accompanied by Dr. Hewitt and myself, at once proceeded through the town and along the high road, which we followed only for a short distance. Then we struck out to the left until we arrived at a small wood, where certain of the French troops were still encamped, but as prisoners.

The night was fine, and would have been pitch dark had not the camp fires shone around numerous and bright. When we came to the house in question, Dr. MacCormac performed several amputations, at which Hewitt and I assisted. In a couple of hours we started again for home, but being both hungry and thirsty, turned aside into a little cottage, where we told the poor woman in occupation that we had been attending the wounded, and had had nothing to eat all day. We were willing to pay for anything she could give us. At first she looked at us sternly; but when we told her on which side we had been engaged, she melted, and received us with a welcome, which, if not effusive, was, under the circumstances, cordial.

Out of her larder she offered us bread, and a

quantity of what she informed us was beef. We could not be particular; and it was not without enjoyment that we made our doubtful, but much needed supper on her viands. No further incident delayed our return to the Caserne D'Asfeld.

CHAPTER VI.

I DO not intend entering here into full details of
our work during this eventful period. But, to
give unprofessional readers some idea of its
nature and extent, I may state, that after the
battles of August 31st, and 1st September,
we had 72 amputations of upper and lower
extremities, the great majority of which operations were performed by Dr. MacCormac.
Besides these, there were scores of equal magnitude—ligatures of arteries of the neck, arm, and
thigh,—and a host of operations, which, in com-
parison, are usually termed minor, most of which,
especially when very serious, were accomplished
by the same skilful hand. After the hurry and
rush of the first few days, we adopted a general
routine of work, and divided the number of
wounded equally among the staff of surgeons and
assistants. We were eighteen, all told. Dr.
Marion Sims was our head, Dr. MacCormac
our chief operator, Dr. Webb our *comptable,*
and Mr. Harry Sims our storekeeper. As I
stated before, Drs. Frank and Blewitt managed

a branch hospital in the Château Mouville, where they rendered to the victims of fire, sword, shot, and shell, of bullet and bayonet, the most signal assistance at the imminent peril of their lives.

Thus for our three hundred and eighty wounded at the Caserne D'Asfeld we had but twelve men, six being surgeons, and six assistants and *sous-aides ;* so that the number of wounded which fell to the share of each surgeon and his assistant was sixty-three. Almost every case occupying a bed in the hospital was of a serious nature, such as to require much time and care in dressing it daily. But, besides, we had to dress the lightly wounded who came to our hospital for inspection, and who were quartered in the town wherever they could find room. The work was simply enormous. We rose at six and breakfasted at half-past seven upon horseflesh soup, or coffee and condensed milk (Mallow brand) with musty bread, for our special supply of provisions was exhausted, and neither bread nor beef could be obtained at any price. The duties to which we then applied ourselves are easily imaginable ; they included the setting of fractures, extracting of bullets, ligaturing arteries, resecting bones and joints, and assisting at the operation table. This last was frequently my province. I was under Dr. May, an experienced American surgeon, who, as I have mentioned earlier, had served in the Confederate Army. No one could be more considerate.   We worked most agreeably together, and soon were the best of friends.

During the press of the first few days, we juniors had lots of bullets to extract and plenty of minor surgery; for although we were not supposed to perform any operation, yet under the strain of necessity we could not but often neglect this otherwise wholesome arrangement.   Every day numberless operations were gone through, at which we assisted in turn; and thus had what we sometimes thought more than enough of practical surgery.   I spare the reader details; yet only perhaps by such ghastly touches as are here omitted, can the nature and ravages of war be truly described.

At one o'clock the meal which we took resembled our breakfast, with the addition of a little brandy; then we fell to work again, sometimes not giving over until six, when we had supper, which was a repetition of our other meals,—coffee or horseflesh soup, and sometimes horseflesh with black bread and brandy.   Then each took his turn of night duty.   It was very important to keep strict watch on the infirmarians, all soldiers under the direction of a sergeant who remained in the guard-room when on duty.   We still owed allegiance to the French, and were nominally under the Intendant Militaire, M. Bilotte.   This gentleman paid us a daily visit, and laid under requisition all the provisions he could get in the neighbourhood, which was not much, considering that the presence of 200,000 men had involved the consumption of every particle of food in the town and the surrounding villages.

Being junior member of the Ambulance Staff, I came first on night duty and took my position on a stretcher in the guard-room, where it was all I could do to keep myself awake. My eyes would close in spite of resolution, and I sometimes awoke just in time to escape a reprimand when Dr. Marion Sims came round at midnight to make his inspection. As a veteran in the American War he kept the strictest discipline, and occasionally made our blood run cold by a description of the penalties inflicted during that lively time for the smallest dereliction of duty. However, except that a dozen or so of poor sufferers required morphia to tranquillise them, nothing occurred until the small hours of the morning, when it struck me that some of the *infirmiers* might be, like myself, inclined to doze. Accordingly, I went round and looked them up.

All were stirring, except the infirmarians of wards 2 and 5, who were stretched out, one on a bench, another on the ground, fast asleep. I kicked them up to attention, and left them certainly more frightened than hurt. On my reporting the matter, as I was bound, next morning, the sleepy delinquents were put in the cells for twenty-four hours.

Later on, one of them had twice as much punishment for the same offence. Poor fellows, I could not really blame them.

A source of disturbance during the night was the droves of loose horses, principally Arabs, that kept neighing and pawing the pavement outside the building, in their endeavour to reach the water which was stored in buckets near the open windows. Every night, as their thirst increased, they became more frantic; and during the daytime they came in dozens, drawn by the scent of water, all the while kicking each other furiously. Some had bridles, some mere fragments of their trappings, and the rest had got quit of all their furniture. It was novel to see these chargers careering about in demi-toilette. In a few days, however, all the wounded animals, now become useless, were shot; the others were brought together—chiefly by the sound of the trumpet, to which they quickly answered—and were picketed in the valley beyond the Meuse and above Donchery.

One morning Hayden and I made an expedition, and secured two of them. Mine was a fine chestnut Arab, which I kept tied to a tree in our enclosure, while one of my *infirmiers* contrived to get fodder for him outside the ramparts, in addition to what I could procure myself from the ambulance stores. Mounted on our captures, Hayden and I used occasionally to explore the country during our hours off duty. Afterwards, when leaving Sedan, we turned them out again upon the plains, where, doubtless, they enjoyed a short-lived freedom. Some of the unsound horses, which the Prussians did not require, they sold for a trifle to the inhabitants. I saw a remarkably useful pair of horses, apparently sound and in good condition, which were sold by auction in the Place de Turenne for twelve francs, that is to say, ten shillings the pair. But we must bear in mind that, with a little vigilance, and by evading the Prussian pickets, horses might then be had on the plains for the trouble of catching them.

What had become, meanwhile, of the defeated and entrapped army of prisoners? After much trouble, their officers had got together all that remained of the regiments, and had sent in a return of their strength to the Prussians. For three days our enclosure was not clear of them. One afternoon, when the prisoners had been shut up into their Island "Park," the Isle d'Iges, Hayden and I paid them a visit. It was a melancholy sight. That imposing army, which included the best soldiers of France, had been marched ignominiously, though 85,000 strong, out of Sedan, and penned like sheep in this island, formed by a bend in the Meuse. There they were kept in view by Prussian sentinels and mounted pickets. We passed the guard without difficulty, for there was no prohibition against Red Cross medical men entering the camp. In addition to the French rank and file, those officers who refused to take the parole were confined upon the island. We saw them to be in a miserable plight, the mud up to their ankles, and their clothing scanty and torn. Many had lost everything and were wholly without kits. The rain, which had succeeded to that brilliant sunshine of the 1st, had now been coming down in torrents for twelve hours, and was drenching them to the skin; for their tent-accommodation was altogether insufficient, and failed to shelter them. Men and officers alike looked miserable.

This open-air prison, I have said, was formed partly by a bend of the Meuse, and partly by a broad, deep, and impassable canal. Within such narrow limits we observed the captives, who were walking up and down in batches, trying to get a little warmth. Some endeavoured to light a fire —no easy task with wet sticks—others were making coffee, or busied themselves in cutting timber to throw on their smoking branches. Their food was a scanty supply of bread and coffee, served out every two days; and for this there was quite a scramble, which ended in many failing to secure more than enough for a single meal. Thus they were condemned to starve until the next supply was served out. We may well ask how such a multitude could exist during those weary days, at the mercy of the weather, and in a sea of filth. But many died, and the sufferings of the rest were deplorable. These poor fellows told us that hundreds of them were victims of dysentery, and begged us to give them such opiates or astringents as we might have about us. Unfortunately, we could do but little under the circumstances.

Whilst I was speaking with a knot of soldiers, my friend fell into conversation with a captain of the line, M. le Marquis de ——, of the 4th Chasseurs d'Afrique. He, too, was suffering from the effects of wet and exposure. Hayden, with that generosity for which he was remarkable, promised to come the next day, and to bring all the medicine required. In return, the captain pressed upon him a fine grey Arab, with bridle and saddle, which Hayden accepted, but could not take away then, for the guard would not have passed him out. However, when he came the day after, with a plentiful supply of medicaments and brandy, he rode an old grey *garron* which he had picked up somewhere, and on his departure went off with the captain's beautiful mount;—a change of steeds that the Prussian did not trouble to remark.

Every day we saw from our quarters regiment after regiment bundled off (there is no other word for it) into Germany. As we watched the whole French army slouching away to the sound of Prussian music, I confess that some of us had strong language on our lips and still stronger feelings in our hearts at the shameful sight. We anathematised the enemy, who now seemed to be pursuing their advantage so unrelentingly.

Yet, candour compels me to add, that when I looked at the Prussian sentinels guarding our gates and pacing our ramparts, I could not help admiring their stern, yet frank and honest countenances, and their stalwart physique. A notable contrast, indeed, they presented to the stunted, nervous-looking, and worn-out French soldiers, who, however, it is only fair to add, were suffering from the effects of long exposure and privation, and whom we had seen at their worst. Still, there was a difference in the men themselves which no one with eyes in his head could fail to observe. What was the explanation of it? He that can reply to this question as the truth demands, and he alone, will explain why the French campaigns of 1870 and 1871 were such a dismal series of misfortunes. The break-down of the Commissariat, the peculation in high quarters, the confused plans, and the military disorder must be ascribed to causes which were long in action before the French entered on their struggle with the Fatherland. I am convinced that those causes were moral and intellectual ; and that they still exist. The future of France will depend on how the nation deals with them.

CHAPTER VII.

MORE WOUNDED. — SIGHTS AFTER THE BATTLE. — A
COUNTRY RAMBLE.—HEAVY HOSPITAL TASKS. —
L'EAU DE ZOUAVE.

EVERY day Sedan became more and more crowded with the soldiers who were hurt; and on the 12th we found ourselves so much pressed for room that we had to put up thirty-six auxiliary tents, which, for this humane purpose, we had stolen from the French.

The first contingent arrived from the neighbourhood of Bazeilles. When they came in we saw that the poor fellows were in a bad way, many still groaning from the pain of their wounds, which had been much increased by their being jolted about in waggons, with only a scanty supply of straw beneath them. Some had fractured limbs; others had undergone severe surgical treatment, such as amputations; and these latter suffered inexpressible torture.

All were craving for food and water, neither of which had been given to them during many hours. Some, altogether exhausted, died on the night of their arrival. One detachment of the sufferers

(79)

had been allotted to Dr. May and myself; and I heard from a soldier that he, and a number of his companions, several of whom had lost their legs, were permitted to remain on their backs upon a little straw for whole days, in a deserted farmhouse outside Givonne. Their dressings had neither been removed nor changed; they had had only water to drink, and a small quantity of musty black bread to eat.

Another suffered from a terrible bed-sore, which arose in the same way.

But what was our surprise, when, on the following day, the Germans sent us up from the town 130 French wounded, to make room for their own in Sedan! They had them conveyed on stretchers; and, as it happened to be a pouring wet day, the unhappy men arrived in their new quarters drenched to the skin and shivering with cold, for many of them had nothing but a light shoddy American blanket to cover them or their tarpaulin.

These new comers, the victims of neglect, exposure, and overcrowding, became soon the victims also of fever, secondary hemorrhage, dysentery, pyæmia, and hospital gangrene. It cannot be surprising that they died every day by the dozen. One morning, in particular, I call to mind that there had been fourteen deaths during the night.

Whether it was that the Germans had more

wounded of their own than they could conveniently attend to,—which I believe was the case,—and were therefore unable to look after the French wounded, or that they were unwilling to do so, I cannot tell, but I know, from personal observation, that large numbers of French soldiers died from the neglect which they had undergone previous to entering our hospitals.

I am aware that the Germans have been blamed, on more than one occasion, for the fearfully neglected state of the French wounded in the districts occupied by them.   But I think the true explanation may be found, first and foremost, in the great desire which the peasants had to convert their houses into ambulances, outside of which they could hang the Red Cross flag.   Thereby, they exempted themselves from having the invaders billeted on them.   But also, it was owing to the reluctance which these same peasants felt at parting with their wounded, which would have put an end to their own immunity.   Furthermore, we must take into our account the undoubted fact that the Prussians were themselves anxious to leave them with the inhabitants, and so get quit of the trouble which it involved to transport and treat them surgically. Besides this, so great was the dread which the French wounded experienced, of being handled by German doctors and taken to German hospitals, that, in many instances, they persuaded their own people to conceal their presence as long as possible. And, all through, we cannot but remember the appalling disorganisation and incompetence of the French voluntary ambulances, which were never to be found when wanted, and which when they did appear, brought with them little or nothing that was necessary to make a battlefield ambulance useful. They possessed no stores; they had few willing hands or cool heads, and discipline was unknown to them.

I think it but right to add, that once the French were transmitted to a German hospital, they invariably (as I can testify from experience) met with the greatest kindness at the hands of the military surgeons, and had all that science and good order could do for them.

During all this time we were virtually prisoners in the hands of the Prussians, and they kept a regular guard upon our quarters, while numerous sentries paced up and down the ramparts beside us, as we went to and fro. Nevertheless, far from interfering in any way they gave us help in every possible manner, and showed us the most marked deference. But the sentries who, after nightfall, were placed every fifty yards in the streets, were, at first, constantly challenging us, until they came to recognise our uniform, and knew who we were.

An incident, which I ought not to pass over, occurred one evening as Hayden and I rode out for an airing. We were going along the road which led through the **Prussian artillery camp** outside Donchery, and we **met** a carriage or landau, accompanied **by a strong** guard of Uhlans, **in which** was a **French** officer, evidently wounded, **for he** lay on his back, propped **up on pillows.** Another officer of rank **sat beside him. We were in-**formed **that the** wounded prisoner was Marshal MacMahon, and that **he was on his way to Ger-**many through Belgium ; **but I have found since** that this could **not have been the case, for Mar-**shal MacMahon **was taken away early on the** day of Sedan **itself. Next we trotted on to the** cottage at Frénois, where, **a few days previously, the** Emperor **had met Count Bismarck.** We then rode **to the Château Bellevue in which** Napoleon had had **his interview with the** King **of Prussia and the capitulation was signed.** Here I was shown, and sat **upon, the chair in which the fallen** Emperor had **been seated. The pen** and ink were shown us, also, **with which, as it** was alleged, the articles had **been** written. **But I felt by no** means sure **of this and told my** companion so. **It** was amusing to see his indignation, and the vehement way in which **he put** down my scepticism, as detracting from the interest of **our pilgrimage.**

Our next move **was to** inspect some of the enemy's positions **on the** heights **of** Marfée. Here **we** could trace no débris of any kind,—a sufficiently **striking contrast to what** we had observed **on the other side, where** one might conceive that myriads of the French had come together for a death struggle. Over many of the Prussian graves were erected small improvised crosses, with the numbers of the dead marked in black paint. Of these graves not a few were afterwards opened, and the bodies buried deeper down ; for they had been lying so close to the surface that the odour became most offensive. The Prussians wisely got their dead out of sight quickly, and buried them hastily, without caring how imperfectly the work was executed at the time. This they did lest the sight of the dead might have a demoralising effect upon the living. As we took a zigzag course towards home, we passed close by the railway station, and perceived that it was full of wounded men. The Salle d'Attente and all the offices and rolling-stock had been converted into ambulances. In many of the carriages the partitions had been removed, so that they now presented the appearance of a hospital upon wheels.

The sight was interesting to me, for I had been one of the last who had travelled in those carriages and alighted on that platform. As we passed on we skirted the French camp, and scanned the remaining occupiers—now reduced to a handful—of this plague-spot. And before returning, we inspected the pontoon bridge which the Prussians had thrown across the Meuse upon the evening of the 31st. I had never seen a bridge of the kind, and was naturally struck with this wonderful result of an hour's labour. By-and-by, fortune gave me an opportunity of seeing a still more marvellous bridge of boats, constructed and destroyed on the Loire at Orleans.

Next day, when I had finished my work, which consisted, as usual, of dressing wounds of every conceivable description, I was despatched by Dr. Sims to Dr. Frank at Bazeilles, in order to ascertain what additional surgical material was required to carry on his hospital at that place. Passing through the town, I noticed that the streets of Sedan were no longer overflowing with French soldiers. They were filled with Prussians, wearing that grave or stolid expression which marked them out so clearly from their adversaries. All the shutters were up, the doors closed, and not an inhabitant to be seen. One could imagine that the town had been completely deserted before the hostile troops had entered.

Such, however, was by no means the case. The inhabitants had shut themselves up as a silent protest, and that their eyes might be relieved from the spectacle of the invader rejoicing over his victory. For, true it is that with a Frenchman, to be out of sight is to be out of mind. A few days later came a decree from the German Commandant, obliging the citizens to open their doors and shops, and to resume the ordinary traffic.

I left the town by the Balan gate, stepped off the high road, which was blocked with transport and Commissariat waggons, and took my way through the fields. In this short journey of less than a mile, I unwittingly stepped over many a grave, and was sometimes made unpleasantly aware of the proximity of its occupant to the surface. Having arrived at my destination, which was easily found,—for the château was an ancient mansion, standing in the midst of fine woods and gardens, and had an avenue leading from the village through a handsome entrance.—I delivered my orders, and then looked round the hospital. It was airy, clean, and commodious, was evidently worked on system, and not overcrowded. In attention to this latter point, lies the secret of success in a field hospital.

I was privately made aware of an interesting fact, that the pleasant old man who went about dressed in a rustic costume, blue blouse, loose trousers, and rough shoes, and made himself generally useful, was the owner of this pretty place. He had adopted the disguise as a safe-guard against the Prussians, and in order to keep an eye on his property. From time to time, he produced out of his secret stores wine of an old vintage and corned meat,—both welcome delicacies during those days of horseflesh soup and black bread.

Having done my errand, I walked through a

plantation which communicated by a wicket with the road leading to the village. More than a week had elapsed since our attention was being drawn in the direction of Bazeilles by those continued volleys of musketry, and the fearful conflagration which had been so conspicuous in the darkness. Yet some of the houses were smouldering as I passed through. One of our Ambulance surgeons who had been present at the street-fighting, gave a vivid description of the scenes enacted there under his own observation ; but to these I have already alluded, and I shall relate only what I saw. Here it was that the dead lay in such heaps that they had to be cleared away before the cavalry could pass. Now all were decently buried, except such as lay beneath the burning ruins, and of these, people said, there were numbers. As the weather was again very close, the odour was in some places most disagreeably perceptible. Strewn about was débris of every kind ; arms, accoutrements, broken furniture and household effects, portions of bedding, and shreds of women's and children's clothing. I pulled at one piece of a garment which was visible through the débris of a ruined house, and fancied that its wearer was lying only a few inches beneath. It was a child, so far as I could judge from the dress. That thought made me hurry away from the spot with a feeling of sickness. Before its downfall, Bazeilles had been a pretty little town, each house having its own trees and garden ; but now, with the exception of a few flowers and shrubs at the Mairie, all had been destroyed. There were statues and vases still standing in their place ; but not a single thing which could lead one to suppose that, a few days previously, this heap of ruins had been a thriving village, its streets lined with comfortable houses, and its people flourishing.

The village church, standing in the centre of the Square, was a total wreck. On entering, I perceived that here, too, the shells had done their work effectively ; for the altar seemed as if it had been struck and shivered to pieces by a mighty hammer. The stone font set in the wall was broken to bits, the glass hung in cones from the windows. I have kept some of these as memorials to this day. Among the rubbish of the altar and tabernacle, I came upon a piece of shell,—the same, no doubt, that wrecked the sanctuary. This I have also preserved.

For some time I wandered about the deserted streets, taking in the sad sight. So fierce had been the conflagration that the trees were burned down to the bare trunks. On turning a corner, I espied at the top of the street, facing me, a man with a portfolio and easel in front of him, hard at work sketching the ruins. As I approached he gave me a searching look, and resumed his work. Later on he came up to the Hospital, and I found he was an artist on the staff of the *Illustrated London News.* In that paper I saw afterwards the sketch he was taking ; and a very excellent one I judge it to be.

On the way back to my quarters I saw a crowd of children at a convent door, from the steps of which two nuns were distributing bread from a large basket. These children, I was informed, were some of the innocents who had fled with their mothers from the burning village. It made my heart ache to see the eagerness with which these half-famished little creatures snatched at and began to devour the bread. And now as I slowly trudged up the steep path which led to our Hospital, I could not but reflect how terrible a curse is war, and what a very faint idea he will have of it who has not seen the detestable thing face to face.

Our Hospital work, hitherto very heavy indeed, was now increased by our thirty-six tents. All were filled with wounded ; and we should soon have overtasked our strength, but for the timely assistance which the English Society lent us. About the 11th September, Drs. A. O. Mackellar, Sherwell, Beck and Warren, and two dressers, accompanied by two English nursing Sisters— Miss Pearson and Miss McLoughlin—arrived, the former from Metz, the latter from London. They brought a supply of Mallow condensed milk and potted beef—a welcome supplement to black coffee and horseflesh soup. Up to this we had quite forgotten the outer world; and we knew little of the great events which had passed, and were passing, outside our own limited experience.

Some days previous to being thus reinforced, several of us were attacked by intestinal disorders, from which I, among the number, suffered severely. In a few days, the origin of this malady was accounted for. The body of a Zouave, in a state of semi-decomposition, was drawn out of the well which alone supplied the Hospital.

His presence there was discovered by the bumping of the bucket against something soft, when a grappling iron was let down and brought up the dead body. . . . This poor fellow had, we supposed, been wounded slightly on the 1st; and, during that night, or the night after, had dragged himself to the edge of the well, and had fallen in, probably owing to his efforts to procure some relief from his thirst. There was no other way of accounting for his presence. Dr. MacCormac christened this well "L'Eau de Zouave". I resolved never again to complain of the coarse and scanty fare upon which we subsisted; but my blood curdled at the thought that this unsavoury and deadly beverage, in the shape of a cold infusion of Zouave and brandy, had for some days past been my chief drink. Such is war!

The weather, which had been fine and warm since we left Paris, had now become wet and stormy. In spite of all we could do, the misery and wretchedness of the wounded under canvas was beyond description. For the rain came through the tents and soaked their scanty bedding. I occupied a small tent in the middle of the others; and to give some notion of the weather, I may mention that one night, when I had taken off nearly all my clothes (by no means a usual, or always possible, proceeding) and had got between the blankets, being stretched on a straw mattress, I awoke to find myself in the open air, with the rain and wind beating fiercely upon me. The tent had been swept away by a gust of wind. I started out of bed, and, standing in the dark, up to my ankles in mud, drenched, and not half-dressed, called to the Hospital guard. One of them brought a lantern, and guided me to the main building close by, where I found some dry clothes, and made up a bed with a few benches in the mess-room. With the help of a tumbler of brandy and hot water, and a dose of chlorodyne, I had an excellent night's rest in my new quarters.

But this bad weather, exposure, and over-crowding—all things beyond our control—brought disaster into our camp. Pyæmia and secondary hemorrhage showed themselves everywhere. All our secondary operations died, and I regret to say that their places were immediately filled up by the Germans, who turned all the French

wounded that they could out of the principal
buildings of the town, and sent them up to us, in
order to make room for their own. Though the
position of the tents was changed, and disinfectants used as far as possible, numbers of these
new invalids had been hardly with us a couple
of days when they were seized by the same infection. The Hospital had become a centre of
the plague, and threatened to be a death-trap to
all who should be sent thither.

CHAPTER VIII.

THE number of wounded in the care of our Ambulance was at this time, roughly speaking, about 500. There were 218 in the Caserne; each of the thirty-three tents held 4 patients, and Dr. Frank had in his Hospital 150 Bavarians. This will make the total given above a fairly accurate estimate. During and after the battles of the 31st August, and the 1st September, the number of men whose wounds we dressed and attended to, without receiving them into the Hospital, was calculated by us at about 2000. Nor can this be thought excessive, when, within rifle range around us, there were of French wounded alone, over 12,500.

A further insight into the magnitude of our labours may be gained from the fact that in our Hospital at Sedan we had a total of 436 primary operations,—152 for injuries of the upper, and 284 for injuries of the lower extremities. Another interesting fact worth recording is, that during

the battles about Sedan, not a single case of
wound by a mitrailleuse bullet was met with
by any member of our staff.

Dr. Marion Sims assured us that the hardships we endured, and the amount of work we
actually got through, went beyond the limits of
his varied experience. To enter at length into
details would, besides involving obscure techni-
calities, be tedious to the general reader. I will
confine myself to a brief account of our Staff and
General Management, and select from my observations a few interesting cases. I have named
the original members of our Ambulance, and those
who had recently joined us. Nor must I forget
Père Bayonne, the Dominican Friar, who was
a general favourite, and untiring in his efforts to
deal with the religious wants of the dying soldiers
—no easy task among Frenchmen. Neither ought
I to omit M. Monod, our Protestant chaplain,
a quiet, gentlemanly man, who moved noiselessly
about, and slipped little pamphlets with stories
of the usual type, and sheets of paper with Bible-
texts printed on them, into the patients' beds as
he went along.

But I have yet to mention, at such length as
he deserves, one of the most notable characters
in our Ambulance, our *chef de cuisine* and stud-
groom, "Nigger Charlie". He was coal-black,
and he and his forefathers had been Virginian
slaves in Dr. Pratt's family. When the slaves

were enfranchised, and slavery abolished, Charlie came to Paris with his master, whose family were ruined by the emancipation, for all their wealth had consisted in their slaves. At Paris, Charlie served Dr. Pratt faithfully for years; indeed, he often told me that he loved his master more dearly than his life. Dr. Pratt, on the other hand, knew and said that in spite of his undoubted devotion, Charlie would sometimes steal his money and pawn his plate, after which he would take to his heels, coming back only when all he had gained in this unrighteous fashion was spent. But, though chastised not too leniently with the whip, nothing would induce him to run away for good. It was, in fact, impossible to get rid of him.

When, therefore, the negro heard that his master had joined the Ambulance, although he had a good salary as courier in an American Bank in Paris, he packed up his traps, and, without saying a word, landed himself into the train by which we arrived at Sedan. He was a wonderful cook, and knew how to serve up horseflesh soup and steaks so as to defy detection. He was also a wit of quite a brilliant type, a great rider and judge of horses, and as a liar beat all records. But his most decided characteristics were hatred of the Yankee, contempt for black men, and a chivalrous devotion to white women. I had many a pleasant chat with him. His descriptions of slave life in Virginia, as he said it went on in nine cases out of ten, and of the happiness of their domestic situation and surroundings, were extremely vivid and even touching. I presume he was, at any rate, a true witness in his own behalf.

Now, as to the exact nature of our Hospital work and its results. It is to me a constant subject of regret that our knowledge of the antiseptic treatment and drainage of wounds was then only in its beginning. Although lint and *charpie* dressings were used, saturated with carbolic solution, yet covered as they were with oiled silk and a bandage, their effect was spoiled. Neither was any serious attempt made to render the instruments, operating table, and surroundings of the patients, aseptic. Hence the high rate of mortality which ensued. Startling, in fact, as the statement may appear, I am convinced that if we had refrained from performing a single secondary operation at Sedan, our results would have turned out far better.

There was associated with every individual in this great host of patients an interesting story,—how, when, and where did they receive their wounds? And among the number some cases could not fail to be exceptionally romantic or affecting. The sketch I have already given of Louis St. Aubin's adventures,—that brave Chasseur d'Afrique who was thrice wounded on the 1st,—may be taken as an instance; and I will now add what happened in the sequel.

St. Aubin came into the Hospital under Dr.
May's care and mine. Two days afterwards, Dr.
MacCormac performed resection of both his
joints. But so afraid was Louis that advantage
might be taken of his induced sleep to amputate
his arm (a mutilation to which the poor fellow
would in no case submit) that he refused utterly
to be put under chloroform. Throughout the
operation, which was of necessity a protracted
one, he bore up with amazing courage. When
the bones had to be sawn through, he clenched
his teeth on the fold of a sheet, and, except to
give utterance to a few stifled groans, neither
flinched nor moved a muscle. His powers of
endurance were wonderful. Day after day I
attended at this brave fellow's bedside, and he and
I became much attached to one another. I took
him little delicacies when I could procure them,
and I was determined not to let him die if I could
help it. Dr. MacCormac visited him very often;
but he was quite jealous of allowing any one but
Dr. May or myself to dress his wounds.

For some time he went on favourably,—a progress which I observed with pleasure; but then
fell back so much that we almost despaired. At
this time his sufferings were intense; and I had
much to do to keep him in bed. One day he
implored of me to put him altogether out of his
pain; I expostulated with him as firmly as I could,
and pointed out how unmanly it was to use such

language, whatever he might be enduring; when he said, with an agonising earnestness, "Tell me, doctor, is it possible that Christ suffered as much as I am suffering now?" I answered, "Your pain is as nothing to His," and he calmed down and went through his agony in silence.

Happily, it was not long until he became better; and when in course of time, I was obliged to leave with the Ambulance and go to the front, he was rapidly recovering. Our parting was sorrowful, for I honoured and loved the noble spirit of that dauntless soldier. He begged for my address in Ireland, that he might write to me; and he has done so several times. I subjoin the translation of one of his letters sent to me while he was in Hospital after I had left Sedan.

"SEDAN, Oct. 10th, 1870.

" Monsieur le Docteur,

" I do not wish to delay any longer before giving you an account of myself, and once more expressing my gratitude for the interest you have taken and the care you have lavished on me. What am I to tell you about my wound? It is slow in healing, and since your departure, I have had to undergo treatment very different from yours; but I have not given up the hope of a complete recovery, although I suffer a good deal, and am obliged to stay in bed.

" I should be very happy if I could see you at my bedside, M. le Docteur. In spite of the pains

taken with me, I feel your going away ; you were
so kind and patient. Shall I ever see you again,
and thank you with my own lips? I hope so with
all my heart. I will never forget you.

"Please accept, with the expression of my
deepest gratitude, my entire devotion.

"LOUIS ST. AUBIN.

"I take the liberty of sending you my address,
and I hope you will do me the honour of letting
me hear from you. Thanks to the kindness of
M. de Montagnac, I shall receive your letter
direct."

The address given was that gentleman's, at
Bouillon.

I insert this touching note, less on account of
the generous acknowledgment which Louis St.
Aubin makes to his doctor, than to show what
fine qualities were in him, and how gracefully his
French courtesy enabled him to express himself.
Indeed, when his Colonel came to see the lad, he
declared that Louis was the best and bravest
soldier in his troop, and that he did not know
what fear was.

Another young fellow, quite a boy, Peyen of
the 50th Regiment of the Line, had been shot
through the wrist, and Dr. May considered that
amputation was necessary. He was a bright
young fellow, with a beaming countenance and a
twinkle in his eye ; and when I came to let him
know our determination, and take him to the

operation ward, I found him smoking a cigar. Not a bit dismayed, he got out of bed, slipped on his trousers, and tripped briskly up the cloister, smoking his cigar all the while, until he mounted the operation table. His arm was amputated; but when he recovered from the chloroform state, he declined to go back to bed until he saw his comrade's leg cut off. "I want," said Peyen, "to tell him how it was done." This might be an incident in *Le Conscrit* of MM. Erckmann-Chatrian.

He quietly smoked another cigar which I procured for him, and attentively watched every step of the operation; after which, he and his companion returned to their ward together.

Peyen wrote me a letter, which I still possess, and will here append, to show me how well he could write with his left hand. Nothing but a facsimile could do justice to the quaint and brave caligraphy of this letter, which I am sorry not to reproduce in the original. It read pretty much as follows:—

"At SEDAN, September 18th, 1870.

"On the 4th of August, took place the Battle of Bixembourg (*sic*) from 9 in the morning till 9 at night. The *division Douai*, composed of about 8000 men, too weak to resist an enemy six times their number, was forced to beat a retreat to Hagenau. In this sad engagement General Douai was killed at the head of his Division.

The battle was won by the Prussians,—that is true, but the honour remains with France, the Division having stood against 60,000 men all that day, and having even prevented them for five hours from ascending the slope of Bixembourg.

(Signed) "PEYEN, LOUIS,

" Ever your devoted servant.

"To M. le Docteur of Ward No. 5."

This plucky young fellow recovered without a single bad symptom. But, alas! it was not so with a vast number of our other patients; for, about the 14th, many of them were in a bad way, and nearly all our staff complained of not feeling well. Dr. Sims noticed one day that the work was telling on me, and ordered me off duty, sending me out for a walk.

Accordingly, I went into the town, and saw the French guns which had now been stored in the Park, or exercise ground for the troops during times of peace. I never shall forget that sight. There were 400 pieces of artillery of all sizes, including 70 mitrailleuses packed close together. The question suggested itself, Would an army of 100,000 Englishmen, with this amount of guns and ammunition, submit to lay down their arms and skulk into Germany? Could any combination of circumstances make such a thing possible? I do not believe it. An officer on duty about the place kindly took me through the Park, and showed me the working of the mitrailleuse, as well as a number of heavy cannon. He warned me against picking up unburst shells, for they had been known to explode as long as seventeen days after being fired—a statement which I thought unlikely.

Standing beside this plateau was a large building which belonged to the Nuns of the Assumption, and in which a sister of mine, who is in that Order, had until recently been living. I paid them a visit and the Mother Superior received me cordially, telling me of their labours on behalf of the wounded, and pointing out where a shell had struck one of the doors leading into the garden. There was also a round hole in another door, as clean cut by a bullet as if it had been done with a punch.

The refectory of these good Sisters was now made the operation room ; and many of the lightly wounded were limping on crutches up and down the cloisters, their faces beaming with contentment, as well they might, for the Nuns were indefatigable in attending to their wants. Having bidden adieu to the amiable Superior, I directed my steps to the Place de Turenne. Here the church, theatre, public schools, and extensive buildings of the cloth and silk factories in the Rue Marqua, were crowded with invalids, as was every second house in the town. All these showed the Red Cross flag—under Prussian management, and I looked into some of them, thinking that **the** Church especially, was an **un-canny** sight when turned into **a** hospital and full of the wounded.

I now passed **on** through the town, and out by the **Torcy** Gate, and so **home** again. It **was** four days before I **was** allowed another ramble, as Dr. May **had a** slight attack of blood poisoning, and his work was given to me. Most of our *infirmiers* had **been** drawn **by the** Prussians. Those that **remained were** French ambulance men ; and, **if we except three, were** altogether ignorant, **lazy, and** good-for-nothing fellows. They **had** received no technical **training ; and the task, therefore,** which devolved **upon me taxed the energies of** mind and **body.**

Some of our patients were wounded in three, **four, five, and, in one instance, in** six places, which made the dressing **of their wounds a** tedious affair. I had also **to dress** ten **or a dozen** amputated limbs. **At one time I had** in my charge **eighteen** of these, **a couple of** resections, **no end of** flesh wounds **from** bullet and shell, **numerous** fractures —**most** of them compound ones—**and all** varieties of lacerations **and** contusions. **About this time** there were **some** forty **secondary** operations, **in all of** which **conservative** surgery **had** been tried ; but owing **to the** overcrowded state and vitiated atmosphere of **the** Hospital, these patients nearly **all** succumbed. **From** the commencement our **lightly** wounded **men** were removed as soon as possible, and sent to some French or Belgian Military Hospital. The result was that, after a few days, we had none in our care but the severely wounded. I cannot conclude without mentioning the kind way in which Dr. Marion Sims dealt with me. Nor shall I ever cease to recall with gratitude, his invariable consideration for one so much younger than himself and wholly without experience.

CHAPTER IX.

I FORGOT to mention a curious story told me by a French soldier, who had a bullet wound through his arm. To account for it, he said that it had been received from the pistol of a Prussian horse-man, to whom he was in the act of handing a piece of bread, which the fellow had asked of him. Could this be true? It seems to me incredible, and, for the honour of our common humanity, I hope was false.

A strange encounter which one of our new arrivals, Dr. Warren, had with two Prussian sentinels caused some excitement, and not a little amusement, among the rest of us. Dr. Warren was returning after dark, with some arms that he had secured as trophies, and secreted a few days previously. When he was passing beneath the ramparts a sentinel from above halted him, and challenged him to give the word. Dr. Warren, who could then neither speak nor understand French or German, shouted and made such explanations as he could in English, which it is needless to observe the sentinel did not comprehend. How unsatisfactory they were to him our friend was quickly convinced, by the sentry raising his rifle and firing at his head. He heard the bullet hit the bank close beside him, and, as it was dusk, the flash revealed two other sentries on their beat near by, one of whom followed suit; but luckily with no better success.

A yet more extraordinary method of assault was now resorted to by a third, who, being conscious, no doubt, of his incompetence as a marksman, began to hurl large stones over the ramparts at our stranger. Thus far, Dr. Warren had been standing petrified with astonishment, but now realising his position he made up his mind to run, which he did at the utmost speed, for he expected every second to feel a bullet through him, the only doubt being where he would get hit. He escaped, and the whole affair was reported to the Prussian commandant. This officer had two of the sentinels mildly reproved for their excess of zeal, and the hurler punished in that he had adopted an unsoldierly method of attack. Dr. Scott suggested to me that this last man must have been by descent from Tipperary.

Misadventures were in the air just then; for,

a morning or two afterwards, Drs. Parker and
Marcus Beck happened to ignite some cartridges
which were lying on the ground near the Hospital,
and thereby caused an explosion. The guard
turned out, arrested our two heroes, and took
them before the commandant, who, upon receiving their explanation, set them at liberty. As
time wore on, our relations with the Teutons became more and more friendly. At first they had
looked upon us with distrust ; but, when they
found that our organisation was thoroughly international, that we were independent of the French,
and our staff and management as complete and
efficient as they proved, the invaders seemed to
take unusual interest in us. Their surgeons came
in numbers to the Hospital, where, of course, they
met with all civility ; and we, on our side, had
nothing of which to complain.

Not only so. Their surgeon-general, the
great Stromeyer, condescended to inspect our
hospital, and complimenting the Chief on its details
and management, invited him to visit his own
Ambulance at Floing. Dr. MacCormac did so,
and was highly pleased with all he saw. The
success of the Prussian surgical operations was
very striking. It contrasted most favourably
with our results ; but this depended, in great
measure, on the Floing Hospital having been
a temporary structure, consisting of improvised
shanties, boarded all round in such a way that

the sides could be opened at will in louvre fashion, so that, weather permitting, the patients were treated practically in the open air, yet without subjecting them to chill or exposure. I conceive that this was the explanation of their low death-rate, for the surgical methods of procedure were identical with our own. And I may anticipate here a remark which my experience at Orleans afterwards confirmed, *viz.*, that such open-air treatment is the only effective protection against blood-poisoning.

This was the first introductory step to our transition from the French to the German side, but the change was slow and gradual. Hints, indeed, were constantly thrown out that our services would be well received, if we followed on in the track of their army. At first we firmly asserted our neutrality. But we were made to understand that the attitude we had assumed was impracticable; we must make up our minds to be on one side or the other. These warnings did much to determine the line of action upon which we finally resolved. Our movements were also influenced by the fact that while, as regarded the majority of our staff, our sympathies were undoubtedly French, yet later on, when we came in contact with the Prussians, and got to know them thoroughly, the admiration with which we started for the other side was very much cooled down. We looked on the belligerents with less prejudiced eyes, and, in the long run, had no decided leaning one way or another.

In a few days from the time of which I have spoken above, Dr. May was sufficiently well to resume duty. There was a fresh addition to our staff in the person of Dr. Sherwell, and our duties becoming less laborious, suffered us at length to breathe. We could now go down frequently in the evening, for an hour, either to the Hotel de la Croix d'Or, or to a first-rate café in the Rue Napoléon, where it was possible to enjoy a smoke or a drink, and a game of billiards upon a table without pockets. This was a great recreation, and I found it did one good after the labours of the day. There we met the French officers who were on parole, and not a little surprise did we feel to see them smoke, drink, and crack jokes as if the capitulation of Sedan were ancient history. There also we came across the surgeons and assistants of the Prussian Military Hospitals, many of whom knew French fairly well, and not a few spoke English. We, however, had to be back again by nine o'clock, before our drawbridge was taken up; for the standing order had been issued that any one found in the streets after that hour was liable to be shot.

On one occasion I happened to be returning with a fellow "Chip," who, after the labours of the day, had partaken rather too freely of "bock" and "cognac de café". With no small difficulty I had induced him to start, and we found the streets dotted with sentries on night-duty. Hence, every few minutes we were halted, and made to advance until their bayonets almost touched our shirt-fronts. This would not have made me nervous, had not my friend, who was a good deal more noisy since he tasted the open air, objected to being stopped by the sentries in so rude a fashion. He declined, in short, to account for himself. Fearing unpleasant consequences, I came forward on the approach of every sentry and gave the name of our corps, specifying our quarters, and adding gently, " Mein Freund hat zu viel bock getrunken ". They invariably met the palaver with a laugh, and let us pass on, for some of them knew who we were. One fellow, either a little more inquisitive than the rest, or else not recognising our uniforms, put us through a regular examination, upon which my companion began to speak roughly, and even made a clutch at his rifle. Fortunately, the sentinel perceived what was the matter, and was willing to let him pass ; but my man wouldn't stir an inch. Here was a predicament ! As he could speak a little German, he used his knowledge to abuse the good-natured sentry, and when he had come to the end of his vocabulary, began again in French (of which language he was perfect master), winding up at last in English. The soldier presented his rifle,

I daresay with the intention of frightening my comrade ; and I thought it time to seize him by the collar and get him along by main force.   Thus we arrived within regulation distance of the gates of the Citadel.

The bridges were up, and the sentry on duty refused to let us advance any further.   By this time my friend had quieted down, and was beginning to realise his position ; for here we had to wait fully half an hour while the sentry was hailing the others, who in their turn hailed some more, and so on, until the officer of the watch came on the scene.   His business was to call out the guard, when, after much shouting, shuffling, and shouldering of arms, the drawbridge was let down and we were admitted.   I was glad enough to get my obstreperous friend safely landed within.   It was a parlous incident, though my friend's drollery and witty *sotto voce* remarks—for he was not really overcome by the " bock " to the extent of intoxication—have often made me laugh heartily since.

I have thus brought my readers to the middle of our third week at Sedan ; and it was with feelings of sincere regret that we now bade adieu to Dr. Marion Sims, who, in so short a space of time, had won the regard of every member of our staff.   He appointed in his place Drs. Frank and MacCormac as co-surgeons in chief—Dr. Frank for the Balan and Bazeilles division of our Ambulance, Dr. MacCormac for Sedan.

As our work was growing gradually less, we now had time for a ride nearly every afternoon. There was one in particular which I enjoyed much, and often took in company with my friend Hayden. It was from Sedan to Bouillon, conveying or bringing back the post. This was the only channel through which we could receive letters from home. Bouillon, as is well known, is a very picturesque town, about six miles from the frontier, and twelve from Sedan. The road thither goes through Balan, Givet, and Givonne, over hills and dales, and through a finely wooded country, partly lying in the Forest of Ardennes, from which there stretches a vast succession of woods for twenty or thirty miles. As we near our destination the road winds circuitously, and turns at last into the Valley of Bouillon. When I saw it, the autumn colours were all abroad, and no prospect could be more enchanting. There, beneath us, nestling amid the foliage, now rich and golden, which clothed its hills, lay in the noonday sun, the ancient town of Bouillon, through which a rapid and boiling river, the Somme, flowed over a rocky bed, and was leaping and dancing round one huge boulder, above which rose the ivy-mantled turrets of Godfrey's once mighty fortress. The steep and grassy slopes seemed to come down sheer to the water's edge. It was a place of sunshine, quiet and secure ; and, at first sight, one would have thought it inaccessible.

I may mention that it was in this little expedition, when passing by Givonne, that I espied, lying on his side and basking at full length in the sun, a beautiful black and tan hound, identical in appearance with the old breed of Kerry beagles. My companion was amused that I could feel excited about Kerry beagles. But I had my reasons, and I asked the owner of the house to whom the dog might belong. He replied that it was the property of a Marquis in the Ardennes, who kept a pack for hunting deer and wild boars, and he added that probably such a dog would not be sold under 500 francs. The " Black and Tans " are an old-established pack in my neighbourhood, with which I have long had very close associations ; and it made my blood run faster to be reminded of them in the neighbourhood of the Forest of Ardennes, which for the world at large has other memories, less personal, if more poetic.

Having arrived at our destination, and delivered and received our letters, we had a good dinner and a smoke. None of my readers can know the pleasure of a good dinner if they have not lived in a situation like that which was then allotted to us. We went to see the old castle, with its corridors hewn out of the solid rock, and its manhole in the parapet leaning over the river, from which highwaymen and robbers—if not others less guilty—were hurled into the waters beneath.　Lingering about the place for hours after we ought to have started, the evening came on so quickly that we shirked the long journey in the dark.　We thought it better to stay the night at Bouillon, and take our chance of getting off a reprimand by means of this explanation.

At first light next morning we started, but on arriving at the Hospital, Dr. May, without asking why we had come after time, informed us from the chief that we must consider ourselves as under arrest until further notice.　This was not exactly pleasant.　But we had our work to do, and there can be no doubt that the strict discipline kept in our Ambulance was what made it so successful.

Many members of the French Hospital staff, whom I met here and elsewhere, assured me that jealousy and want of discipline among them were potent causes of their failure ; their supply of material—which was generally very short—in some cases outlasting the final disruption.

I had one other most interesting expedition, to the Château Bellevue and along by the hills where the Prussians established their heavy guns on the First.　It commanded the whole valley, and as we looked down upon the Plateau of Floing, the Bois de Garenne, the slopes of Givonne, and our hospital standing on its huge embankment above the ramparts of Sedan between them and us, the only wonder was that a single man of us remained alive.

It was now time to think of a fresh field for our labours. Dr. Parker and I were deputed to visit Arlon, a town in Belgium about thirty-five miles distant, to consult with Capt. H. Brackenbury, who was secretary to the English Aid Society on the Continent. We made the journey in a two-horse open carriage by way of Bouillon in about ten hours; and with such charming scenery, and in agreeable companionship, the journey could not fail to prove delightful.

On the next day, Sunday, we had an interview with Brackenbury's secretary, for he was not at home himself; and we then started off again for Sedan before there was a soul in the streets, so that my recollections of Arlon do not amount to a great deal.

On our return the staff held a meeting, at which Dr. MacCormac gave in his resignation as chief in favour of Dr. Pratt (son-in-law to Marion Sims), who succeeded him. Dr. MacCormac was engaged, as we knew, to deliver an inaugural address at the Queen's College, Belfast, about the middle of October; and his pupil, Scott, accompanied him on his departure. As Dr. Nicholl also wished to return to America, it was arranged that Wyman and Hewitt should continue with Dr. Frank for some time before we disbanded, for the Hospital at Bazeilles had to be wound up with our own. The following members were then selected to proceed to the front,—our new chief, Dr. Pratt, and Drs. May, Tilghman, Mackellar, Parker, Warren, Hayden, Sherwell, Wallace, Wombwell, Adams, and myself. These formed the staff. With us went, of course, Nigger Charlie, and a Turco named Jean. This Turco had received a bullet in the back at Metz, during an effort (which proved successful) to get water from a well which was guarded by a Prussian picket, who had already bowled over four or five others intent on the same enterprise.

The 4th of October, which was the day appointed for starting, arrived. We said good-bye to the few patients now remaining, who were to be taken over by Dr. Frank. Among them was my friend Louis St. Aubin. The poor fellow on taking leave of me, in his weak state, sobbed like a child, and I felt equally grieved at having to part from him. We bade farewell to Dr. Mac-Cormac with much regret; and then the draw-bridge was let down, Dr. Pratt gave the word to start, and the Anglo-American Ambulance made its exit from the Caserne, slowly wending its way down the rugged path, *en route* for Paris.

The first chapter in my experience of a military Hospital, and of the battlefield, was closed.

CHAPTER X.

DR. PRATT was of opinion that, if the Germans
did not require our services, they might perhaps
allow us to get into Paris, where, as it was
rumoured, medical men were scarce. With this
object in view, we had determined to go round
by Belgium, and now made for Bouillon, the
nearest frontier town. It was a lovely evening
when we arrived. As we came near the custom-
house —" *la Douane*," the meaning of which
I now understood—we were in a state of trepida-
tion lest, on the waggons being overhauled, our
trophies of Sedan should be discovered and taken
from us. For my part, I had hidden my chassepot, pistol, sword, and lance-top from the Plain
of Floing, securely beneath some sacks of
corn. But the officers allowed us to pass with
only a formal scrutiny. As it was late, we stayed
that night in Bouillon at the hotel. All our
baggage, waggons, horses, and infirmarians were
quartered in the old Castle yard ; and, having

(117)

given my horse to the groom to be picketed (for I had turned my grey Arab loose again on the plains of Sedan), I joined Hayden, and went down into the town to look for quarters. When we had secured them, we dined very comfortably at our hotel with the rest of the staff. This was the first meal we had enjoyed for many weeks in a neighbourhood free from war's alarms, and we found it pleasant.

After a sound night's rest we arose at three, and had our horses and men together at the appointed time, which was an hour later. But more time elapsed before all was ready, and it was quite five when marching orders were given. We reached Libramont after a pleasant five hours' journey through a pretty and very interesting country. Here all our staff, with the exception of Hayden and myself, took the fast train to Brussels.

We two had been told off to stay in charge of the *infirmiers*, waggons, horses, and stores, which we were to take on to Brussels in the evening, by luggage-train. This was a heavy task, and occupied nearly all the afternoon. Moreover, we had to get our ten horses fed, watered, cleaned, and boxed, which was far from easy, considering that few of the *infirmiers* knew anything about the management of horses, while their boxing and conveyance by train were quite beyond them. Here my experience of boxing horses for the world-renowned Fair of Cahirmee, near Buttevant, stood **me in** very **good** stead. Three of our waggons were heavily laden with stores and corn, and required a truck each for themselves. The fourth **was** a light covered fourgon which contained our personal luggage, and **in** this we resolved to travel up **to** Brussels.

Having dined on mutton and fruit in a clean little inn near the station, at 7·30 **P.M.** we started, comfortably stretched out at the bottom of our fourgon, and covered up in rugs and coats. The night wore on, **and we** were suddenly aroused from our slumbers by feeling the movement of our waggon upon the truck, which latter was only a sand **train. As we went** along, the line became more **and more** uneven ; our van rolled several times backwards and forwards, and was kind enough also to sway from **side to** side in **a** most uncomfortable manner. I crept **out** and found **its** moorings loose. The night was dark **and misty,** and we had no light, nor the **means of getting one** ; and, as the wheels of the fourgon were **high, and** the edges of the truck low, while the motion **of the train** was very rough, we thought **it** would **be** dangerous to **try** our hand at putting the concern straight. **We** discussed our chances **of** being pitched overboard ; but concluded that the risk was small, although the jolting and swaying from time to time vexed us not a little. However, **at one in** the morning, we found ourselves **at**

Namur, and were told we should have to stay there four hours.

Accordingly, leaving men, horses, and waggons at the station, my friend and I strolled into the town. It was a beautiful moonlight night. After some wandering we saw a gleam in cne of the restaurants, and roused up the landlady, who kindly gave us some hot coffee and braised mutton. Thus fortified we settled down in a couple of arm-chairs, and slept for some hours. At half-past four we took our places again in the waggon ; but not until we had seen it firmly secured.

We arrived in Brussels at 10 A.M., having been *en route* more than fourteen hours. When we alighted we were in a sad plight,—sleepy, hungry, and disreputable-looking, bearing upon us all the marks of the hardships which we had gone through since entering on the campaign. Not many minutes after our arrival, Dr. Pratt came up, and expressed his satisfaction that orders had been carried out punctually. There was a conveyance waiting, he said, to take us to the Hôtel de France ; and there we should find breakfast and comfortable quarters ready.

After the wear and tear of the last couple of months, one may fancy our joy at this sudden return to the comforts, and even the luxuries, of civilised life. No longer the din of armed men on the march, or going to their exercises ; no longer sentries at every step ; no longer the streets thronged with military !   Yet, the sight of an occasional French officer limping about on crutches, or with his arm in a sling, reminded us that the seat of war was not far distant. When breakfast was over, we turned in and slept until evening.   Then, with some others of the staff, and certain friends of Dr. May's who had fled from Paris, we took a box at the Circus, and enjoyed ourselves thoroughly.

Next day it was our business to report to Captain Brackenbury.   After filling up forms, answering questions, and submitting to a deal of red tape, we were handed our pay up to date and a month in advance.

Here we learned that the French Society, under whose patronage we had started from Paris, was now disorganised, and had stopped supplies. Not only were its funds exhausted, but its Ambulances had failed to render efficient service on the field of battle.   Although we had now joined the English Society, and, in consequence, were associated also with the Prussians, it was a graceful act on the part of the Vice-President of the French Association to make his acknowledgments, as he did, for the assistance which we had given to his countrymen in our Hospitals around Sedan.

At noon on the 8th of October, we received orders to hold ourselves in readiness ; and great excitement arose when it was noised abroad that the Prussians had cut the line between Lille and

Brussels. Thus, we might have to go round by London, in order to reach Paris. We ascertained, however, that the line had not yet been injured, although the enemy had come into its immediate neighbourhood near the town of Lille.

In the evening, therefore, we quitted Brussels by train, taking with us stores, waggons, and horses. The journey to Lille was a short one, and from thence we travelled by Douai and Arras to Amiens, where we halted for a few hours to eat and sleep until the next train set out for Rouen. At daybreak we resumed our expedition, and as we entered Normandy the whole aspect of the country, which had been hitherto flat and monotonous, changed for the better. The red-brick houses, some tiled, some thatched, reminded me a little of villages I had remarked in my journey from London to Holyhead ; but here most of the houses had timber built into them, which made them more quaint and picturesque.

CHAPTER XI.

WE arrived in Rouen at four o'clock in the afternoon of the 9th, and found the town full of Gardes Mobiles, who were marching about in civilian dress, but armed to the teeth.

Our few hours of sight-seeing next day were not long in coming to an end ; but on going to the Railway Terminus, we heard that a telegram had just been received, saying that the Prussians had torn up the line to Paris, and we could travel no further.

However, in a couple of hours, we succeeded in chartering an engine,—four waggons and a carriage—in which we determined to proceed as far as we could. Our advance, when we had started, was so slow and deliberate that we felt sure our conductors were only waiting to pull up at the first opportunity, and jump off the train as soon as they saw danger ahead. After going no faster than a horse could have trotted for two hours or so, we came to a dead stop at a little country village called St. Pierre. Beyond this point our guard and driver stoutly refused to carry us; and, as it was now late, we thought well to stay there for the night. We occupied the village inn and a private house close by. As we had orders to start at daybreak, we were up betimes next morning. I went out as soon as it was light, and took a stroll through the village, in which many of the houses seemed to have been deserted. On inquiry, I found that, since the first intelligence, a few days back, that the Prussians were coming, the owners of these houses had packed up their moveables and gone north, leaving their dwellings to take care of themselves. The situation of St. Pierre, over-looking the Seine, was pretty enough. On the heights above stood its quaint little church, built of flint-stone, and as black as coal in appearance. I went inside, and saw that it was unadorned, but scrupulously clean.

In another hour we were on our journey again, this time by road. We took the *route Impériale* through the valley beside the river, and it would be difficult to do justice in description to the varied and picturesque scenes that came repeatedly into view, along the many miles which we pursued of its winding course.

About midday we gained Gaillon, where we halted to refresh our horses and ourselves. Gaillon is a large village, with a refreshing air of comfort and cleanliness about it, and has a broad central street, lined on each side with handsome trees. Having rested a couple of hours we pushed on for Vernon, which was, perhaps, some ten miles distant,—a long journey, during which we had to accommodate our pace to the jaded horses with their heavy-laden waggons. Our way took us through vast orchards, and, from an elevation at one part of the road, we could see nothing for miles round us but fruit trees. But as we were now in constant expectation of meeting the Prussian outposts, our Chief picked out Hayden and myself, being the lightest and keenest horse-men in the party, and sent us ahead, my friend to reconnoitre on one side of the road, and I upon the other.

For a long while not a soul did we meet, and Dr. Pratt came to the conclusion that Vernon was unoccupied, whether by the French or the Prussians, as had been the case at St. Pierre. Believing that it was so, Hayden and myself received orders to push on thither, and report our approach at the Mairie, where we must secure the necessary accommodation during the night for all our party.

With these commands we started, I on a mare of Dr. Pratt's, which we had got from the Prussians at Sedan, and Hayden upon a black belonging to Dr. May. As evening came on, it grew so dark that we could hardly see a few yards in front of us. On we went gaily for some miles, chatting unconcernedly on various topics, until our road entered a thick and gloomy wood, with high forest trees towering up on each side. The darkness was now such that we could not see one another. It was necessary to slacken rein, and let our horses go at a slow walk, lest they might leave the road and get us into unexpected trouble.

My friend here remarked to me cheerfully what a helpless condition we were in, should any accident happen to us, or supposing we fell in with the French outposts. The words, which echoed through the woods (for he was speaking at the top of his voice, and it was a still night), had hardly passed his lips, when suddenly we heard, first a rustling, and then the sound of voices; shouts were raised on every side of us; and through the brushwood in all directions we could hear men crashing headlong towards the place where we stood entrapped.

We held our ground, for to attempt escape was certain death. We should have received a volley before we had gone many yards.

The challenge now came to us on all sides in French, "*Qui vive?*" We replied, "*Deux officiers de l'Ambulance Anglo-Américaine*".

They seemed not to be satisfied, and challenged us twice, finally shouting, as if we were half a mile away, though but a few short paces from them, "Advance, two officers of the Anglo-American ambulance, twenty paces, and halt!"

We had no time to obey, for, in a moment, we were surrounded by armed men.   One seized my wrists and another my horse's rein.   In a moment a lantern was produced, wherewith having examined us and found that we were unarmed, they let go their hold, but roughly hustled us out of our saddles.

We watched these men, whom we knew by their uniforms to be Francs-Tireurs, as they carefully examined our horses by the light of their lanterns.   All this time Hayden and I were kept apart, and, on my attempting to speak to him, I was told that if I did so, I should be shot straightway.

By a dim light, which some one held behind me, I discovered that I was standing in a circle of these irregulars with bayonets set.   This was the less assuring that we had heard much of their lawlessness, and in what fashion they dealt with those who fell into their hands.   I now made a motion towards the breast pocket of my tunic, to get my official papers, when a musket was pointed at me and I was told not to move.   Having held a council of war over the horses, some of the men now came up and informed their comrades that they had at last caught two Prussian spies.   For they had discovered, on my mare's flank, the Prussian brand, and, moreover, we spoke French with a German accent; while our uniforms also were not French but Prussian.   When they had come to this conclusion, I need hardly say that the treatment we received was not the most courteous. They cursed and swore at us, and flourished their bayonets about as if they had been walking-sticks. They marched us along separately, often threatening that if we stirred or spoke, except by their direction, they would shoot us. Two of these brigands (for they were nothing else) marched behind me, two in front, and as many on each side with fixed bayonets, as if I were likely to overpower them unless guarded by the whole eight. Even when I put my hands into my trousers pockets, the flourish of a bayonet near my stomach (from a fellow whom I discovered to be more than half drunk) compelled me to take them out again.

What distance we marched before arriving at Vernon we could not even guess, so much upset and, I must acknowledge, so daunted were we at the possible fate in store for us. We knew too well that these ruffians were capable at any moment of hanging us from the nearest tree. Indeed, before we entered the town, I came to the conclusion that several of the band were under the influence of drink. I believe there was quite as much risk of our being shot accidentally as on purpose. They appeared to have no officer among them; nor could any of them, I suspect, so much as read or write. They would be admirable judges, therefore, all considered, of the difference in speaking French between the Prussian and any other foreign accent!

We must have tramped some three or four miles, when we got into the town; and there it was an advantage to have even these drunken bullies as our escort, for crowds gathered in the streets as we passed along, and taking us to be Prussian spies, stared and scowled fiercely—some even menacing us with clenched fists. Had not our captors guarded their prey jealously, I am confident that we should have had a rough handling from the populace.

When we were taken into the principal barrack, I supposed that we should be allowed to see the officer of the guard, to whom we could show our papers, and then pass out. But nothing of the kind; the officer of the guard was not to be found. He had gone into town to dine with the Commandant of the place. We were put in the lock-up at the rear of the guard room, with two sentries over us. Our courage now returned, and we opened fire at the fellows on guard. Hayden, who spoke French fluently, gave them his mind concerning the Francs-Tireurs individually, and the whole French Army collectively, in such scathing language that they must have thought we were most certainly Prussians. I, not being of so excitable a temper as my friend, gave them to understand that such an exhibition of military ignorance and *gaucherie* as we had witnessed that night would have been impossible anywhere but in France; and I think with good reason.

We had been in the lock-up for about an hour, when the officer of the guard appeared and examined our papers. These he forwarded to the Commandant Militaire, who inspected them once more, and immediately ordered our release.

The Commandant came down himself to apologise for the manner in which we had been treated, and added the information that the Francs-Tireurs were *canaille*, who had neither military status nor any organisation. But he assured us, as we did not need telling, that it was a mercy we had not been shot by them.

We were never in a thorough passion until now. My companion repeated his strong language, and shook his fist at this gentleman; but he, measuring the situation like a true Frenchman, became very civil and declined the contest. After that, I begged him to overlook anything discourteous that had been said in the heat of provocation; and our interview ended by his ordering two gendarmes to escort us to the Mairie. We had just time to secure the requisite quarters when our corps arrived.

I need hardly say how concerned our friends were about this ugly incident, or how great was their satisfaction at our having escaped a fate which had befallen others at the hands of this undisciplined but armed rabble. It is a matter of history that the Francs-Tireurs showed no respect even for the property of their own countrymen; and we must not be surprised if they were relentless towards any of the invaders whose ill luck it was to fall in with their companies. They reminded me a good deal of what I had read about Italian brigands, whom it is certain they resembled. And their very existence, in such a province as Normandy, was a striking proof that France had sunk into the utmost disorder. The Empire had perished; the Republic, established on the 4th September, was struggling feebly for its life.

Another incident of a different nature, but of considerable interest to me, occurred next morning, just as we were on the point of continuing our journey.

I was standing outside my quarters ready to march, when I noticed a smart-looking, well-dressed young man, more like an American than a Frenchman, eyeing me at a little distance off.

There was something about him that excited my curiosity. As he approached rather timidly, I smiled, and said, to relieve his embarrassment, " You are not a Frenchman, I presume?" upon which his hesitation disappeared, and, in unmistakable Tipperary accent, he exclaimed, " No, indeed, Mr. Ryan. I'd make the queer Frenchman, born and reared as I was in the parish of Cullen, and educated near your father's place in the Street of Kilteely, by Mr. William Lundon."

As the speaker had uttered all this in one breath, my amazement was considerable. Suddenly, and under such circumstances, to meet a man at Vernon who came from the village of Kilteely, and was acquainted with me, gave me, so to call it, a shock; and I stared at him for some seconds without speaking. The new-comer went on to inform me that his name was Timothy Nihil; that he was an enforced exile from his native land; and that, at the time of the Fenian rising in 1867, he had been the leader of that party which attacked and fired on the Glenbane Police Barracks, near Cullen. He was, in consequence, obliged to flee the country. He had come over to this place, and, being a man of some education and intelligence, had found a situation as Professor of English in the Pension of Vernon ; which appointment, he told me, was worth nearly £100 a year to him.

Timothy Nihil had been brought up in the National school; and, indeed, went through his classics, as he had said, under Mr. William Lundon, a teacher of great ability in his own line. To him, perhaps, it was owing that my Fenian had a very polished address. Poor fellow ! his face lighted up with pleasure when he spoke of "the Old Country"; and when, in answer to his inquiries about different friends, I told him all I knew, he beamed with delight. Rebel though he had been, he was yet a fellow-countryman; and as such I gave him the hand of friendship, and could not but sympathise with him in his exile. With tears in his eyes, he repeated that he could never go back to Ireland again.

He was particular in asking about my brother John, for whom he had from his earliest youth a warm affection; neither did he forget the Black and Tan hounds at home, in which I have already expressed my own interest. When he had walked out of the town with me a couple of miles we parted, after an earnest request that I would give his people news about him on my return, which I did very gladly. During our conversation not a little amusement was caused among the party by an English officer, Captain F——, of the Carbineers, who, when he heard that my new acquaintance had been a Fenian, became much excited, and was with difficulty kept from laying hands on Nihil. I explained, however, under what circumstances he had spoken to me, and the Captain cooled down. His strong feeling against these men was in itself not unreasonable, as he had been on active service in Ireland during the winter months of 1867, and had commanded a flying squadron there.

During these four days of our journey to Paris, the weather continued very fine, and our walking tour through so pleasant a country was most enjoyable. Sometimes we chatted with the peasant folk who crossed our footsteps; and I am bound to say that, in these districts, numbers of those with whom we talked were loud in praise both of the Emperor and the Empire. "Look," they often said, "at our beautiful roads,—the *route Impériale*, for instance, between Rouen and Paris —look at our towns and villages, with their magnificently wooded streets, and their public buildings and monuments; look at the fine bridges and aqueducts which you see all round! Whom have we to thank for these things but the Emperor? Who has given work to the millions of the labouring class throughout France? Who has made Paris one of the most beautiful cities of the world, and the Capital of Europe? Who ruled France when she was the most rich and prosperous of nations, with a trade and commerce more extensive than ever before?" Such were the facts on which these humble people became eloquent. Were they altogether in the wrong? Let others decide.

The country between Vernon and Mantes is very hilly, and some parts of the road were rendered almost impassable by the deep trenches which the French had cut across them to hinder the German progress. Strangely enough, although they went to such great trouble to destroy the road, they yet left a narrow causeway, over which a waggon might pass, with a few inches to spare. Afterwards, round about Orleans, I saw this business of making the roads difficult for the enemy, much more cunningly contrived, as I shall relate in its place.

CHAPTER XII.

A TOWN CAPTURED BY FIVE UHLANS.—MANTES TO VERSAILLES.—WE ARE ANNEXED BY THE GERMANS.—GENERAL SHERIDAN AND NIGGER CHARLIE. —SOUTHERN EXILES.

OUR horses being fatigued from the long journeys and heavy roads, we made but slow progress. On coming to Mantes we put up for the night at the Hôtel de France. This famous town is a wonder of cleanliness, with streets as tidy as they are kept in Holland, and not a disagreeable nook anywhere. Much consternation had been caused the day before, by five Uhlans coming into the market-place with a train of waggons, and carrying off all the corn and fodder they wanted for the troops about Versailles. After they had satisfied these demands, the Uhlans proceeded to set the station house on fire, as also to saw down the telegraph posts and cut the wires. "What pluck these five must have had!" will be the reader's exclamation. "Imagine such a force riding through a populous town and carrying away with them half the produce of the market, while the people looked on and never dreamt of molesting them!"

But the feat was not so daring, after all. Every one knew that, if the inhabitants had interfered with these Uhlans, the place would have been visited the day after, and reduced to ashes. Such was the punishment inflicted upon whole villages of innocent and peaceable inhabitants, sometimes in revenge of what had been done by a few individuals. I shall give, by-and-by, a proclamation which was posted up on the walls of Orleans, describing such an execution, and threatening to repeat the like under similar circumstances.

Here it was that Pratt, who was anxious to get a vehicle in which most of the medical staff could travel, produced an order which he had got from the Prussian authorities at Sedan, requiring the Mairie of any French town through which he passed, to provide him with whatever horses and vehicles he might need for the use of his corps. Hayden and I were sent to carry out this unpleasant task. Armed with our peremptory document, we made a tour of discovery through Mantes, and, by throwing a couple of francs to a lad, were informed of a large, private, four-wheeled omnibus,—the very thing we wanted,—and a dashing, stoutly-built pair of greys that might draw it. The yard gate stood open, so in we walked, with the boldness of highwaymen, and asked to see the owner. I knew by the servant's face that he suspected what was in the wind. He retreated without uttering a syllable; but soon came back, followed by his master—a middle-aged man of gentlemanly appearance. He seemed very uneasy; but, when we showed him our requisition, and told him that we had come to relieve him for a time of his carriage and pair of horses, his face wore an aspect of the blankest dismay.

We, however, gave a sign to our own ostlers outside the gate, and directed them to harness the horses and put to, which they did with as great alacrity as if they had been Prussians, the owner looking on in sullen silence. But what were his feelings, when, twenty minutes after, he saw us driving his team through the gate and out of the town, I dare not guess. This carriage and pair, I may here subjoin, we used until the end of the war, when they were returned to the Mayor of Versailles, with a request that they might be given back to the original owner at Mantes, minus, however, one of the horses, which died from over-work and hardship.

Thus it is, that, during times of war, the sacred rights of property are violated, and systematic robbery is held to be justifiable by those who can successfully practise it. In this instance the property was ultimately restored to its rightful owner; but, in how many cases is that never done? To be sure, the Government is supposed to indemnify any individual who can produce the counterfoil of the requisition : yet it would be interesting to hear from such injured persons, the story of how much they asked and how little they got.

We pushed on rapidly towards St. Germain, for Dr. Pratt was in haste to get there as soon as possible. Curious to relate, we had not thus far fallen in with a single German outpost ; neither did we, until our entrance into the Forest of St. Germain, when we were challenged, and had to give up our papers for inspection. A few miles outside that town we passed through the village of Mézières, which had been burned to the ground a few days previously, and was now a smouldering heap of ruins. One burned village is like another, and I might have fancied myself in Bazeilles. Whole streets in the suburbs of St. Germain, through which we passed, had been plundered, and, in some cases, the soldiers had gone from house to house by means of holes, which they had picked through the partition walls. I rambled over a pile of such buildings, and certainly the wanton destruction within them was astounding. The Germans, I must say, when not watched, are rare good hands at pillage ; but they were kept down by such rigid discipline, and so severely punished for every offence, how trivial soever, that they were, and are, I suppose (although not with their goodwill), the best conducted soldiers on active service in Europe. In the matter of discipline, nothing appears to have been changed, at least in the way of relaxation, among the Prussian rank and file, since the good old days of Frederick the Great and his eccentric and brutal father.

Soon after leaving St. Germain we came upon the heights of Marly, just below the aqueduct. From this position we commanded that historic view which is too well known for me to think of describing it, even if I could. Beneath us we observed the Palace of St. Cloud, destined in a few short hours to be a ruin; and beyond, towering gloomily above it, the fort of Mont Valérien. Nor was the garrison of the latter idle, for it kept up a brisk cannonade in our direction, even as we were looking towards it.

Presently we noticed a number of men descending beneath its guns. Evidently, something unusual was about to take place. Of this fact we were soon made certain by the shells dropping much nearer to us, some bursting at the other side of the road beneath;—which, for a moment, led us to imagine that the fort had mistaken us for an ammunition train. The shells came very close; and the ladies who were with us felt, as was not unreasonable, a good deal of alarm.

Just then two bodies of Bavarian cavalry and a regiment of infantry passed us in hot haste, doubling down the hill, along a by-road, to join other troops of the Line which were concealed in the woods beneath us, and under cover of them were advancing. Directly to our left and below us, the Prussian batteries opened fire from their positions, which covered their cavalry and infantry on the right and left flank. For some time the booming and rattling were kept up vigorously, reminding us of the 31st August and 1st September on a small scale. But in about an hour all was quiet again, and the French had retreated within their big fort.

This was only one of numberless little skirmishes, which were constantly taking place between the besiegers and besieged, according as either made excursions in the country around them in quest of provisions, fodder, or fuel.

Early in the afternoon we entered Versailles, and reported ourselves immediately to the Prussian General Commandant of the place. We established our headquarters at the Hôtel des Réservoirs, in the street of the same name. There Dr. Pratt and one or two others secured apartments, which was a troublesome business, for every room in the hotel seemed to be occupied by a Baron, a Prince, a Duke, or some high officer of King William's household. I have heard that in the Hôtel des Réservoirs alone there were four or five such magnates, among them Prince Pless, and that Prince of Hohenzollern whose candidature for the Crown of Spain was the pretext on which Louis Napoleon had declared war. This latter I used to see

constantly about the Conciergerie of the hotel,—
a gentlemanly, gay, and handsome youth, wearing the uniform of the White Hussars, and
certainly the last man in the world one would
picture to oneself as having originated this tremendous conflict.

Staying at the same hotel were two American
Generals of great, but unlike celebrity,—Sheridan,
the famous cavalry hero, and Burnside, who lost
the battle of Fredericksburg. They made most
friendly advances towards the Americans of
our Staff; but their attentions were received
by the latter with the utmost indifference, as
they might have anticipated; for our men, with
the exception of Hayden, were Southerners,
and hated the ground these Yankees trod upon.
Nigger Charlie, whom their efforts had made
a freeman, gnashed his teeth at Sheridan
when that General condescended to notice
him. It was an honour of which the darkie
felt by no means proud. I may here state
that no one who has not lived for some time
among a number of Southerners can realise how
bitter was their hatred in those years towards the
North. So great was it, indeed, that, when they
could avoid it, they would not even eat at the
same table, or have any social intercourse with
them. I must add my suspicion that this was
strictly true only in the case of men like my
confrères, who had been large slave-owners and

landed proprietors; and who, having been completely ruined by the war, had gone into voluntary exile.   On such as these the indulgent policy of the United States Government, after the ruin of the Southern cause, had no power to efface the memory of what they had lost. Wherever one travelled in Europe twenty years ago, one still found Southern exiles, as deeply imbued with hatred of the Yankee as if their subjugation had taken place only the day before. But that feeling was not likely to outlive them. And I am told that the gentlemen of Virginia and South Carolina have acquiesced now in the abolition of slavery, against which they fought so fiercely and to such little purpose, although we have just been witnessing the renewal of their efforts to disfranchise the coloured voters, and restore the local and State government to their own class.

But I am wandering from my subject.   As I have already said, our chief's private wish was, if possible, to get into Paris; and, with this object in view, Dr. Pratt held a long consultation with Colonel Lloyd Lindsay, R.A., president of the English Society, from whom we now awaited our orders.   He declared the project impossible, and placed our contingent at the service of Prince Pless, Inspector-General of the German Ambulance Corps, who told us that we were wanted very badly indeed at Orleans, where there had been some days' severe fighting, with great loss on both sides. The town was full of wounded, and the medical staff quite insufficient to take charge of them.

Ostensibly, therefore, under the direction of Colonel Lloyd Lindsay and the English Society, but, as a matter of fact, under German orders, we had henceforth to carry on our mission. This change of control was disagreeable to us; but there was no help for it. We had been at first exclusively in the service of the French, but were always international; and we could not, in honour or conscience, refuse to enlist in the service of the Germans. As it had been rumoured about Versailles that we wanted to get into Paris, there was felt a certain amount of suspicion regarding our neutrality; and to have hesitated at this moment would have been fatal to our usefulness in the forthcoming campaigns. We made preparations to start as soon as might be. Colonel Lloyd Lindsay objected to our present Ambulance uniforms, and thought them too French. The Francs-Tireurs who had captured us, it will not be forgotten, had taken them to be Prussian. At his suggestion, we were to wear the undress uniform of the Royal Artillery while attached to the German Field Hospital Service; and a supply was ordered immediately from London. We received them, and wore them until we left Orleans. Such were the circumstances under which our transfer from the French to the Germans was effected.

CHAPTER XIII.

As Dr. Pratt had arrangements to make for our transit, and stores to lay in, and as our horses sorely required rest, our departure was delayed for two days, during which I had ample opportunity of seeing everything that was worth while at Versailles. My quarters were comfortable; and I ought not to pass over the circumstances which enabled me to come by them.

A Polish lady of great wealth, Madame Urbonouski, who lived in the Rue des Réservoirs, hearing that our Ambulance corps had entered Versailles, came out in person and accosted Dr. Mackellar; telling him that it would give her much pleasure if he and two others of his companions would accept the use of her house and the hospitality of her table, whilst they were staying in the city. So generous an offer could not be refused. Mackellar, Hayden, and myself were only too well pleased to accept such agreeable lodgings. Our apartments were exquisitely furnished, and provided with all manner of luxuries, to which the sorry plight wherein we had come from Rouen hardly allowed us to do justice. Nothing could exceed Madame Urbonouski's kind attention during the couple of days that we lodged under her roof. Provisions were scarce and costly ; but that did not prevent her from giving us the best of everything to eat, and the choicest of wines at dinner. Before I left, my hostess, understanding that I was an Irishman, and being well aware of the sympathies which have existed between her own nation and Ireland (countries alike in their religious history and their long disasters), insisted that, if ever I returned to Versailles, I should pay a fresh visit to the Rue des Réservoirs. I promised, and should have been glad to have kept my word. But I did not see Madame Urbonouski a second time, nor do I know if she is still living.

On the day after our arrival every one was talking of the burning of St. Cloud, which occurred the previous evening. It was the unhappy result of that fighting which we had witnessed, and, thanks to the shells from Mont Valérien, had as good as shared in, on the 13th. Next morning we visited the Château of Versailles, and saw the picture galleries and the Chapel Royal. Here, too, the tokens of war made themselves conspicuous elsewhere than in the smoky battle pieces which stared at us from the walls. All the galleries on the ground floor had been turned into a Hospital, and were filled with wounded Germans. And a first-class Hospital they made,—commodious and airy, the arrangement and general organisation as nearly perfect as possible. But on the well-tended grass plots in front of the Palace, I saw numbers of the King's horses exercised, where, but a short time previously, it had been almost a crime to set foot.

I must not speak of the Grand and Little Trianon, the trim walks, or the fountain which I beheld playing into the basin of Neptune. It was all new and delightful to a raw youth, whose reading of French history had been neither extensive nor profound. Mackellar and I took a drive through the Park, out of Versailles, and enjoyed a distant view of Paris from certain heights whence now and then we could hear the booming of cannon as the forts discharged their thunder. On our homeward journey we met the old King driving in an open landau. He was accompanied by the German Chancellor. When I saw him another time, General von Moltke was in the carriage. Thus I had now set eyes on the man at Sedan who had lost one Empire, and on those who were destined, in the halls of Louis XIV., to set up another ere six months should have passed.

But, indeed, it would seem that half the inhabitants of Versailles consisted of Princes, Dukes, Barons, and commanding officers. I counted nine of these notables at the Hôtel des Réservoirs; yet some were such shabby-looking specimens of their class, that for the time they extinguished in me the respect which I had supposed myself to entertain for Royalty and its surroundings. A Prince, a Duke, or a General who walked about the streets munching alternately a piece of raw ham or sausage from one hand, and a junk of bread from the other, was not exactly one's idea of feudal, or even German dignity, and modern civilisation. Yet such were the manners of not a few whose high-sounding names read well in the " Gazette ".

I have been offered a share of these rude repasts, and, famished as I might be at the time, my self-respect, nay, my very appetite, revolted ; and it was not without an effort that I was able politely to decline. The proverb runs, " A la guerre comme à la guerre ". I do not mean to imply that in a campaign the decencies of life can be always observed ; but there is such a thing as a gentlemanly bearing, and, out of that great assembly which boasted of the oldest German blood in its members, I saw few that came up to the standard which English officers are expected to fulfil, as they do with the rarest exception.

I must confess that, when I looked at several of our *attachés* in the German Court, and contrasted them with their perhaps more intellectual, and certainly more uncouth and burly, cousins from across the Rhine, and from the Mark of Brandenburg, I could not help feeling proud of that sister country which gave them birth. But, alas! when we compare, not the officers and men individually, but the English army with the German, we can no longer boast: our methods of training, until lately, have been old-fashioned; our military science lags behind; and our neglect of the training, to which all young men in town and village might, with the greatest advantage, be submitted, is, I venture to think, no less short-sighted than imbecile.

On the evening of the 15th, I saw 12,000 men marched through Versailles. These were new levies from Germany, coming to reinforce the army of investment around Paris; and a splendid body of men they looked. The general topic of conversation now was the fighting about Orleans, the taking of that town, and the defeat of the Army of the Loire, news of which had just reached us. Fresh combats in the neighbourhood were expected, and Dr. Pratt made all ready to start on the morrow. At Versailles it seemed to be the general opinion that Paris could not long hold out; and, with its capitulation, the war must end.

On the same night, we had orders to report

ourselves next morning at headquarters, and to be ready to start at a moment's notice.

October 16th was Sunday. I was up at cock-crow, heard Mass at the Grande Église, and bade good-bye to my amiable hostess. Our staff was assembled at headquarters, in the midst of the Princes, Barons, Dukes, and the rest whom I have already mentioned. When everything was ready, and the waggons and stores had got into line, those who had horses rode forward, while we others drove in the comfortable private omnibus we had—borrowed, I suppose, is the word,—at Mantes. Our departure created a little stir in the town. As for Prince Pless, he made himself agreeable to all of us, and was even so thoughtful as to give us a supply of cigars.

Moving along in procession we made somewhat of a display. From the foremost of our Ambulance waggons floated the flags of England and America on the breeze. Just as we arrived at the broad avenue in front of the Mairie, which is the way out of the town, a Prussian regiment passed us in full marching order. As they approached, we heard orders passed along among officers and under officers, in loud harsh tones, with the result that, as each Company went by, it presented arms, our chief and those who rode with him returning the salute.

We were soon clear of Versailles and on the way to Longumeau, at which place, after a pleasant journey, we arrived towards evening, and secured quarters for the night. Before we were in the town very long, it appeared that our arrival had created a commotion among the Prussian authorities, who had no knowledge as to what we were, and whither we were going. On these points several of us were questioned repeatedly by the German officers. This was the case. Our chief, finding Longumeau such a trifling village, did not think it necessary to report himself to the Commandant. That such was not this dignitary's opinion we soon discovered by his coming down to the hotel where we had put up, and storming in most vociferous and unparliamentary language at all and sundry, but especially at Dr. Pratt, for not reporting to him as soon as we were in his jurisdiction.

However, the matter was made straight by the production of the Doctor's credentials, signed by the authorities at Versailles, upon which our boisterous little friend, who wore a uniform of rusty gold lace, fell into a surly silence. Before it became dusk, I went out with Dr. May to buy such odds and ends of eatables as might eke out what was provided for dinner. We went into a store, which was crowded with German soldiers. While I was waiting to be served, I watched the different purchases that were being made. One of our Teutons was buying butter, old and rank, another lard, another candles, another fat pork or bacon.   All were investing their groschen and small change in something or other greasy.   One of these fellows took a piece of butter in his fingers, weighing about half a pound, and then asked the price of it; but while the poor French shopkeeper was looking in another direction, the hero slipped out and decamped to his quarters.   I felt inclined to follow him up, but judged it wiser to control my indignation, as I had to do many a time before and afterwards.   Within an hour from our arrival, the towns-people learned on what errand we were going, and became, in consequence, most polite and communicative.   One of the most respectable among the bourgeois went so far as to ask us into his house to tea and supper.

Some four of us accepted the invitation.   We slipped across the street, after dark, to our good friend's abode, and spent a pleasant evening over an excellent cup of coffee, with fair bread and butter.   No one, who has not served during a campaign, can conceive how impossible it is to get anything like a comfortable meal, or to procure good and eatable bread, not to mention good butter, which was a rarity indeed.   And I am afraid the same must be said of beef and mutton, —in fact, of all the ordinary articles of consumption.

Next morning we made an early start.   Our road still lay through a finely wooded country, each side lined with cherry, apple, and pear trees, to the fruit of which we helped ourselves abundantly. The weather continued open. And, as before, we had to keep a sharp look-out for the Francs-Tireurs, rumours of whose wanton doings were rife amongst the peasants, who bore them a cordial hatred.

About midday, we arrived at the little town of Arpajon, where we made our luncheon. What struck us, in passing through the hamlets and villages on our route, was the utterly deserted and forlorn aspect of their houses, streets, and public places. The country seemed to have become a wilderness, so far as inhabitants were concerned.

Early in the afternoon we reached Étampes, a clean little town, with wide boulevards, and a prettily planted square. Curious to tell, we did not find a single German in occupation, and had no difficulty in getting quarters. I took a stroll through the town with Mackellar and Warren. The first building which drew our attention was the parish church, standing in the principal street, and not inelegant. We entered, expecting to see everything in that state of gaudy neatness which is characteristic of French country churches ; but what was our horror to find the air laden with a foul odour, and the floors of the aisle and transept littered with straw ! It was evident that a troop of cavalry horses had been quartered here, some having been tied to the benches, which supplied the place of mangers, and others secured to the railings of the side-chapel.

It was also plain that the stalls in the Sanctuary had been used in like manner, judging from the amount of stable débris that lay about on all sides; many of the benches, too, had been broken up, and fires lighted with them in different parts of the church. The steps and the altar showed signs of having been used for the purposes of eating and sleeping upon them. At the foot of the altar, which was flashy and splendid, lay upon straw a ham bone picked clean. All this was very revolting. Hitherto, we had indeed seen the churches in and around Sedan and Versailles turned into hospitals; but no one will describe that as an improper use of them. It was quite another thing to make of the Sanctuary a noisome den.

On quitting the desecrated church, we crossed the railway to the old Château, which stands on the hill above Étampes. It is a place of historic associations, but the Prussians had ransacked it, and all was confusion within. When we came back it was reported to our chief that the mayor had made some objection about giving fodder to our horses; so that my friend Hayden was forthwith deputed to call on him and put the matter straight. To him the mayor abruptly reiterated his objection, little knowing the character of the man whom he had to deal with. Hayden resorted to his store of strong terms, and warned him, with the audacity of a Yankee, that if the provender was not forthcoming and sent in before night, he would have his worship publicly hanged next morning from one of the trees in his own garden.   Panic-stricken at the energy with which Hayden announced his doom upon the morrow, the poor man, without more ado, gave orders to have the fodder and corn delivered at once, which was accordingly done.

There was something not a little daring in this procedure of Hayden's, though nothing, perhaps, really courageous ; for M. le Maire had no soldiers, and not so much as a gendarme in the town at his command.   Hence his instantaneous surrender.   We had a great laugh over the whole affair.

Next morning we resumed our march, and pushed on briskly, for we now heard, from two Ambulance couriers who came against us, that fighting was going on about Orleans, and that our services were much needed in that town.

As the day advanced, we could distinctly hear the ceaseless booming of cannon many miles ahead.   Towards evening, when we had passed by Artenay, we found the road and the plain on both sides covered with the débris of a battle.   Numbers of torn uniforms, knapsacks, arms, accoutrements, dead horses, and newly-made graves,—all were tokens that the neighbourhood had lately seen severe fighting. An unexploded shell lay beside the road, but we avoided touching it. Many of the trees were severed midway up their trunks, and nearly all had small branches broken here and there, showing that the fighting was not confined to artillery. Some of the tree trunks were grooved in a most curious manner, evidently by shell or shot.

During the whole of this day, 18th October, we pushed on as fast as we could, arriving late at the village of Chevilly. We heard from the Mayor, who kindly gave us quarters for the night, that a fierce and bloody battle had been fought both in and around the village during the previous week. His little flower-garden had been the scene of an infantry charge; and I marked by the trampled and uprooted plants, and the scattered earth, the very spot where several deadly struggles had taken place. The ground was furrowed, and the branches of the trees broken by bombshells. Our hostess, who had retreated with her husband into a cellar during the fighting, gave me a vivid description of the affair. The whole village was a heap of ruins. But I shall remember the poor lady and her kind husband, who gave us so hospitable a welcome, despite the agitation which their late experience and the spoiling of their dwelling place had caused them.

It was a problem what would become of the inhabitants in these country districts, where the

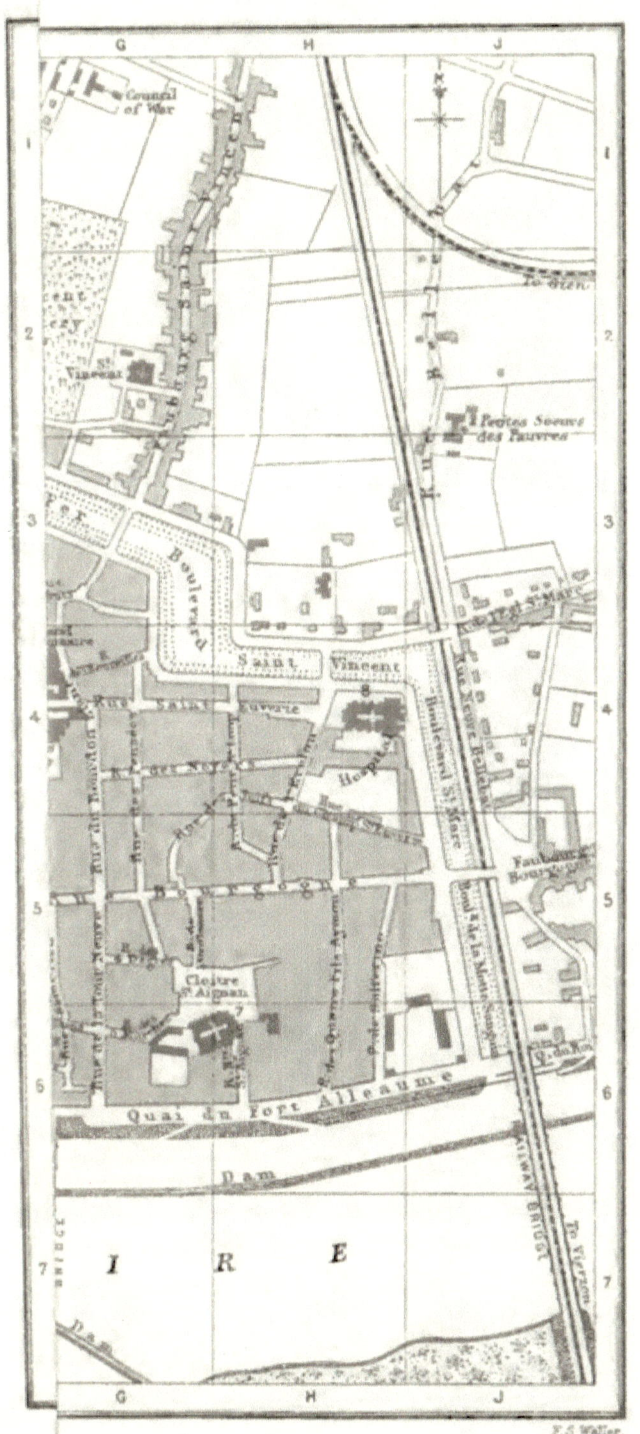
Council of War
St. Vincent
Petites Soeurs des Pauvres
Boulevard
Saint Vincent
Rue Neuve Ballu
Boulevard St Marc
Rue Saint Fauvrie
Rue des Noyals
Hospital
Faubourg Bourg
Cloitre St Aignan
Quai du Fort Alleaume
Dam
I R E
Dam
To Gien
To Vierzon
RAILWAY BRIDGE
F. S. Weller

Prussians (as my host and hostess informed me) had eaten up their meat, bread, and vegetables, had carried off their cattle, their hay, straw and corn, and in many instances had finished up, when they thought the people had balked them of supplies, by burning the houses over the heads of the Frenchmen. Such things, we were assured, had come to pass round Orleans. On several occasions since leaving Longumeau, we had encountered waggon-loads of women and children, who told us piteous tales how their houses had been destroyed, and themselves obliged to fly; and, perhaps, the saddest part of their story was, that when we asked whither they were going, they seemed, in some instances, not to have the faintest idea. They were wanderers on the face of the earth, and dazed by the calamities which had fallen on them so unexpectedly.

We left Chevilly for Orleans on the morning of the 19th. Our road still lay through the heart of the battlefield; and innumerable horses, knapsacks, broken muskets, and military trappings of all sorts, were lying about on every side. The frequent graves told their own monotonous tale. It had become a strange and painful journey; but our adventures were not yet over.

CHAPTER XIV.

ABOUT midday we entered Orleans by the Faubourg Bannier. All this time the cannon had been actively engaged at the other side of the town in the direction of Châteaudun, and, as we passed in, we met several companies of German regiments marching along some by-roads towards the quarter whence the sound of firing came, doubtless with the intention of joining in the fray. Orleans had fallen into the hands of the Bavarians ; but at present the garrison was small, for all the available troops had been sent to the front, where they were now pursuing the Army of the Loire in its retreat upon Tours. In passing through the Faubourg Bannier, we saw convincing proofs of a severe and very recent conflict. Whole lines of houses were burned to the ground, while others had been partially demolished by shell, or had their doors and windows riddled. Many of the doors bore marks of having been broken through by the crowbar, or the hatchet of the sapper. In the streets the litter of the bloody battle which had been fought in the previous week, lay scattered about; and, judging from appearances, the street fighting must have been a very hot affair indeed.

We reported ourselves at once to the Commandant; for I need hardly say, that during the time of war, this is the first thing to be done by every sort of men entering a town, be they Regiment, Ambulance Corps, Couriers, or any persons whatsoever. Even a stranger whose business is not well known is at once taken by the Military Police before the General Commandant, and required to give a full account of himself; which if he cannot do to that officer's satisfaction, he is placed under police supervision, and compelled to report himself every morning at headquarters. This regulation I mention, because a certain auxiliary member of our staff was compelled to do the like, on account of his speaking unguardedly of the position of the forces to· some of the townsfolk.

Our Ambulance train came to a standstill in the Place Bannier, while Dr. Pratt was making his report, and getting our quarters assigned to us. In the centre of the Place stood a large drinking fountain, around which were congregated a troop of horses, jostling each other in their anxiety to get at the water. They appeared so fatigued, that I judged they must have returned quite lately from the field. While our Ambulance was awaiting the return of Dr. Pratt, Mackellar and I strolled round leisurely. The excitement of the people was at this period remarkable; for they imagined that, in spite of all their recent reverses, the Army of the Loire, which was still fighting at a short distance outside the city, would beat the Germans back, and again occupy the place.

Hundreds of men, women, and children flocked about the bridge of the Loire, and kept a steady look-out down the river, in the direction of the fighting. But their expression was that of scared sheep; and when we ventured to ask one intelligent-looking young fellow why he was not fighting, and driving the invader from his country, he answered, "Sir, we have no arms, and no leaders". It was manifest that they did not think, as others in the like circumstances have done, of improvising either.

The beautiful statue of Jeanne d'Arc, which seemed to be gazing on the battle from afar, had been entwined with wreaths and garlands, placed there by townsfolk who desired thus to win her prayers for the success of their army.

Soon after, we were informed that Nos. 66 and 68 Quai du Châtelet, on the bank of the Loire, had been allotted to us as our quarters. On arriving there we found two very spacious and elegant houses, commanding a beautiful view of the city opposite, as well as of the river, and the two famous bridges, which are among the finest monuments of the Imperial rule. Up to this date, the larger of the two houses, No. 66, had been unoccupied; and the owner, probably not knowing that we had a billet from the Commandant, was at first unwilling to let us take up the whole house. He showed a sullen countenance, and was proceeding to lock up his best suite of apartments, when our chief informed him quietly that if he gave any further trouble, and did not at once surrender the keys of every door in the house, he, Dr. Pratt, would convert the whole of his charming mansion into a hospital, and make an operation theatre of his drawing-room. This was a stern, but necessary, warning, which cleared up the situation. Monsieur yielded to *force majeure* thus vigorously threatened, and ever after behaved towards us with the civility which in the French nature is inherent, and which our mission at Orleans might fairly be said to demand.

Our chief had many interviews with the authorities on the two days succeeding our arrival. The question was, whether we should take on ourselves only the duties of a stationary Hospital, or follow in the track of the army. A middle course was fixed upon. We were to have a Hospital in town, and, when required, were to take the field with the German Ambulance Corps. Our services were gladly accepted by the Surgeon-

General, and two large Hospitals were at once handed over to us; the first—a sick and fever Hospital—containing 150 men; the second, consisting of the railway terminus, with its waiting and refreshment rooms, stores and offices, in which lay 65 wounded; and there were beds to accommodate 150 more. We received, therewith, Hospital plant, and a staff of trained military infirmarians. We were also given a liberal supply of provisions, which were dealt out to us and our wounded by requisition. On the morning of the 21st, Surgeon-General Dr. Von Nussbaum was present at the chemin de fer d'Orleans to make us acquainted with the former staff, who were now handing over their charge to us. Our installation was a very formal proceeding. The German Guard turned out, and saluted as we passed in.

This was the beginning of our labours at Orleans. As I have stated, it was at the railway terminus, which had been converted into a Hospital by the Prussians the day after they took possession of the town.

Entering from the Place in front of the station into the principal waiting-room, we passed through two lines of soldiers, drawn up at attention, and out on the platform. There were no carriages within the precincts of the terminus, but some dreary-looking trucks might be seen scattered about on the sidings, and, except a few men on guard at the coal depôt, there was not a human being within sight.

The terminus was covered, and of great extent. All the buildings connected with it were spacious, and fitted up in the ordinary way. We made ourselves at home immediately in the first-class waiting-room. Its sofas were placed back to back in the centre; and there were lines of beds at each side, every bed occupied by a wounded man. The second- and third-class *salles d'attente* were arranged in like manner, and as full as they could hold.

The next room was the Bureau des Inspecteurs, or the office of the railway directors. Here also there was a single row of wounded.

In the buffet there were double rows, and, as it was very spacious, the numbers it accommodated were proportionately great. In the ticket office were kept all the medical and surgical stores and requisites. In the telegraph office was the operation theatre, and in the station-master's private bureau the instruments to serve it were kept; there the surgeon on night duty remained during the period of his watch. In this room there was always a good fire, and outside the door paced up and down a German sentinel on guard.

At the other side of the platform, approached by the level crossing, we found the goods department, and the carriage, waggon, and engine depôt, which latter, in its general appearance, was nothing more or less than an immense shed, with open archways at both ends. In this most airy apartment lay, also, numbers of wounded.

When we pointed to several large holes in the roof (which had been made by falling shells a few days previously), and then to the open archways, suggesting to our friends that they were, perhaps, a degree too airy to be beneficial, Prof. Nussbaum informed us that the wounded in this place got better more rapidly than those in the Salles, who were kept warm, and completely protected from the weather.

We remained there nearly two hours, seeing the more interesting cases dressed, and then looked on at an operation by Nussbaum. As several of the parcel and lamp offices were also occupied by wounded, it may be conceived that the whole mass of buildings around the platforms made a very extensive hospital. It was a curious and novel sight, and for a long time afterwards I never entered a large terminus of the kind without speculating on the numbers of wounded that it would accommodate.

We were received very kindly by our German friends ; and before evening were in charge of the whole place, having an efficient staff of nurses to assist us, and to look after the wants of our invalids.

As we had now enjoyed a considerable experience in the working of a military field-hospital, it took us but a few hours to get into the routine ; and the Germans were evidently pleased at seeing how briskly we fell into line, and took up from them the whole management.

With regard to the Barrack across the river, which was full of sick and fever patients, it had been, I say, assigned to us ; but we never actually took it over. The German surgeons who were in charge had to join their field-hospital, which was about to move in the track of the army. Nor did the Bavarians possess any medical reserve in Orleans at this time, so that we came to their assistance at a juncture when we were much needed ; and they showed themselves extremely grateful. When, however, they were on the point of delivering up the second hospital to us, their orders to move were rescinded ; and we were saved, thereby, an amount of labour and responsibility, to which our limited staff would have been altogether unequal.

CHAPTER XV.

I WAS now promoted to be Assistant Surgeon by
our chief, and was given charge of seventeen
patients, under Dr. Mackellar. As much of the
doctor's time was employed in registering and
taking notes of the cases in Hospital, except when
he performed operations, I was virtually in sole
charge of my section, though under his supervision.

We breakfasted at 7·30, dined at 12·30, and
supped at 6·30; all our meals were abundantly
furnished at our quarters in the Quai du Châtelet.

With such hard work in hand, there was certainly need of substantial food, or we could never
have got through it. Every day brought us fresh
batches of wounded, and with them news of fresh
encounters, and skirmishes in the field.

On 23rd October, I had to perform my first
amputation. It was the removal of a portion of a
foot, which had been crushed by a waggon wheel.

The patient, I should explain, lay in a private house, at the rear of the Quai du Châtelet. Dr. Mackellar, who had kindly given me the operation, and Jean the Turco, assisted me. But when I had made the first incision, Jean bolted out of the room, and then tumbled downstairs in a faint.

I went on with my task ; but no sooner was it completed, than we were both taken aback on finding that my subject had been given an overdose of chloroform : his face was livid ; and it seemed that he had already ceased to breathe. In a moment, we flung the windows and door open, and were slapping him with cold wet towels, and using artificial respiration.

To my great relief, in a few seconds the poor man breathed freely again, and before long came back to himself. He made a very prompt recovery ; was convalescent, and able to hobble about on crutches in a fortnight, and had still a useful limb.

My patients increased daily, until from seventeen they became double that number. And at this time it was my duty to stay up every fifth night.

Three or four days now passed away in constant hard work, part of which consisted in rearranging and cleaning up the whole Hospital, which our predecessors had left in anything but an orderly state.

Later on, when I had time to go out, I saw

numbers of the Bavarian troops returning from the recent fighting,—dirty, foot-sore, and jaded ; they reminded me, in fact, more of French than of German soldiers. The campaign seemed to be taking an unfavourable turn for them. Occasionally, in the evening, the bands played in the Place Martroi, where the German officers and men were wont to assemble to smoke and chat. This was one of their customs at home which they had imported into France ; and by no means a disagreeable one. I heartily enjoyed the musical treat which they gave ; but I liked still better to listen while whole companies were singing glees in perfect harmony, during their bivouac under the trees on the Boulevards. There we saw them awaiting the assignment of their quarters with stolid patience, and cooking their food in cauldrons over wood fires, all to this delightful accompaniment, which showed them at their best.

All the German soldiers had a knowledge of music, and more than half were fairly well trained to sing. Nearly all the Infantry regiments in Orleans at this time were Bavarians ; but several detachments of the Prussian Cavalry regiments were likewise quartered in the town. I could never have imagined such a variety of uniforms and colours as I have seen among the hosts of the Emperor William. Let me recall a few of them.

There were Bismarck's Cuirassiers, in scarlet
and gold; a gorgeous uniform, the undress of
which (pure white) is, I think, no less becoming.
Then there were the Black Brunswickers, whose
uniform is like that worn by the Royal Irish
Constabulary, but who wear on their shakos an
emblem representing a death's head and cross
bones. Again, besides the dark blue with red
facings of the Prussian Infantry, and the Bavarian light blue with green facings, I could count
up Hussars of all colours, red, black, and white,
light blue, dark blue and gold, and the Würtem-
burg green. The German soldiers are certainly
a magnificent body of men, and, although at the
bottom of my heart my sympathies and affections
are altogether with the French, despite their
shortcomings, I am bound to declare the superi-
ority of their adversaries, as men of fine physique
and manly bearing, and of cool undaunted courage;
and I need not repeat how admirable is the
discipline under which they have been brought
to such perfection.

In 1870, the French did not realise that they
had to deal with an army the rank and file of
which not only was composed of the muscle and
sinew of the German people, but included their
best brains also. Perhaps the more observant of
the French writers, such as the late M. Renan,
or George Sand, might have summed up the war
as a contest of science against civilisation. Cer-

tain it is, that the highly wrought intelligence of the invaders was a force against which the Republic and the Empire alike contended in vain. The general run of soldiers from beyond the Rhine were well educated, and few, indeed, were unable to read and write. Those few might be found among the Bavarians—in my judgment, a slow, dull race, yet accustomed to fight in a dogged fashion, who neither went into action with the dash and ardour, nor ran away with the alacrity, of Frenchmen. Their movements were on system, and according to rule : they fought because they were bidden to fight, and mowed down the enemy, not from hatred of them, but because such were their orders ; and, if they did not take to flight, it was in the same spirit of passive obedience.

I should give the result of my impressions, therefore, somewhat as follows : Take no notice of a German soldier, and do not molest or interfere with him, especially when he is carrying out the orders of his superiors, and he will be as harmless as a child, and as easily pleased. But if, on the other hand, you do meddle with him, and stir up his rage on any pretext, his revenge will be no less prompt than terrible. In the battle-field, when once he is excited, he will use his bayonet and musket as a Zulu his assegai, or an Indian his tomahawk.

As for his manners, they are, at the best of

times, uncouth, **not to say** detestable, and when at meals, disgusting.   **He** is **an** enormous eater, caring not so much about the quality of what he devours, **so** long **as** quantity is provided; and though he drinks an amount of beer that would make any **other** European helplessly intoxicated, **he** is seldom drunk.   Nothing irritates him like hunger and **thirst; in** which circumstance **he** furnishes the **most** unpleasing contrast **to a** French soldier,—always patient, and commonly cheerful under such privations.   **When** suffering in this **way,** physically (which **seldom** occurred under the admirable organisation of **the** German commissariat), **he** would pillage **and plunder all** before him **to** get food or beer.   **For such de**-predations, when caught, **he was** mercilessly punished.   **And the** German soldier submits impassively to this treatment at the hands of his officer, **as if he were** a dog, without seeming to resent it.   I have seen officers and their subalterns on the quays of Orleans **strike their men re**-peatedly, and on parade drill make their recruits dress in **line, with the flat of** their broad-swords, —a disgraceful procedure, **to** which neither **an** English nor a French lad would **submit.   All** these features of the German system, as **brutal as it has** proved effective, I observed, long after **I had seen them at Orleans, in** the vivacious and sparkling pages of *Barry Lyndon.*   So little does the world change in a hundred and thirty years!

For some days no one but the military had appeared in the streets. All the shop windows in the town were closed, all business suspended; and the place, in these circumstances, had anything but a lively aspect. The Commandant, however, issued an order to all shopkeepers, obliging them, under pain of severe punishment, to take down their shutters, and open their establishments. In accordance with this regulation, on a certain day, before the appointed hour, down came all the shutters; but the display of goods in the windows amused me very much. In one, exhibiting a frontage of perhaps twenty feet or more, where silks, satins, and the most costly stuffs were usually spread out, now appeared in a tasteful arrangement several pieces of glazed calico, which were, it seemed, the only goods one could purchase in that establishment. Another equally large shop in the Rue Royale, a hardware house, exhibited as its stock in trade some dozen or so of rusty kettles, saucepans, and gridirons. In like manner did nearly all the other shopkeepers.

The pastrycooks, however, drove a roaring trade; their counters were crowded at all hours of the day with the conquering heroes, for Germans eat sweetmeats and confectionery as a cow munches young clover in the month of May. But the owners of these establishments were not at all particular as to the quality of the articles they provided.   I once walked into such a place, and was about to eat of some tempting-looking things in the way of tarts, when the man behind the counter recognised me, for we were acquaintances, and whispered that he would give me in a moment something more agreeable, instead of those greasy things, pointing to what was before him, which were made only for Prussians.   I ought to remark on the characteristic way in which Frenchmen, who are the most ignorant people in the world with regard to foreigners and their languages, called every stranger a Prussian, no matter of what nation he might be.

Meanwhile Orleans continued in a state of siege, and strict watch was kept on every one who moved about during the daytime.   After dark no one could walk abroad without being liable to be shot down by the sentries, who were placed at every hundred yards along the streets, unless he carried a lighted lantern.   I took great pleasure in listening to the bugles sounding the order for citizens to retire indoors at nine o'clock. Standing four abreast at the top of each street, the musicians sounded their call, which was a most plaintive and melodious strain.

Before going on with my narrative, I ought not to omit the curious proclamation, still on the walls of Orleans, which the Bavarian General, Von der Tann, had put forth after his capture of the city, October 13.   It ran as follows :—

" FRENCH CITIZENS!

" As I desire, so much as in me lies, to alleviate the burden of the population now suffering from the evils of war, I appeal to your good sense, and trust that the sincerity with which I address you will open your eyes to the real state of affairs ; and will persuade you to take your stand with the party of reason and peace.

" Your late Government declared war against Germany. Never was there a declaration more frivolous. Nor could the German armies do otherwise than reply by passing the frontier.

" They won victory after victory ; and your own army, deluded upon system, and demoralised, was all but annihilated.

" Another Government has arisen. We hoped that it would make peace. It has done no such thing. And why ? Because it feared for its own existence ; and, pretending that the German conditions were impossible, it has chosen to continue a war, the outcome of which cannot fail to be the ruin of France.

" Now, what are the conditions which they call impossible ?

" They are the restoration of those provinces that belonged to Germany, and in which the German language still prevails in town and country ; in other words, of Alsace and the German Lorraine.

" Is this proposal **too** much ?

" What conditions would a victorious **France** have exacted ?

" You have been told that the purpose of the German armies is to degrade France. That is simply a falsehood, invented to stir up and excite the masses.

" On the contrary, it is your Government which, by its conduct, is forcibly drawing on the German battalions into **the** heart **of** the country, and is leading up to the **ruin** which it will accomplish **if it persists in** itself degrading **that** fair France, **which might have** proved **to be the warmest friend of** the nation it has driven into hostilities.

" Orleans, 13th **Oct.,** 1870.

" BARON DE **TANN,**

" General of Infantry."

The olive-branch of this good General of Infantry, held out at the point of the sword to a people **than** whom a more touchy or sensitive does not exist, was hardly intended **to** produce an effect. Orleans was eagerly waiting all through that month and down to the 10th November, in the feverish expectation **of** succour from without, which **would** rid them of M. de Tann and his proclamations.

But day passed after day, until the monotony **of our routine was** broken **by** the astounding news, long foreseen, yet, when it came, overpowering, of the capitulation of Metz, with Bazaine, 3 Marshals, 66 Generals, 3000 cannon, and 173,000 men. It was the greatest surrender in history,—perhaps, the most flagrant act of treason.

Accounts given by the wounded stragglers, whom we daily received into our Hospital, told us that a desultory warfare, but no regular fighting, was going on between the opposing armies in our front. On one day, about November 3, two Bavarians were admitted, rather severely wounded. They related that in the direction of Blois, a party of skirmishers, with which they were serving, came upon, and surprised, a body of French, of whom, after a desperate fight, they captured two only, but left forty dead on the field. This, they stated, had taken place eight hours' distance (*i.e.*, 24 miles) from Orleans. A few days later, I received three others, who had been engaged in a similar small skirmish with the rear guard of the enemy. All three, by an odd coincidence, were wounded in the upper extremity. One Hussar had received a bayonet-thrust through the upper and fleshy part of his arm ; but, with a beaming smile, he related how he had cleft the Frenchman's head in two, while his opponent was in the act of making his thrust. The other two had bullet wounds in their arms, evidently received at close quarters.

On another day, two men were brought in,

who had been shot by a couple of Francs-Tireurs. These latter wore no uniform, and had coolly potted them from behind a hedge. Yet, as the following notice from General Wittich announced,—and it was a sample of others posted up throughout the country,—all such civilian aggressors were liable to the extreme penalty. "I declare to the inhabitants," so ran this document, "that all persons, not being soldiers, who shall be taken bearing arms against the German troops, or committing other acts of hostility or treason, will be irrevocably put to death. Only those will be considered as military who wear uniforms, or who are recognisable at rifle distance by distinctions not separable from the clothes which they have on."

In the general arrangement of our Hospital, and particularly in the nursing department, we were greatly assisted by a most generous and kind-hearted little Bavarian, named Leopold Schrenk, Captain in a Regiment of the Line. He used to come every day when off duty, and work in our Hospital, ready to help all round, but was of especial service in looking after the patients' rations. I have seen him making the beds of my wounded men, and washing their faces. This devotion to his suffering and wounded fellow-countrymen was admirable; but he displayed a hatred for all Frenchmen and Roman Catholics, and he detested priests, in a way which I could never account for, as it was very unusual among South Germans.   However, he behaved like a staunch patriot, and was a favourite with us all. When I parted from him he gave me his address and his photograph.

Some ladies who belonged to Orleans also came and distributed soup to the wounded; among them one who was by birth from Ireland, Madame O'Hanlon.   Actuated solely by motives of charity, they ministered alike to Prussians and French, with equal kindness and attention.

CHAPTER XVI.

As it is my object to exclude as much as possible professional details of my labours at the bedside, description of wounds, and the like, I shall again merely mention particulars of a few cases, in order to give my reader a general idea of the nature of the wounds received by soldiers in battle.

Take No. 6, for instance, as I find it in my notes. It was a very bad case. A German soldier of the Line had received a bullet wound behind and below the calf of his leg, which passed up, without touching the bone, behind his knee joint, beneath the muscles of the thigh to the joint of the hip. Having pursued this most extraordinary course, it lodged so deep beneath the muscles that neither the German doctors nor ourselves, to whom the case was handed over, could find the exact position of the bullet; yet I laid open its track in four or five places. Despite all treatment, he died eventually of blood-poisoning. On making a post-mortem examination, I traced the bullet actually into the abdomen, and still was unable to find it, although certain of its general position. These particulars I mention to show the unaccountable course a bullet may take after entering an extremity. There were dozens of similar curious cases, for which this may suffice as an example.

In another instance the bullet, having entered the right thigh and fractured the bone, carried along with it, impacted in its centre, a splinter of this bone, and pieces of the tunic and lining, as well as of trousers and shirt. It then entered the left thigh, lodging close to the skin on the outer side, from which I extracted the different fragments in the order just described.

By this time we had evacuated the large shed, which was now only occupied by those who suffered from pyæmia, or blood-poisoning. All the rest had comfortable quarters in different portions of the building; but these unfortunates were doomed to remain in the shed, though exposed to the biting frost and bleak winds of November. The simple reason was that their presence under the same roof with their comrades would mean certain death to all. When they had contracted this dread disease, which they chiefly did by infection, their only chance,—and a poor one it proved,—was to be placed in a current of fresh air. Hence their removal to this shed was commonly but their first step to the deadhouse.

This plague of the Field Hospital made great havoc amongst our men during the month of November in Orleans, as it had done at Sedan in September. The only instance of recovery after it, which came under my notice during the whole campaign, was that of the Bavarian named Martin Dilger; and his was of a very bad type. His thigh had been amputated ; and, when the symptoms set in, I sent him out to the shed, where he quickly became as bad as his comrades. I attended him several times every day ; but he speedily grew worse, until at last, his case seemed more desperate than all the others. The soft parts sloughed, leaving the thigh-bone protruding ; while the patient was almost comatose, and had that violent hiccough which is generally, in such cases, the forerunner of death. Several of my fellow-surgeons, moved by feelings of humanity, advised me not to put him to the useless pain and annoyance of dressing his stump, since he was *in articulo mortis*, and his recovery beyond the range of possibility. However, I resolved that while he lived, I would do as much for him as possible ; and I continued to dress his wounds.

Dilger had prolonged and repeated rigors, followed by profuse perspiration, and was generally of a bluish livid colour,—all symptoms of most deadly omen. I gave him as much brandy as he could take. and chloral every two hours, for the hiccough, which was so violent that it shook not only his whole frame, but the bed on which he lay. Yet, in a few days these rigors subsided ; he opened his eyes, and became conscious. In the face of such a decided improvement, I ventured the opinion that he would recover. He was now taking immense quantities of brandy, which was supplied from the stores, and broth which I had made for him in the town. Under this treatment his wounds took on a healthy action, his pulse and temperature came down, and rational speech returned, instead of his low muttering delirium ; my colleagues now admitted that his recovery was possible. I suffered him to remain in the shed, as I felt that his safety depended upon having him there. Some suggested his removal into a warm comfortable room in the town. Indeed, it was with difficulty that I turned a deaf ear to these suggestions, and overcame my own inclinations, when, on going to visit him on a cold November night, I heard the wind whistling through that goods store in the most melancholy manner, and the rain coming pitter-patter through the holes in the roof. Nevertheless, in this cave of Æolus he outlived all the others, and found himself at last its sole occupant.

This was my first case of pyæmia at Orleans, but it was to be quickly followed by many more. A Black Hussar, in the first-class waiting-room, developed it in a most virulent form, and died in twenty-four hours. That frightened me very much, and I trembled for the safety of the rest. So I had my wards washed out with a strong solution of carbolic acid immediately. What made me still more apprehensive was the awful fact that, out of seventeen patients in a neighbouring ward, all hitherto going on favourably, fourteen died in a very short time of this dreadful scourge. In spite of my precautions, I found a few days subsequently that one of my patients had severe rigors, followed by perspiration ; and bitter was my disappointment to see a case which had been going on splendidly, almost even to complete success, suddenly turn to the bad in a few hours. I had my man at once removed to the shed, and, as I well remember, on a biting November night ; but I had no choice. I would have put him out on the road-side, rather than have allowed him to sow the seeds of inevitable death amongst the rest of my patients.

The poor fellow had now plenty of company in his dismal quarters, for my colleagues had sent just as many out there as I had.

Not three days afterwards, a bright, handsome, fair-haired lad of about twenty, with a quick, piercing eye, and manly countenance, showed also the dreaded premonitory symptoms. I said nothing to him, but asked the Hospital sergeant to get two of his men and have him removed on a stretcher to the deadhouse. Such I can only call the place from which none that entered it came out alive, except in the single instance I have quoted. Shall I ever forget the moment when the *infirmiers* came, and that poor young lad, looking me wistfully in the face, read his doom in my silence? He knew what it meant. He had seen his comrades go, and had learned their fate, which was so soon to be his own. A few days later, I lost a fourth,—a good, pious fellow, who was continually telling his beads. His name was Johann Krum, particulars of whose case have been already given. He was a man that never smiled; and when I discovered that he had left a wife and three children at home, I pitied him greatly.

I am thankful to say that this was the last of my patients who succumbed to pyæmia. Any others whom I lost died from shock, hemorrhage, or the severity of their wounds.

The days went on, until we had reached the second week of November. Skirmishes with the enemy,—that is to say, with the French, who were advancing upon Orleans,—now became an everyday occurrence; and the number of wounded that came straggling in meant a very considerable loss to the Bavarians.

About this time, Dr. Pratt made a journey to Versailles, in quest of stores and money, leaving Dr. Tilghman in command. Inspector-General

Nussbaum made several visits to our Hospital, and expressed himself greatly pleased with the way in which it was conducted. The truth was that nobody could teach our veteran Americans anything new in the management of a Field Hospital. They had all served their time during the four years of the American War, and under a system of military medical organisation which, as all authorities acknowledge, they had brought to perfection. This was the secret of the undoubtedly successful career of our Ambulance. And I must not omit to observe that it was they who introduced the anterior suspension splint for fractures and wounds of the joints, which we were the means of having adopted in many of the German Hospitals.

To turn for a moment, before the Germans evacuate Orleans, to a subject on which their presence and behaviour often set me thinking. It was a fine sight when the Bavarians heard Mass in the great Cathedral, to mark them fully equipped in heavy marching order, as they stood in close military array in every available portion of the church, with sabres drawn, glittering helmets, and waving plumes. The officers, too, stood with drawn swords during Mass; and at the Elevation they gave, in their deep sonorous tones, the word to present arms. Altogether the spectacle, though not calculated to inspire devotion, was most impressive.

The Bavarians are, as a rule, good Catholics, and large numbers of them were to be seen at daily Mass, reading their prayers attentively, and going up to receive Communion. In the Hospitals also, they showed the same devout temper. Their Chaplains were zealous men, always at work among them, sharing their fatigues, and seeing that they attended to their religious duties. One of the infirmarians in the ward next to me, a common soldier, was in Holy Orders, though not yet a priest ; and a more saintly young fellow I never met. He was light-hearted and merry, had a pleasant word for every one, and fulfilled punctiliously the duties devolving upon him as a soldier, and as a minister of religion. In this matter, as in other things of less importance, the Bavarians struck me as very unlike the French. When you saw a French soldier in church (which was but seldom), he never seemed to utter a prayer. And I feel bound to set down my experience, that so long as I was among them, I never noticed a French soldier with a prayer-book ; nor did I ever hear one pray when dying. Others may have been more fortunate ; but such was the fact in my case, and I think it deplorable. But the average French citizen appears to think nothing at all of religion.

Far otherwise was it with the Bavarians. And I have seen large numbers, also, of the Prussians and North Germans, who belonged to the Evangelical or other Churches, reading their prayer-books and their Bibles in the Hospitals, and praying earnestly as a matter of course. These manifestly had religious convictions ; they served God with zeal and courage according to their lights. But in France the decadence of religion had been complete. No wonder, therefore, if she has fallen. Such, indeed, was the judgment of Europe a few months later, when the Commune, breaking out like a volcano, startled men from the Voltairean lightness which, during too many years of frivolity and thoughtlessness, had been the fashion. For a moment all were agreed in proclaiming the necessity of a return to the beliefs and practices of their Christian forefathers,—was it, perchance, too late ?

CHAPTER XVII.

ON 28th Oct. the inhabitants of Orleans had read
with dismay and amazement the official report,
printed and posted up as a placard on their walls,
of the surrender of Bazaine with his army, and
the capitulation of Metz. The majority were
of opinion that the Marshal was nothing but
a traitor. Many, nevertheless, whom I met,
scorned to entertain such an opinion; whilst
others went so far as to declare that the whole
thing was a German lie.

But to return to the subject of our Hospital.
The wounded, as I have already stated, came
straggling in by twos and threes, bringing with
them reports of numerous skirmishes, which, according to their accounts, invariably terminated in
victory for the Germans. On the 6th and 7th
November, large caravans of wounded came into
Orleans; and we now became aware, through
information gained from them, that the great

Army of the Loire, so much vaunted by the French, and which up to this moment we thought had existed only in the imagination of the townsfolk, was no myth, but a reality; while these convoys of wounded were the result of something far more serious than skirmishes between the outposts.

With all this there was very little excitement in the town; and the evening of the 8th arrived without anything happening to disturb the ordinary routine of our Hospital work. About eight o'clock our Chief was summoned to the head-quarters of the Bavarian Commandant. Here he was privately informed that the troops were going to evacuate Orleans that very night; that there would most likely be a general engagement on the morrow outside the town; and that, as they would be obliged to withdraw their Field Hospital corps and their surgeons, they laid upon our Ambulance the task of looking after all the wounded in their absence, and thus formally delivered them over to our charge.

When we heard of this most unexpected move, we were, as may be supposed, not a little excited. We could hardly believe that such a thing had happened to the ever-victorious armies of the Fatherland as a set-back, compelling them to give up this important position; and to describe our state of mind during that night would be difficult. I had gone to the Hospital about seven o'clock to see some patients, and all seemed quiet and peaceable. Now, I could not help thinking that it would be a sterling proof of the admirable organisation and discipline of an army amounting to 15,000 men, if, at a couple of hours' notice, it could evacuate, during the dead of the night, a large town like Orleans, carrying away arms, ammunition, and a heavy train of guns, without the knowledge of any but a few among the citizens. Some must have had their suspicions aroused by the preparations which were already being made in the Parks. But, until the appointed moment, when the bugle sounded, and the whole garrison turned out to join their regiments, by far the greater proportion of the inhabitants suspected nothing. Eleven o'clock P.M. was the hour appointed to commence the evacuation.

At half-past ten I took my stand at the door of 64 Quai du Châtelet; and as the clock tolled eleven, I saw the sentries on the bridges leaving their posts and filing off in the direction of the Place Martroi. Presently, battalion after battalion marched past, on their way from the quarters in the side streets which adjoined the Quai. To our great grief we found that our infirmarians were also ordered out, leaving not a soul in charge of the Hospital, except the two surgeons on duty and their assistants. These had to minister, as best they could, to the wants of the poor deserted patients. The truth was that the Germans

could not **spare a single man, and** were compelled
to take them along with the Army.

Some days before **this, the bridge** next us
had been mined, **and the** powder **laid ; we ex-**
pected that it would **be** blown **up** during the
night. As this bridge **was no** more than a
hundred yards from **my bedroom** window, I
retired **to rest with** such pleasant anticipations
as may be supposed. But, in spite **of the** excitement, I **was** quite **overcome by** fatigue, **having**
been at work all that **day, and on duty** the
previous night ; so that, in my **drowsy mood,**
I seemed to **care** little whether the bridge **or**
myself took an aerial flight. **Next** morning I
repaired **to the** Hospital at six to **look after my**
wounded. **On my way** through the **town I** was
astonished **to meet several** pickets marching
along the **streets ; but not** another soldier, save
a few sentries, was now in the place ; the latter
being left, as I **afterwards** heard, merely **to** keep
up appearances. Everything **that they** did not
want **to carry** away with them **the** Germans put
into a luggage train, which **started from** the
platform of **our Hospital** during **the** night.

Great excitement now **prevailed** among the
townspeople, and they **moved** about the streets
in crowds. All this **time** a heavy cannonade
was going **on at** the North-West **side,** in the
direction **of** Orme ; and the **din** and roll of battle
apprised **us** of the **fact that a** hot engagement

was being carried on not far off. Multitudes surged up on the bridge, and kept their gaze fixed in the direction of the fighting, which was indicated, not only by the booming of cannon, but by the wreaths of smoke which we could see many miles away, ascending in the still air. All these spectators chattered and gesticulated vehemently; nor could anything exceed their emotion. They ran about shaking each other by the hands in a fever of excitement, as the hour of their deliverance drew on apace. Once again I saw wreaths of *immortelles* placed upon the statue of the Heroic Maid, which stands with drawn sword by the river.

When we had got through our Hospital work, we received orders to prepare for an expedition to the field of battle. It had been determined, however, that, in any circumstances, we should return to the Hospital that night, and take up our medical duties again.

It was only now that we realised the awkwardness of our situation. Bound to stand our ground, no matter who might be victorious (though none of us anticipated the defeat of the Germans), the possibility of a French victory and a fresh occupation of Orleans by the latter, filled us with disquietude. We were under the direction of the foreigners, identified with their cause, receiving our orders from them. Our sympathies were supposed to be Prussian, while our Hospital and ourselves had been maintained by requisitions on the town. Hence the question arose, what kind of treatment should we receive at the hands of our new masters, when the last of the Germans had quitted Orleans? Would they, in the flush and the tumult of victory, overlook the fact that we were neutrals, engaged simply in alleviating the horrors of war? It seemed not to be impossible, so far as the population was concerned. But again, would the French military admit of our claims to be an International Ambulance? or take us prisoners and send us beyond the frontier? for they could not detain us under the Convention of Geneva. Such were our speculations when we left the town about 9 A.M. in our Ambulance waggons, and with our flags flying. Drs. Parker and Warren were left behind in charge of the Hospital. We took the road to Coulmiers, where the firing was heaviest, and from which place it appeared to be rapidly extending northwards.

As we passed along, the crowd on the bridge gave us a friendly cheer, and I cannot recall a salutation that caused us more pleasure. The town was still in the possession of the Germans, although their only representatives were an under officer and a handful of men on sentry duty, who could at any moment have been easily overpowered by the mob. As our conveyances rolled through the gate of the Faubourg St.

Jean, leading out into the open country, we were surprised to find a solitary German on guard, who saluted us as we passed. Probably he was even then convinced of his approaching fate; but he knew his duty too well to abandon his post. There, as Dr. Warren afterwards told us, he remained until the French came and relieved him of his guard for ever.

In half an hour from our exit, we came up with a Bavarian battalion, consisting of a regiment of 2000 men, about 300 cavalry, and a battery of guns. Many of the officers were old friends of ours, and received us very kindly. They were short of surgeons, and prevailed on us to stay with them; saying that every minute they expected to be called into action, and to receive their orders to advance. Our position, at this time, was close in the rear of the fighting Bavarian army, and within sight of the field of battle.

Thus it was that we were placed on the high road, upon a little rising ground which commanded a view of the country between Baccon and Coulmiers. Thence we saw that a fierce battle was raging, a host of above 60,000 Frenchmen giving fight to perhaps some 15,000 Bavarians. The result of so uneven a match became evident very early in the day. A short time after noon, the South Germans had retreated from their position in the woods and village in front of us, and the

French were appearing in **force** on the ground that their opponents had occupied an hour previously.

The firing was now vigorous and incessant: the din **and** roar of **battle were** something **tremendous**; and the French bombshells fell short of us only by a few hundred yards. Our party, **which was** halting in ambush, and as yet un**perceived by the** enemy, **every** moment expected **the** order **to** advance. For ourselves the **sus**pense was most painful, and yet **we** had to remain there stationary **for** as much as **an** hour. During all this time the men **were** in their ranks, ready for action. In **that vast** concourse not **a** word was spoken: all appeared sullen and out of spirits; but that sullenness was usual with **them.** Some, overcome by fatigue and hunger—for they had not tasted anything but the bread which they carried since the previous night—slept soundly **just as they** were, leaning back on their knapsacks. While these **slept,** the others watched their **comrades** being picked off on the plain below, apparently without **the** smallest concern **or** excitement. Thus did they placidly view the **course of the** battle, awaiting their turn **to** join **in** the fray, and add to the number **of** the dead or dying.

About three o'clock the artillery fire slackened, and **we** joined in the general backward movement which took place along the whole line. The rattle **of musketry** resounded on every side of us, **and** was kept up without intermission. The Bavarians, though fighting hard, were now rapidly losing ground; and the French were not only advancing as fast as they gave way, but threatening to close in upon them all round. They were likewise striving to outflank them on the right; so that, by half-past three, the German soldiers found themselves compelled to retreat, though fighting still, lest the enemy should effect this object. Thus, with the Loire at our back, we had only a narrow strip of country between us and Orleans, by which to make good our escape. The French, who swarmed along in every direction, fought desperately; and, in particular, one regiment of Chasseurs à Pieds and Gardes Mobiles made a most brilliant charge against the trained Bavarian veterans, who were occupying in force the heights of Renardier. From this place they dislodged the Teutons, who had then to join our force in the general retreat.

By four o'clock on this autumnal day it was quite dark. The firing gradually ceased, and the French remained in possession of all they had captured. Now on the Bavarian side there was a general order given to retreat; it was obeyed with alacrity. We followed the defeated army for some distance; but when we learned that Étampes was their destination, and that the German troops were utterly to abandon Orleans, we parted company with them; for under any circumstances, and at all risks, we were bound to return to our Hospital. From the first sound of the retreat, which was carried out in quite an orderly but still in a precipitate manner, we expected every moment to hear the French Cavalry coming down upon us. It had been rumoured that they were present in great force. This pleasant expectation compelled us to hasten our steps, but neither we nor (as it turned out afterwards) any of the German troops experienced the least molestation in our rapid retreat. What was the explanation of so remarkable a pause in pursuit, considering that General d'Aureilles de Paladine had a host of mounted men at his command? We were told by the French that it was the result of interference on the part of M. Léon Gambetta, who forbade Paladine to follow up his victory. M. Gambetta suspected that the flight of the Bavarians was a ruse to entice the French into a trap. He dreamed that they had an auxiliary force somewhere in the neighbourhood, which might surround the Army of the Loire, and bring about its irreparable ruin. Whatever may have been the reason, certain it is that the Bavarians were saved from annihilation. They retreated that night in perfect safety, and were joined next day by the Grand Duke of Mecklenburg. They had allowed the French to gain a victory, which proved to be their first and last in this sanguinary contest.

CHAPTER XVIII.

AFTER THE BATTLE.—ORLEANS FROM WITHOUT AND
WITHIN.—THE MOB AND THE AMBULANCE.—
THE BAVARIAN GIANT.

OUR duty was now to return to the battlefield,
and render all the assistance we could to the
wounded, so forthwith we retraced our steps ;
and, though our day's experience, owing to circumstances over which we had no control, had
not been very fruitful of work, it was fraught
with much strain and anxiety. The night was dark,
but we had no difficulty in making out our way,
the numerous camp fires in front serving us as
beacons. We pushed on to the scene of the
day's conflict, Tilghman and Sherwell riding
ahead, to see that the route was clear.

One part of the road had a shrubbery at the
left hand side ; and, just as we came to the
corner of it, we perceived a figure standing
amongst the bushes. As we approached, the
man stepped forward, and the light of our
waggon lamps revealed the uniform of a French
soldier. He challenged, and brought us to a halt.
The difficulty of our situation was now apparent.

We were about to enter the French lines, having served the Germans all day in a medico-military capacity, and having come from their headquarters at Orleans.

A patrol on outpost duty quickly appeared on the scene, and we were detained some time until an officer was brought up. Having questioned us about all these particulars, and heard our replies, he informed us that it would be necessary to conduct us to headquarters, and take us into the presence of the General, before he could permit us to go on our way. At the same time he showed us the utmost courtesy. We were now surrounded by a strong escort, and had no choice but to follow. We soon came in sight of the French camp, and as we passed by the rows of cheerful blazing fires, around which were clustered, in merry groups, the victors of the day, the ring of their mirth and revelry contrasted with the deep gloom which had hung both upon ourselves and our German colleagues since morning.

This great army was reckoned at 100,000 men, who now lay in the open plain under canvas. We passed along through several regiments of the Line, of Turcos, Zouaves, and Gardes Mobiles, all in excellent trim, and as jolly and pleasant as possible. They did not at all appear to be the undisciplined rabble which the Germans had represented to us. A rare opportunity was now given of contrasting the relative strength of these opposing armies; but on this subject no inquiries were made. On the contrary, we received orders not to exchange a word on the matter.

Singing, eating, and drinking, appeared to be everywhere the business of the night. Presently we came to a halt before M. de Paladine's tent; and our chief, Dr. Tilghman, was conducted alone into his presence. The doctor told him exactly what our position was; and how we had left our quarters at Orleans to come and assist the wounded on the battlefield. Our duty had been to pick up any that had escaped the notice of the military surgeons, and to get them into the neighbouring houses. But, said Dr. Tilghman, we were bound to return to Orleans next day, and resume charge of our wounded. This was a difficult matter to settle; for, as the French had not followed up their victory, they were still under the impression that Orleans was in German hands, nor could we undeceive them. The question was, would it be safe to let us go back when we had been through the camp of the French, and had made observations on their position? Upon this head Dr. Tilghman speedily received a satisfactory answer. General de Paladine observed courteously that, in dealing with us, he had to deal with English and American gentlemen, who had already given abundant proof of their honour and the integrity of their word. In short, when Dr.

Tilghman had shown all his papers, and the testimonials of past services rendered to the French,
the old General was profuse in his acknowledgments, being evidently in high good humour over
his day's success.

When the interview came to an end, the
members of the 5th Ambulance received us most
cordially, and invited us to mess with them.   But,
after some deliberation, Dr. Tilghman, thanking
them for their kindness, and deeming our position
an awkward one, determined immediately to re-
trace his steps to Orleans, from whence he could,
on the following day, send waggons to take as
many of the wounded as possible into the town.
He had good reasons for thus acting, and without
waiting for a morsel of bread or a glass of wine,
we moved out of the camp on our way home-
wards.

In a large space, near the General's quarters,
lay the bodies of several Bavarians—perhaps a
dozen, some of whom had their faces turned up as
they were lying, and looked very ghastly.   Outside the camp, the ground was strewn, in some
places quite thickly, with the Bavarian soldiers
who had fallen on that day, which had proved so
disastrous to their arms.   The sight, though no
longer strange, was all the same a sad one to us,
for we had begun to look upon the wearers of the
light blue uniform with friendly fellow-feeling,
and we seemed (so fast does the time run in a cam-

paign) to have been long associated with them. I shall not here describe the battlefield, since my view of it, by the light of our lamps and of the moon (for a beautiful moon arose just in time to show us the way home), was, of necessity, rather limited. But, in any case, I doubt the possibility of depicting, as they really present themselves, the details of a battlefield. Who can do justice to the heartrending scenes of warfare as carried on with modern weapons, the chief excellence of which seems to consist in the degree of mutilation which they can inflict on the bodies of those against whom they are directed?

Before relating our entrance into Orleans, I will give Warren and Parker's account of what had happened in the town after our departure.

As the day advanced, and rumours were spread of a French victory, the excitement of the townsfolk knew no bounds. They rushed frantically about in all directions, but did not dare to interfere with the few soldiers on guard at the gates of the Mairie and at the Hospital.

In the afternoon, however, when it became generally known that the Germans were retreating, not towards the town but in the direction of Étampes, the populace became most riotous, and from the manner in which they menaced the unfortunate guards, it was plain that their lives were in great danger. At our Hospital, indeed, where there were ten men on guard over some Ambulance waggons at the door, the mob met with a stern opposition. The German soldiers stood together, with their swords drawn, and, bidding defiance to the crowd, were determined not to budge an inch, but rather to die than relinquish the charge assigned to them.

These brave fellows, who stood so resolutely by their post, would most assuredly have met with a violent death at the hands of the Orleaners, had not the Mayor sent out a *Parlementaire*, accompanied by a body of the Gendarmerie of the town, and requested them, in the name of the Government of National Defence, to lay down their arms. This they did willingly, as they saw the danger of their position, and so they were taken off as prisoners to the Mairie. A great crowd followed, howling and yelling in the most disgraceful manner during the whole journey.

Just about the time when the sentries were removed, the blue blouses rushed into our Hospital and seized all the rifles which they could lay hands on. The wards and other offices of the railway terminus now presented a scene of unutterable confusion. Drs. Warren and Parker, like true Britons, in spite of all this, remained at their posts ; they refused to allow any of the mob to enter our store-rooms, or private Bureaux, and, although repeatedly threatened, would not submit to the intrusion. But their demeanour was so calm and steady that they experienced no rough usage. Their situation during that tumultuous day was certainly far from enviable. In the forenoon, several officers who had been wounded, and were in consequence left behind, came to our men entreating them to keep their swords for them, or else to let them hide them in our store-rooms. This request we were bound to refuse; but they succeeded in putting their weapons away among some bedding, which was lying in the waggon sheds at the terminus.

A very amusing incident occurred at this time. There was a young Bavarian officer, the tallest man I have ever seen except one (who was, of course, an Irishman), who had been slightly wounded in the hand. For this reason he had been left on duty in the town, and not seeing any way of escape, slipped into our Hospital in the afternoon; but, finding that the mob was becoming riotous and might at any moment discover him, he divested himself of his helmet, cuirass, and uniform—he belonged to the house-hold cavalry—which Drs. Warren and Parker consented to stow away in a corner. But in vain did they search for a bed long enough to cover the prostrate form of their giant; and it was only by stratagem that they succeeded at last in concealing him. The young man spoke English well, and was evidently by birth a gentleman. I cannot recall his name. Hardly was he settled in his hiding-place when, as Dr. Warren told us, some of the mob rushed wildly through the Hospital; whereupon the doctor sat down leisurely on the bed beneath which our hero lay half smothered. When the tumult had somewhat subsided, and darkness set in, our brave cuirassier, bruised and sore from the hard boards, at length was allowed to creep out.

He now donned a suit of peasant's clothes, or rather two suits, for it took all that to cover him, and even then, as the Irish proverb has it, he looked " like a crane in a crate ". All this notwithstanding, he appeared in his disguise every inch a soldier, and a German to boot. For a heavy bribe he procured a donkey cart, in which he seated himself, with legs crossed on some bundles of fuel, and a carter's bullock whip in his hand, and thus set out on his perilous journey. Having arrived safely outside the town, he took to his heels, and by-and-by chartering an old worthless animal from a peasant, reached the German headquarters in Étampes. It will be of interest to state that, subsequently, at the retaking of Orleans, this officer was one of the first to greet us on entering the town ; and his satisfaction at recovering his helmet, cuirass, and accoutrements was unbounded.

CHAPTER XIX.

OUR AMBULANCE RETURNS.—ENTRY OF THE FRENCH.
—THEIR DISHEVELLED APPEARANCE AND DIS-
ARRAY.—WE ARE SENT OUT OF THE RAILWAY
STATION.

Now that I have given a rough sketch of some
of the experiences of Drs. Parker and Warren,
to whom I am indebted for the foregoing particulars, I must return to our Ambulance cortège,
which I left in the moonlight making its way
back to Orleans at the dead of the night.

About an hour after our interview with the
General we found ourselves in the open country,
whence we could see the glare in the sky thrown
up by the numerous fires in the French camp
which we had just quitted. The early part of
the night had been bright and fine, but ere long
we had to encounter a storm of wind, hail, and
rain. For some time we had much difficulty in
picking our way, as the roads were narrow and
winding, as well as rugged. Calling at the few
peasants' houses which we passed, in order to
get directions, we found the inhabitants in a
frenzy of fear, and either unwilling or incapable

of assisting us.   We learned, subsequently, from the **owner** of Château **Renardier**, that they **took** us **for** Prussians, and **our** French *infirmiers* for spies.   When we had gone past **these** scattered dwellings, **we** came at length on the **broad** *route Impériale*, which we needed only **to** pursue in order to arrive at our **journey's** end.   Frequent were our surmises **as to whether** the **French or the** Germans, or either, **were in** occupation **of Orleans.** After what had **happened** that day, **and** especially as the **Army of the Loire** seemed **to be** making no effort **to advance, we** could **none of us** tell what the case **within the city might be.   We** drew **near** anxiously, but observed that **no** pickets had been set, **nor were we** challenged by **outposts** or sentries.   **This led us to imagine that** the **place was no longer in** the **occupation of** the Germans ; **for** otherwise we never should have come thus **far** without being halted by their numerous sentinels.   Outposts, we knew, would have been planted along the **roads for** miles outside **the town by** them ; **whereas** experience told **us** that the **present state of things** was not **in** the least incompatible with **a French** occupa-tion, and with French military tactics.

We passed **on unmol**ested until we got to the **same gates** by which we had come out that morning.   Then, **at last, as** we entered, the challenge **came, and we** were brought to a standstill.   **We all now tried to** catch a glimpse of the sentry in the darkness; we advanced slowly, and our lamps revealed a slight, well-built man, in a grey tweed uniform and tan leather leggings, with a Tyrolese, or kind of wide-awake hat, surmounted by a feather, set on the side of his head. Clearly this was no German. With his rifle slung across his shoulder in the most nonchalant manner, he put his questions to us. Who were we, whence had we come, and whither were we going? Having satisfied himself upon these points, he leisurely blew his whistle, and quickly brought to his side about half a dozen men similarly clad, accoutred and armed. One of these turned out to be an Englishman, who conversed freely with us, and was most polite, giving our chief the password. He informed us that they were a body of Francs-Tireurs, who had come from the country across the Loire, and had occupied the town a few hours before nightfall. They numbered only a hundred, and with the exception of a company of Gardes Mobiles, there were no regulars in the town. On the way to our quarters we were several times challenged by pickets patrolling the streets, but giving the password we were allowed to go forward, and so reached our quarters, thoroughly worn out, at three in the morning.

Dr. Sherwell and Mr. Adams were immediately sent to the Hospital to relieve Parker and Warren, who came back to the Quai du Châtelet and reported the thrilling incidents which had happened while we were away, some of which I have endeavoured to set down above. We were given only a brief interval for sleep. At an early hour we had to be up and about the Hospital, dressing and attending to the wounded, who had suffered considerably in our absence, not so much from lack of surgical aid, as from want of food and drink. For all the military nurses had been drawn away; and the onerous task of giving them food and looking after them had devolved on Parker and Warren, a duty which, in spite of all difficulties, they did their utmost to fulfil. Much credit is due to these gentlemen for their brave and noble conduct upon that memorable day. By their coolness and determination they made all safe for their helpless patients, and protected them from the violence, which might easily have gone to great excess, of the rabble of Orleans.

About ten o'clock on the morning of the 10th, Mackellar, Wallace, and our acting chief, Dr. Tilghman, went out with their waggons to the battlefield about Coulmiers and Baccon, and picking up some thirty-three badly-wounded men brought them into the city. We were much distressed to hear from them, how, on going over the battlefield, one of the first bodies which met their gaze was that of a young Bavarian surgeon, who used to work with us at the railway terminus when we first came. The poor fellow lay on his back, his face turned up, stripped of his boots and trousers, which no doubt had been appropriated by some plundering Frenchman, who was in need of both. It is incidents like this which bring home to one the horror and the waste of war.

That same morning, when business required me to go through the town, I was astonished to see the motley collection of French soldiery which had flocked in from all quarters. It was not their numbers which surprised me,—I had set eyes on the Grande Armée of Sedan,—but the variety of uniforms, and the quaint un-military get-up of the individuals who composed this array of M. Gambetta's. Many in the first regiment that passed along seemed to be half in German and half in French costume. One fellow had put on a pair of Bavarian trousers and boots, another had a complete French costume all but his helmet, another German sidearms and belt, or a French uniform and a Bavarian plume. The trousers and boots of the enemy appeared, how-ever, to be in greatest demand. Fully one third of the new-comers were raw recruits, and little more than boys. To complete the incongruity of the scene a large *American* flag was borne upon a staff as the standard of this regiment, having the words " Liberté, Egalité, Fraternité " stamped on pennants which hung from each corner.

One could not help smiling as one watched this miscellaneous rag-tag collection marching past.   We asked one fellow where they were going; he answered gravely, " To Paris, in order to crush (*écraser*) the Germans ".   After these came a regiment of poorly clad boys, looking cold and weary, as well as homesick.   Some of the latter had wooden shoes, in which they clogged lamely along the pavements, in a slouching style that was by no means soldierlike.   Then followed, by way of a redeeming feature, one of the regiments of the Line, in which every man bore himself splendidly.   After these, we remarked companies of Francs-Tireurs, and detachments of the Garde Mobile, who marched along in the haphazard manner of civilians during a public procession.   One youth, possibly a half-witted fellow, or a volunteer who had joined *en route*, made me laugh heartily.   He was dressed in full Bavarian costume, plume and all, and marched along bearing a most impassive countenance, quite unaware of the ridiculous figure he was cutting, in a uniform that was much too big for him, and in a helmet and plume which no doubt became their original broad-faced owner, but certainly never were meant to adorn the head of a thin and sharp-featured Frenchman.   How it came about that these fellows were permitted by their officers, for very shame, to make such a spectacle of themselves, I did not understand, until an intelligent townsman let me into the secret of the soldiers' wardrobe, by assuring me that the men's boots and clothes were made for sale rather than use, and were all thoroughly rotten.

The excitement and enthusiasm of the towns-people were, as I need hardly say, beyond description. They rushed about shaking each other by the hands, and swearing to do terrible things on the Prussians, when their troops had once got into Germany.

Early in the afternoon, during the entry of the French divisions, no less amusement than bustle was created at our quarters on the Quai du Châtelet, by our Turco Jean rushing wildly up the town, in his white apron and cap, with a rifle in his hand, to meet the regiment of his fellow-Turcos, which, as some one had told him, was among the arrivals. He went as on wings to the Place Martroi, and finding that such was indeed the case, threw himself into the embraces of his companions. These were also in a fever of excitement. They crowded round the statue of Joan of Arc, and waving turbans on the points of their bayonets, yelled as loudly as their throats would suffer them : " Vive l'Empereur ! A bas la République!" Had they been natives they might have been shot for sedition. In this little episode Jean cut the most ludicrous figure, entering into the demonstration heart and soul ; for like every Turco, he dearly loved his Imperial master. Even now, when all was over, the Turco was still his devotedly attached friend, and scorned to conceal his loyalty towards the man for whom he had fought with such valour and desperation. It may perhaps be asked whether to introduce these Algerian barbarians into civilised warfare was not as great a crime as the employment, during the last century, of Red Indians by the English and French in North America. Their appearance at the statue of the Maid was certainly in a high degree picturesque.

I am, of course, incapable of describing the varied scenes of excitement which greeted the soldiers on every side. How long would such an army keep its hold on Orleans, I asked myself as I moved about, bewildered by the seething crowds. Not long, it seemed to me. When later in the day, every café was crowded with soldiers, they appeared to be feasting freely in order to make up for past short commons. All seemed thoughtless, gay, and oblivious of danger. Nor did they care one jot, apparently, what had become of the Germans. Truly, these French are an astonishing people!

In my short walk from the Quai du Châtelet I could not have seen less than ten thousand men, and again I was struck by the contrast between the soldiers of the two nations. In the stunted and undeveloped make of these youthful French levies, any observant spectator, though not a physician, might have beheld the offspring of parents who had overtaxed their vital energies by dissipation and luxury. Physical degeneration had set in among the inhabitants, not of the large towns only,—such as Marseilles, Lyons, and Paris, or Roubaix and St. Étienne,—but in the rural parts of the country likewise, ever since the days of the Revolution. Napoleon's wars had consumed the men of France during his twenty campaigns. But that was not all. I have spoken of the decay of religion; it was a patent fact; and, with religion, morality had seen its own influence decline. Legal restrictions on the disposal of property had given strength to the system, whereby married persons limited their families according to their means and social position. That is the undoubted cause of the estrangement between the average layman and the Catholic clergy that has so long prevailed; for against this system the clergy have set their faces, as they were bound to do. With such parents, and especially when their fathers set them the example, it was not to be wondered at if the growing lads had put away religion at an early age, and so lost the moral restraint which would have enabled them to turn out valiant men, sound in mind as in body, and a match for any Germans. Their sunken eyes and pinched faces, their whole bearing, indeed, told a very different tale. We were looking on, in those unhappy days, at the wreck of a population which, in shame and defeat, was paying the penalty of laws not to be broken with impunity.

So much for the rank and file. As regards the singular want of courage no less than competency among their officers, it may with truth be affirmed that one of the main factors, in addition to those already mentioned, was the total neglect of early training, and the absence of that physical education which tends to a manly development. This system, which characterises public school life in England and Germany, and which results for the most part in a straightforward character, and an undaunted temper, had not then been introduced into France. It is now not unknown there, and will perhaps change the disposition of the coming generations. Many tokens there are to prove that such a change is greatly needed.

Towards evening equal confusion and consternation was caused by our receiving an order from the French Commandant to evacuate the railway station in two days. We were told that we must by that time have all our wounded taken away. Dr. Tilghman protested that we could not complete the evacuation of the buildings in less than four days, and we were allowed the time required, but informed that as traffic would recommence immediately, our business was at once to clear out of the stationmaster's and superintendent's offices, which we did forthwith.

On the next morning, the 11th, a long train

full of people arrived on the platform. They were the first passengers we had seen since our coming to the place. The change now suddenly wrought was wonderful. Where up to this we had been masters, and where the profound silence had for a long time been broken only by the chat of the medical staff, or by the groans and cries of the wounded, we were now jostled about on a densely crowded platform, and could hardly hear our own voices, so great were the din and clamour of passengers endeavouring to secure seats in an outgoing train, or to get their luggage from the one which had just arrived. I enjoyed the novelty of the thing much, although the shrieking of railway whistles, and the hissing of the steam-engines were no pleasant sounds to have continuously in one's ears.

While we remained, I saw numbers of French soldiers going round to the beds of our wounded Germans and shaking hands with them. These friendly enemies tried to convey their meaning by signs and gesticulations ; they gave away their tobacco ; arranged the beds ; and did many other little acts of kindness, which were received with no less good will by the Germans. It was a pretty sight. On one matter French and Bavarians seemed of one opinion, which the latter expressed in their quaint phrase of " Bismarck Caput ". "Caput," that strong man armed undoubtedly had proved himself to be.

It was whilst standing on the platform awaiting the arrival of a train when I had finished my Hospital work, that I saw the new Dictator, M. Léon Gambetta. I knew him at once from the description that had been given me. He was speaking in low, earnest tones to an elderly gentleman, a member of the Provisional Government, and when I had surveyed his by no means elegant form, and caught from beneath a pair of prominent and bushy eyebrows several glances of his dark piercing eyes, I came to the conclusion that his appearance was not at all prepossessing. His military discernment on the day of Coulmier, which had saved the Bavarian army from total ruin, I have mentioned in its place. I never saw him again.

Our chief was now busily engaged looking out for a building, public or private, in which we could establish our Hospital. After much difficulty, a large and spacious mansion, belonging to a gentleman named D'Allaine, was placed by him at our disposal, and thither we determined to transport our wounded as soon as practicable. The house was situated off the Place du Grand Marché, behind the Quai du Châtelet ;—that being the old market-place, and one of the most ancient parts of the town. It had one great advantage ; it was only a few minutes' walk from our quarters. The authorities also put at our disposal the Caserne St. Charles, a large building across the river. We despatched the greater part of our invalids into that caserne at once.

The first man to be sent out of the railway station in order to make room for the traffic was Martin Dilger, the surviving tenant of the goods-shed, to whose successful battle for life I have already alluded. His almost miraculous recovery made him better known to my colleagues than all the rest; and though I had upwards of twenty at that time under my charge, he commonly went by the name of "Ryan's man". I had taken particular care of his food, getting him meat, wine, and fruit as I could, and even that great rarity, a chicken, which latter was not easy to come at, especially if there happened to be Turcos about, for at stealing poultry these Africans are worse than foxes. Dilger was quite strong and merry when I removed him to D'Allaine's house. He showed his delight and gratitude in every possible way, often alluding to his condition when in the shed at the railway station; and he had a somewhat German habit of making me laugh by hiccoughing in order to recall to me that painful symptom from which he had suffered. He has since written to me several times, and I will give a specimen of his letters in due course. The poor fellow had left at home a wife and children, which was no slight addition to his other troubles.

As great numbers of wounded were being brought into the town, and it was difficult to find accommodation for them, we hastened to get the Caserne St. Charles ready, and received into it a large batch of them. These were principally Germans, sent to us by reason of our previous association with their armies. When we had got everything here into working order, conceive our amazement and wrath on hearing that Dr. Tilghman had been told immediately to evacuate the Barracks! Room was to be made for the Foreign Legion. There was no alternative; remonstrance would have been waste of time ; and we put our hand to this fresh and most provoking move. While it was being carried out, as the wounded must be taken to our Hospital at D'Allaine's, Dr. Parker and I were busily employed in transporting them across the town, using for this purpose every available conveyance. Thus we were compelled by the French authorities to take out of their beds, as best we could, men in dire agony, some even at the door of death, and all severely wounded.

I could not recall without pain the details of the scenes which accompanied their transportation. As I have said, their wounds were all of the gravest character ; some were mortal, the majority were amputations, and the remainder compound fractures, or severe lacerated shell wounds. To shake the bed of many of these patients, or even to move them gently, was to cause them acute suffering. One may imagine the agony of these brave fellows when they were hauled out on their mattresses and put, two or three together, into a cart or waggon, which, no matter how carefully driven, had to jostle them along the weary streets to their place of destination.

I went successively into several of the waggons where some of the worst cases were, and did all in my power to mitigate their dreadful pains; but, in spite of everything I could do, they moaned most piteously as the wheels bumped over any roughness in the pavement. I thought a bullet through the heart was preferable to such agony as they endured. Even to look on at it was too much.

About 18th November, we had completely evacuated the Station. The last batch consisted of those who had been lying in the refreshment rooms, and, as these apartments were not required by the railway officials, they did not oblige us to remove our wounded in such precipitous haste. Every day fresh supplies of wounded were being brought in; and not only every available nook and corner in our Hospital was occupied, but also many of the neighbouring houses. It was, however, expressly forbidden by the public authorities that any house should harbour the military, whether wounded or not, unless a declaration of their presence had been made, and leave obtained.

Our work was now very heavy and our energies tasked to the utmost. Besides the evil of overcrowding, we had to contend against the innumerable difficulties consequent on our having been ordered about from one place to another without notice, or sufficient time to make preparations for departure. Then upon getting into our new quarters we had to re-establish our culinary and commissariat departments, on which everything depended, as well as to re-organise the system of Hospital management, and put the whole into working order. Until this was effected (which would take about a week) our whole day's work was nothing but a scramble from morning till night. Our chief was completely distracted from constantly receiving orders to have certain things done, and then (as in the case of the Caserne St. Charles) just when he had accomplished them, and was settled down, getting fresh orders countermanding the first. All this was thoroughly French,—at least, it was quite in accordance with our experience of their system.

For the first few days after the return of the French, the revelry and rejoicings of the townspeople were excessive. From the appearance of the streets, the bustle, and the dense crowds, one would have thought that some great festival was being celebrated. It was astonishing to hear these people talk and boast of their glorious victory of Coulmiers—the first they had gained, and, as it was to prove, also the last. But it would sadden the heart of any lover of France to witness these frivolities, these humiliating follies of her vain-glorious and light-hearted citizens, who never seemed to think seriously of anything, no matter how grave the issue.

Soon, however, the bustle in the streets subsided, and the military became comparatively few in number; many had gone to the front. But there was an evident intention of making a stand at Orleans, should the main body of the army be compelled to fall back again. I saw hundreds of men hard at work erecting barricades and earthworks across the faubourgs ; while trenches and rifle pits were cut in all directions through the vineyards which lay about the suburbs of the town. An order was issued by the Commandant to leave the tall vine stakes standing, so that they might hinder the progress of the enemy, should they re-invest the place. If I may be allowed to anticipate, these very stakes were a most serious impediment to their own retreat before the Germans during the following month. Wherever they are abundant in vine-growing districts they make the country impervious both to cavalry and artillery, and form a splendid ambuscade for infantry troops in action. But the disadvantages of them from another point of view seem to have been overlooked.

It was a source of deep regret to me, during this campaign, that I was not better posted on military matters ; for, had I been acquainted even with the rudiments of war tactics, the numerous and important military operations which were carried on immediately under my observation would have been intelligible to me without the aid of an expert, and that blank which now must be left in this slight record might have been filled up with many most interesting details.

The few convalescents who had acted as our *infirmiers* and attendants, and with whom we had been working the Hospital since the evening of the 8th,—at which time, as the reader will not have forgotten, all our regular nurses and *infirmiers* were drawn away for active service— were now sent off to Pau as prisoners of war. This we thought unwise and intolerable ; but it was done in spite of remonstrances on our part that such dealing was nothing less than a violation of the Geneva Convention. What did we get in their place ? Simply a scratch company of French *infirmiers*, whom we had much difficulty in knocking into shape, and whom we found by no means so ready to submit to discipline as had been their German predecessors. One of the new arrivals was a little fellow named Jack, by birth a native of Flanders, but who had been all his life on board a ship in the British Merchant

Service, and who had had the top of a finger shot off.   He had joined the Foreign Legion, not, as he told us, from any liking for war or for France, but in order to be with an old companion who had joined that corps.   He was quite a little dwarf, and unsuited to hospital work ; but his superiors, deeming him, I daresay, no great ornament to his regiment, had handed him over to us as an *infirmier*.   Besides his native language, he spoke English, French, and German fluently, and professed to be able to converse in Spanish and Italian.   This might have been of service to us in an emergency ; but the following anecdote will show what a treasure we had got in our Fleming.

One night Dr. Mackellar and I were on duty with Jack when a case of extensive contusion (with compound fracture of the leg) began to bleed ; and Mackellar came to the conclusion that immediate amputation was the only course possible.   We therefore set about removing the limb.   Dr. Mackellar operated, and I assisted and gave chloroform, while Jack was to hand the sponges, carbolised water and other requisites. In the middle of the operation, our good dwarf, getting nervous at a sight to which he was so little accustomed, lost his self-control and while endeavouring to effect a retreat, fell on his head to the ground in a swoon.   I am afraid we both laughed at the prostrate brave, who was

a regular lion in his own opinion.   Left to ourselves to do the work, we had some difficulty in
finishing the operation satisfactorily.   But that
was the last occasion on which Jack figured as an
assistant in the operation room.

CHAPTER XX.

AMERICAN FRANCS-TIREURS.—PONTOON BRIDGE OVER THE LOIRE.—FRENCH CARELESSNESS.—SOLITARY DEATHS OF THE WOUNDED.

ABOUT this time a small regiment of American volunteers, in Franc-Tireur uniform, passed through Orleans on their way to the front. Their Colonel called on us, and offered a place as assistant surgeon to any who might be willing to join. Had I been at liberty, the spirit of adventure would assuredly have prompted me to accept his offer, and he pressed me hard to do so ; but the required permission was wanting. These men, I afterwards heard, joined General Bourbaki, and having been driven over the Swiss frontier, were detained as prisoners of war.

About the 20th November Dr. Pratt returned, bringing with him two gentlemen, Mr. Olive and Mr. Wombwell, who were to take charge of the commissariat and store department. They had been in London, and brought a large supply of stores. They, like Hayden and myself, had been taken by Francs-Tireurs, not once, however, but twice, and only the French passport which Dr.

Pratt held ever since his departure from Paris, prevented them from being shot out of hand as Prussian spies.

A work of great interest was being carried on by the garrison within sight of our windows on the Quai. It was the construction of a pontoon bridge across the Loire, for the more speedy passage of troops. The Germans, some weeks previously, at the time we arrived in Orleans, had attempted a similar bridge ; but before they had half finished it, a flood came one night and swept the whole thing away, to the intense amusement and delight of the Orleaners. The pontoon bridge which the French now constructed, showed not only the perfection to which military engineering had been brought, but also the acquaintance which the natives possessed with the sudden and violent floods which were wont unexpectedly to swell the current of that great river, causing its waters to rise in a few hours so as to overflow its banks and flood the adjoining country. The bridge was composed, not of pontoon boats, but of large barges, which had been used on the river for the freight of merchandise. These were connected with one another by pine trees, which themselves had been lashed together by spars. A rough idea of the size of the bridge will be given if I state that it took thirty-three such barges to make its length, and that they were about ten feet apart.

Active preparations were now being made on all sides for a determined stand. Every one said that ere many days were over, the enemy would be once more upon them, but they reckoned that an engagement, though sure to be bloody and desperate, would end in a decisive victory for the French army. Such was the gossip of the town, and of officers in the cafés whom I fell in with.

Another event, of even greater interest than the construction of the bridge, was the entrance, one frosty morning, of a body of marine infantry, bearing with them four gunboats placed on long timber waggons, each drawn by eight horses. It is not easy to describe how very novel and curious an appearance this flotilla on dry land presented as it passed slowly down the Rue Royale, each gunboat fully rigged, and carrying on board its bright brass cannons which glistened in the sun.

As I happened to have half an hour to spare, I followed the marines, curious to see what would become of this extraordinary naval procession.

The limber waggons with their cross beams, on which the keels of the boats rested, took up nearly the entire breadth of the street. When they arrived on the Quai du Châtelet, I found myself one of a large crowd that had been drawn there by the same motive, and we wondered much how these unwieldy things could be launched.   It was surprising with what facility this was done by comparatively few hands ; but, presently, when our interest in the performance had yielded to admiration, we saw the last of the gunboats turn upside down as soon as it was in the water, flinging cannon, men, and everything on board into the Loire.   The danger seemed not so great as it might have been, and we were much amused.   There followed a univeral scramble of excited Frenchmen to haul their comrades out of the stream ; but their whole idea of assisting the struggling men was to gesticulate frantically at them, and at their neighbours on shore, and to maul one another in a fashion as ludicrous as it was unseasonable.   Some of the marines, however, let down a boat and brought their comrades on shore.   But it was not until next day that they were able to right the gunboat, and they never fished up the cannon and other materials which had sunk with it.

I often watched these diminutive men-of-war as they cruised about at a great speed, for they were driven by steam, with their guns as bright as gold, and the tricolour flying from their sterns.

On the banks of the river opposite our quarters, there were several cannon placed on the footpath with a sentry on each.   And speaking of sentries, I am reminded how great was the difference between the French and the German method of occupying a town in time of war.   When the

Germans were at Orleans, they set a sentry at every street corner, several at either end of the bridges, one in every public square, and one at the door of every person at all distinguished. A stranger would be challenged at every couple of hundred yards, nor could he pass along anywhere unobserved. Not so was it with the French. During their stay we seldom came across a sentry, and, when we did, he took no more notice of those who passed by, or of what went on in his neighbourhood, than if he had been at a review.

Again, during the French occupation, we missed the noise and rattle of the many hours of morning drill in which our Germans troops were daily practised, no matter how long had been their previous marches, or how severe the hardships they had undergone. During the weeks which the French spent in Orleans I never once saw their soldiers at drill. When they came into the town they simply threw their arms into a corner in their quarters, and left them there until they were again on the move. That such was the case I have personal reason to know; for in a house where I was attending a wounded man, I saw such a collection of arms, and they remained untouched till the regiment to which their owners belonged took its departure.

But this was only in keeping with all that I had seen of the discipline and internal *régime* of their armies. A significant token of their ignorance with regard to the country in which they were fighting was that, immediately on entering Orleans, they requisitioned, by public placards, all maps of the surrounding districts which might be in the hands of the inhabitants, ordering them to be delivered up forthwith to the military commandant. **Thus** did their organisation prove itself in every detail either deficient **or** slovenly. And on all sides there was accumulating evidence **of** something radically unsound in the army as in the people.

About November **22**, the Inspector-General of French Ambulances called to see us **formally at the** railway station **with** Messieurs Crémieux and **Bezoin, two active** members **of** the **Pro-**visional Government. With all three we shook hands solemnly, and received their thanks for the assistance **we had** rendered **to** the French wounded. They signified to our chief that France would be in **a** position, by-and-by, to make some public recognition **of** our services; and after the exchange of other compliments bade us a cordial farewell.

In the midst **of** the excitement and bustle, consequent **on the fact** that Orleans was now the headquarters of the Army of the Loire, **we** continued **our** daily labour at the bedsides of the wounded, caring little about what was happening outside **our own** sphere of work. Many of our wounded were scattered through the town; and these, comfortably established in private houses, we visited every day. As already stated, after leaving the terminus we took up our quarters at M. d'Allaine's in the old market-place. Here we set up our Hospital exclusively for German wounded, as, in the circumstances under which we found ourselves in the town during the French occupation, and taking into consideration the nature of our mission there, we considered the care of the wounded whom the Germans had left to us as our primary duty. For this reason we kept them together as much as possible, that they might not fall into other and less attentive hands; and when we had done our duty by them, we bestowed such time as we could spare upon any French wounded that came under our charge.

At this time our position in Orleans was extremely critical. All knew that we had been in the service of the Germans, and that they had looked upon us as part and parcel of their medical army corps; and we could hear many a subdued expletive when we passed along the streets. It was, however, most likely for this reason that no one dared to molest us. They had learned by a bitter experience how inevitable was the Prussians' day of retribution, and they knew with what severity the invaders punished any outrage on their friends.

Now it was that Colonel Reilly, Captain Frazer and Colonel Hozier arrived in Orleans with the headquarters of General d'Aureilles de Paladine, as *attachés* to the Foreign Embassy. They came several times to mess, and spent their evenings with us,—pleasant jovial men, and as brave as they were agreeable. Nothing could be more welcome, when one was fagged and worn out after a long day's work among the wounded, than to turn in to a comfortable dinner with nearly a score of good-natured fellows, who vied with one another in making the evening pass pleasantly for all. Never a wrangle, never a hasty or bickering word was exchanged; never did an unkind remark or an ungenerous act mar that friendly harmony which existed among the Ambulance corps then working unitedly under the banners of England and America.

I often look back with feelings of satisfaction to the cheery circle we used to form when mess was over, seated round a large wood fire; and I can still see the grinning face of " Nigger Charlie" as he entered the room, bearing in his hand a large wash-hand basin of steaming punch with a dash of brandy and port in it, flavoured with spices and lemon, which we could pronounce with a good conscience to be all it seemed.

Our work was taxing and incessant, but nothing is too hard if one goes at it with a will. Yet my advice to anybody who has a soft drop in him, and who contemplates entering upon a campaign, would be that he had better stay at home.

One of our party was a good musician, and every evening entertained us by playing on a piano which we borrowed from a merchant, as the Scotch would call him, in the town. This was a grand resource after supper when we all came together. And so much for our leisure hours.

In the daily routine of professional work at this time I have nothing out of the way to chronicle. There was one case, however, the particulars of which might be interesting. The patient's name was Karl Melchers, a young artilleryman, who had been shot in the leg at the end of October, and whose thigh was subsequently amputated at the railway station. He had been transferred then to M. d'Allaine's, where, to my grief, he showed symptoms of approaching pyæmia. Reluctantly, but forthwith, I determined that he must be put out of the Hospital ; and I took peremptory orders from my chief to that effect.

Now the difficulty was to find a place where I could lodge poor Melchers. I tried at the neighbouring houses, but all that were not occupied by invalids were full of the rank and file of the army now billeted through the town. Not a nook could I discover anywhere. In the yard, however, there was an empty stable, and into this I had no choice but to have Melchers conveyed. In order to give the place a less dreary appearance—it was dismal enough—I procured some straw, and had it laid on the pavement. He was then brought down on his mattress, and I never shall forget the poor fellow's face when he caught the first glimpse of those new quarters which he felt that he should not long occupy.

When he found himself laid on the straw, alone, and separated from his companions perhaps for ever, the utter desolation of his fate dawned upon him, and he sobbed audibly. Yet he was a fine brave young fellow, with piercing black eyes, dark hair and whiskers, and a very high forehead. We were the best of friends; and I did all in my power, little enough as it was, to comfort him. I persuaded one of our nursing sisters, a native of Luxemburg, who belonged to the convent of Notre Dame de Recouvrance, to sit beside him on the straw, and talk to him for a while. However, both Sœur Berthe and I had soon to go about our own business, and leave him to himself. Day after day he complained bitterly of being where he was, in the damp and cold, but there was no help for it ; his presence in the neighbourhood of any other wounded must have meant the death of many, if not of all. Once he called the sister and me to his bedside, and said : " My end is now not far off ; I should die happy had I but one half-hour with my comrades, behind my gun, with a thousand Frenchmen in front of me ".

Another day and this poor fellow, after having bidden us a touching farewell,—for he knew that we could not help his unhappy position,—died in a manner and in a place that I should not have liked his poor old mother away across the Rhine to have seen.   Yet melancholy as were the circumstances attending the death of this dauntless soldier, still more pitiable was the fate of many others as brave as he, who were condemned to drag out the last few hours of their existence on some bleak and lonely hillside, or in the thick brushwood skirting some silent forest, or in the swampy sedge beside some rivulet.   Such tragedies were not uncommon during that stern winter which was now setting in, as I can but too surely bear witness.

Always we were expecting to hear of an engagement taking place in our neighbourhood; but none happened until Thursday, the 24th November, when we learned from the military in command that hostilities had begun in the direction of Neuville.   During the evening of this day, some of us were told off for field service, and made preparations to depart.   I was among the number.

It gave me, I must confess, no small pleasure to be chosen to go to the front.   There is a fascination in the excitement of the battlefield; and, even in its horrors and imminent deadly perils, a seduction, which one cannot easily resist.

A life of campaigning seems to bring out what moralists would perhaps term a diseased hankering after its uncertainties and adventures. But in the case of the Ambulance officer this not altogether human quality is liable to be merged in one more useful. He is in the field not to give wounds, but to heal them, and to assuage the suffering that makes war so detestable in one aspect, so heroic in another.

CHAPTER XXI.

ON the evening of the 24th, our chief reported himself to the General Commandant, and asked for a "*Feuille de route*," and "*Laissez passer*," which were freely granted, together with instructions to push on as far as Neuville at once ; for no doubt our services would be required there before many hours. Already we could hear the cannon booming in the distance, which satisfied us that this speculation was correct. Early next morning we started with our omnibus and train of waggons, leaving the town by the Faubourg Bannier. Every man carried with him all the portable necessaries, consisting of bandages, chloroform, morphia, lint, tourniquets, and instruments. When we were clear of the town, a good insight into the doings of the French during the past few weeks was permitted us. We saw how they had executed their plan for the fortification of Orleans, and had made an entrenched camp round about it, with ninety-five naval guns manned by the seamen from Cherbourg.

At regular intervals the road was intersected by trenches of great depth and width, running parallel to each other, and extending for miles round the town. They had been driven alike through the woods, the open country, and the vineyards. The cuttings which were thus made in the road had been filled with bundles of twigs and birch tops, packed together and covered with sods, so as to admit of one waggon crossing them.

It surprised me that our horses' feet did not go through; but I remarked that the bundles on the top were made of fine slender maple tops. The sensation experienced when crossing these elastic surfaces was very peculiar. The omnibuses and waggons sprang up and down, and rocked from side to side, as if they had been on india-rubber, until I thought we should be upset; but we were perfectly safe, and the materials proved admirably suited for their purpose. They had, of course, the advantage of being easily removed on the shortest notice. The covering of sods was nothing to speak of, and had by this time resolved itself into a mere crust.

The trenches, however, were not by any means so numerous as the shallow rifle pits and earthworks, which, taking a zigzag course, intersected one another, and seemed to form a network in every direction. It was clear to us that the deep trenches were intended to arrest the progress of artillery and cavalry, while the pits and mounds were for sheltering advancing infantry. All this pointed to the determination of the French to make a resolute stand at Orleans; but we all agreed that we should yet see the Germans making use of those very trenches to defeat the army which had constructed them. And so it turned out.

On our journey we passed through the forest near Orleans, where one portion of the French army had recently encamped. They had cut avenues through the trees, and crossed them again at right angles by others. At each side of these were erected little huts, made of branches set upright in the ground, and interwoven with smaller branches and twigs, while a rough thatch of broom and birch tops covered them. This gave the whole the appearance of an Indian village.

Some of the huts were large and commodious, and if not perfectly strong, made a comfortable shelter against the blast. When inhabited, one could well imagine what a picturesque appearance they must have presented, as seen at night by the blaze of the camp fires. We were told that here had been the quarters of some of the troops from Algiers. The French always kept these wild fellows as much as possible by themselves, and away from the towns, where they are apt to become unmanageable.

Some miles further on, in the middle of an open country, we met an encampment of Zouaves. The ground was all converted into a heavy slush, for it had been raining ; and these unlucky men, stationed here during the past four days, were under orders to move on to the front in the morning. As a group of them stood beside a fire near the road, I was struck with their jaded and draggled appearance. Half famished, and up to their ankles in mud, they gave little earnest of the spirit with which they would go into action on the morrow. Numbers of them were moving about, carrying wood and water, while others were cooking their victuals. I felt much amused at the manner in which some of them performed their morning ablutions. Two fellows whom I noticed were kneeling on a board, washing their faces in some dirty water that had lodged in a waggon track. There were Turcos among them ;—one a dark, fierce-looking brigand, who stalked up with an old barn-door cock in his hand and a turkey under his arm, jabbering to each of his victims a jargon, which they probably did not understand, though they fluttered and screamed in answer to him. These feathered captives were, no doubt, the result of a visit to some old dame's farmyard ; for Turcos never pass through a country without stealing all the poultry and eggs they can lay hands on. Such is the "loot" on which they set value.

16

Further on, we marched through several hamlets which were almost entirely deserted, as were, indeed, most of the farmhouses. Presently, one of the sentinels at an outpost challenged us, and in half an hour we found ourselves at our destination. Neuville is a tidy village situated on the north-east of Orleans, which can boast its little square and town hall, or Mairie, and presented the clean and neat appearance of which I have so often spoken when describing the hamlets I came upon in my French travels. It lies on the outskirts of the forest of Orleans, and has a small but decent church at one end, and a fine corn market at the other. Its central square now afforded a most lively scene, being covered with tents from which the French soldiery were swarming out ; and by their excited manner and,—even for them,—unusual volubility, it was not difficult to guess that some event of the gravest importance was threatening.

We reported ourselves to the Commandant, who looked at our papers, was made aware of our business and destination, and assigned us quarters. This gentleman, who was most courteous and communicative, informed us that there had been a battle on the day previously, in which the Prussians were repulsed, and that, although the engagement had been long and hotly contested, the losses on the French side were trivial; while those of the Germans, if not heavy, were yet not inconsiderable.   We also learned that a few small skirmishes had taken place during the early part of the day, and that the cannon which we heard were further up the French lines to our right. The Commandant said that for the wounded at Neuville he had ample provision in his military surgeons; but added that he expected an engagement on the morrow, when our services would probably be useful.

Such appear to have been the facts. Yet, a few days afterwards, the French journals gave a glowing account of an engagement which had taken place on that very day, and in which a large number of Prussians were killed, with the loss of only one Garde Mobile and half a dozen wounded on the French side. Well and good, if the papers had confined themselves to the doings of the 24th, when there was really some brisk fighting, and some cannonading too, as I can testify; for I saw where a bombshell had entered the mayor's house, and, having passed through the roof, had burst inside, knocking in the ceiling of the sitting-room, and riddling the partition walls so that one could see into the adjoining chamber. But all beyond this was exaggeration or fable.

I remarked that many of the houses in Neuville had received the like treatment, and that, here and there, doors, windows, and sashes had been smashed by fragments of shells. Presently, while wending our way through the camp to our quarters, we fell in with a young corporal, who was of English descent on the mother's side. He had known Dr. May in Paris, spoke English fluently, and showed much refinement and intelligence. He told us that, on the day before, some thousand and odd Frenchmen had defeated in a pitched battle four thousand Prussians; but as the French had had fresh reinforcements that morning, they were now on a more equal footing with the enemy, and could muster, at least, three thousand men. About the movements or position of the other side no one seemed to have precise information, which rather astonished us, since they talked so confidently.

When we had put up in a little tavern, situated in a by-lane, and as clean and comfortable as we could expect in time of war, we went out again to see what was going forward. On one side to the north of the village, our friends had constructed rifle pits, mounds, and trenches just as at Orleans, but on a smaller scale.

We directed our steps to the church, and found there several score or so of wounded, the greater number of whom were German. These latter were in charge of a very uncommunicative young surgeon of their own, who, although I have no desire to misjudge him, did not seem to be very deeply concerned about his patients. They were all gravely wounded, and lay on the flags, with but a scanty supply of straw beneath them, having neither blankets nor anything else to cover them, except their over-coats. Many were in a dying condition, their limbs mangled by fragments of shells, or tra-versed by bullets in some vital part. Two of them assured me that their wounds had not been dressed since they were brought in from the battle-field, and that the bullets were still unextracted; but this may have happened from want of Hos-pital plant and material. We had, however, the gratification of seeing the few out of that dying multitude who could bear removal, transported to our depôt at Orleans; while the rest were left under the charge of their German doctor, let us hope to die in peace.

Some lay in the sanctuary of the church beside the altar; others made use of the steps to support their aching heads; and we noticed others again who were writhing on the ground in the agony of death.

But war had imposed its burden on us, and we took an early rest in order to be fresh for our work next morning. Dr. May was told off to rise at three, and ascertain when we might be expected to be up and moving. The morning came; but no firing had as yet begun, and Dr. May let us lie until seven. When we came down, the village presented a very different aspect from that of yesterday. Not a civilian was to be seen in the streets. A regiment silently drawn up was in the centre of the square. Every man stood in his place, with his hand on his rifle, and ready to begin at a moment's notice. Our forces at this point consisted of a regiment of marine infantry, a couple of regiments of the Line, a few hundred cavalry, and three batteries.

We took our position on the *route Impériale*, immediately outside the town, from which place one could observe how the forces were disposed, and the relation which we bore to the enemy. There was a forest in front of Neuville, some few thousand yards away from the earthworks, and in and beside this wood the Prussians held their ground. The French infantry were drawn up within and in front, as well as on the left of the town; while the artillery had taken up their position on a small hill to the right, from which they could rake the plain before them, should the Prussians give them battle. In the rear of the artillery, and away from the town, were placed the cavalry.

Now, when I talk of the infantry being drawn up, be it understood that they were not ranged in lines on the open plain, as the uninitiated might suppose,—far from it,—for, positively, on looking over the country, it was hard to make out their presence. The French forces were scattered about in farmyards; behind woods, orchards, and hedges; and close to the houses themselves.

The early part of the morning had been wet, but it was now quite fine ; and my reader can imagine with what burning anxiety we kept our eyes on the plain before us, and with a fixed gaze waited for the moment when the familiar rattle at the outposts should declare that hostilities had begun.

Time passed, and no wounded were coming in. Some of us walked about unheeded, observing all we thought of interest. The Prussians were not visible, and we were moving along the road, when we saw the outposts engaged at two different points, as we judged by the smoke and the sounds of musketry.

We now retreated to our lines, feeling sure that this was the commencement of a hot day's work. However, it turned out otherwise ; for after a considerable amount of shifting their position on the part of the infantry, and the advancing of a few companies, there was very little firing on either side save that which was kept up between the outposts ; and they, in the end, got tired of firing in the air in the direction of one another. I should say, from the distance they were apart, that they might have gone on firing till the day of judgment, and done no execution on their respective enemies. In a little time two companies went forward and exchanged a few volleys with the Prussians, whereupon the latter retired altogether from the scene. Thus ended the battle of the 25th, without a drop of blood being shed or a single man being wounded.

Now, it may appear strange that I should have travelled into the details of so bloodless an engagement; but my reason for doing so is simply this, that a few days later, when perusing one of the French journals, I lighted on a glowing report of three brilliant victories which had been gained at Neuville by the French, on the 24th, 25th, and 26th of November, with all particulars at length.

The comments on the battle of the 24th, as I have said, were exaggerated; but in describing the two days subsequent, my newspaper stated that, after a determined resistance of many hours, the Prussians were completely routed, and had left eighty prisoners in the hands of the French, with a quantity of baggage and waggons. I have given the circumstances of this notable victory of the 25th, and the reader may draw his own conclusion. So much for French journalism, which, to my thinking, was not wholly guiltless of many of the disasters that befel the French arms. The facts I have related speak for themselves; they furnish, however, an example of the mania, which, at this period, seized the French press, and led them persistently to falsify the news from the seat of war. Not only did they strain every effort to blindfold their own people, and screen the truth from them,—which was that they were being hopelessly beaten,—but they did their best to persuade the world that they **were** winning, and that their ultimate success **was** certain.

These bare-faced falsehoods, which delayed negotiations, and put off the treaty of peace **until** the country was exhausted, could **be** matched only by a story which **I heard** long afterwards. An acquaintance of **ours**, who was staying at Tours in 1880, **used to** relate how his French host was in the habit **of** saying, when they fell to talking about old times, "*Franchement, nous avons vaincu dans cette guerre, mais les gens ne veulent pas le reconnaître*". No, I say, they hardly could!

We returned **to Orleans on** the night of Saturday, the 26th, and next day, during **a** leisure half-hour, **I wrote** home rather a tame account of these glorious French **victories**.

Wonderful (I **used to** think), **how easy it is to** revive by abundant palaver the **drooping spirits of the** French! **Not two** months **ago they** had looked **upon** their prospects, **if not with** despair, yet with the most gloomy forebodings; but to-day, elated by a few slight **successes, they** were swaggering about **the** streets, boasting **of what** France had done in generations past, and of what she **would do in** the future. It was no uncommon thing **to hear** them in the cafés talking **of the** requisitions they would make when they had raised the siege of Paris, and were marching through Germany, about which they knew little more than **they** did of the interior of China. Nor would it have been safe to hint, at this period, that any Germans would still remain on French territory by that day six weeks.

It was amusing, if also, perhaps, exasperating, to hear them run on in this fashion ; for we non-combatants all expected that ere many days we should see the German sentinels again at our Hospital gates. For ourselves, we were still branded by public opinion as Germans, and had nothing to protect us save our calling, and the flag which hung out all through, over our door on the Quai du Châtelet. Hence we were careful how we moved about after nightfall, lest we might come into collision with the soldiery, or such of the townsfolk as might have been disposed to interfere with us.

CHAPTER XXII.

TIME went by in the ordinary routine of Hospital work, until the 1st December, when the news of a successful sortie from Paris, made by Trochu and Ducrot, put the whole town into a fever of excitement. Report said that the Army of Paris was already approaching Étampes.

Next day, 2nd December, we heard heavy firing going on all along the lines, so far as we could judge, from Neuville and Chevilly on the right, to Patay on the left. A severe frost had set in during the past fortnight, and there had been a heavy fall of snow during the last few days. The ground was hard, and the air clear, so that the roar of the guns thundered in our ears as if they had been only a few furlongs instead of eight miles away. Of course, it was devoutly held by the Orleaners that Trochu was fighting his way through the Prussian lines, and would be in Orleans to-morrow.

(251)

We, however, guessed what the real state of things was. During the last week we had obtained permission from the French authorities to have the old Church of St. Euverte, in the Rue St. Aignan, fitted up as a Hospital, and the Mayor had provided about 300 beds with their bedding. We had been actively employed the past three days in transferring our wounded from D'Allaine's to our new abode; and by the evening of the 3rd all our arrangements were made to receive the wounded. The cooking department was seen to by an energetic Frenchman, M. Bonjour, whose services throughout our stay at Orleans can never be forgotten by us.

Towards the evening of that same day, the firing became fierce and continual; it appeared to come nearer than it had been in the morning. Both sides had heavy guns, eighteen and twenty-four pounders, hard at work. Nor were the mitrailleuses inactive. It was not until long after dark that the cannonading ceased. As may be supposed, no one knew, though every one pretended to know, the result of this long engagement. Some I heard saying that Prince Frederick Charles had been taken prisoner with 20,000 men; while others ventilated equally foolish reports. But ere long convoys of wounded arrived, and we soon had no doubt as to what had happened. The French were evidently getting the worst of it.

Next day, the 4th December, a furious cannonade raged outside the town, making a most terrific din, though still several miles away. It told us that the French were making a determined stand. Early in the morning our Ambulance, minus Tilghman, Mackellar, Hayden and myself, quitted Orleans, and went on to the battlefield. We four were left behind to receive the wounded, as well as to look after those who were already on our hands. I had been under orders to go; but Dr. Warren, who was burning to be in the thick of it, asked me to effect an exchange with him; and I consented to the arrangement, subject to the necessary permission of our chief. My friend had never been among the bullets; and great was his anxiety to receive what Louis Napoleon called in a famous despatch, the "baptism of fire". As I had a great deal of useful work to do, I was quite willing to stay. After my late experience, curiosity alone, without the call of duty, never would prompt me to go again into a battlefield; but I had had my baptism. As regards the success of this expedition, I may add that, when they arrived on the scene of action, they found the French were fighting in retreat, and there was no possibility of establishing a temporary field Hospital. They had, therefore, to content themselves with bringing home as many of the wounded as they could accommodate in their waggons.

The description which they gave of the slaughter was fearful. The Prussian artillery had raked the French lines through and through before their eyes; and Dr. Warren confessed to me that, short as was the time they had been on the battlefield, he had seen sights so horrible that the recollection of them would haunt him till his dying day.

Long before the return of our comrades, we became aware that the French must be fighting in retreat, by the extended convoys of provision and baggage waggons, that streamed down the Rue Royale and across the Loire. For upwards of ten hours the baggage, provision, and ammunition train of the French army continued to pour across that bridge in unbroken succession. It was a sight to fill one with amazement; one could hardly believe that it was not all a dream.

In the middle of the day, while going to see some of my wounded who were quartered in a neighbouring street, I met a convoy of Prussian prisoners being hurried along by a detachment of marines. They must have been some time in the hands of the French, for they looked thin and worn; and it made my blood boil to see the malignant delight which beamed in the faces of the townsfolk as they scanned these famished and half-frozen wretches passing along.

But an hour later, I witnessed in the Rue Jeanne d'Arc a scene, the novelty of which, to

my mind, was without a parallel.   Moving down
the street towards me at a slow hand-gallop,—almost at a walking pace,—came a troop of African
cavalry, from the borders of the Sahara.   I don't
know that anything had ever excited in me so
much curiosity as did the sight of these Spahis ;
and a more strange and wild-looking collection of
men and beasts it would be impossible to conceive.   They halted opposite the Cathedral, so
that I had ample time to take stock of them.
The townspeople displayed as much astonishment
as I did, and flocked after them in crowds, just
as if they had been the outriders of some great
circus.

They were tall, fine-looking men, with bronzed
faces, but of various tints, some light, some almost
black, some handsome, others square-faced, and,
one had almost said, ugly.   There were those
among them who had well-chiselled features, with
dark eyes, and so piercing a look as to give one
the idea that they could see right through one.
Their outer dress consisted of long-flowing mantles
in white flannel, which trailed along the ground
when they dismounted, and were fastened over
one shoulder, somewhat after the fashion of the
Roman toga.   This garment, however, had
attached to it a hood and a short cape.   On their
heads I saw what appeared to be a high coil
of whitewashed rope, entangled in the hair, which,
so far as I could judge, they wore long.   This

coil was looped up about their head-dress like the ordinary turban.   The hood, of which I have spoken, was partly drawn up over the turban or coil, just far enough to catch the apex, and the whole appeared as if each man carried on his head a small turret.   Add to these details, a lean, ugly, big-boned, square-hipped, straight-shouldered Arab horse, with a wooden frame set on a large pad for a saddle, and having a high piece going up behind, so as to reach half-way up the rider's back.   The whole thing looked more like a diminutive chair than a saddle.   The girths by which it was secured passed round saddle, horse and all.   Wooden shoes came out at each side, with strips of hide for stirrups ; there was a strong crupper behind, and blinkers, were set on the bridles of untanned leather.   It was, I think, the oddest specimen of an equestrian turn-out that ever showed on a European battlefield.

These men are supposed to be about the best riders in the world.   As they moved on, I remarked that they all rocked in their saddles in the most curious fashion, and thrust out their toes in tailorlike style.   They each carried a musket about the length of one's arm, a brace of pistols, and a sword, which did not look like a sword, it was so much bent.   Yet this is their favourite weapon. I could well imagine an enemy being taken aback when he approached these mysterious foes, and beheld their grim dark faces peering through a small loophole at the top of a tower of white flannel. They certainly had more the resemblance of cowled monks than of a troop of cavalry, and might have been introduced by Sir Walter Scott in *Ivanhoe*, as Moslem Knights Templars.

When I had seen this curious sight, I went on my way to look after a captain of the Garde Mobile, who was shot through the foot, and a young corporal of the Line, shot through the left lung. The latter was a very bad case, not likely to recover; the ball had descended in the cavity of the chest, and the air which the poor lad was breathing entered and escaped through the perforation. Presently, a boy of about sixteen came in, the friend and companion of the dying corporal. He had but a few minutes to remain, and in this short time he learned from me that his friend's wound was mortal, and that he must now bid him a hasty farewell. The parting scene between them was most touching, for they were attached comrades.

Among the number brought in to-day by our ambulance was one who came under my charge, and whose case was of interest by reason of his tender years. He was a fine lad, only seventeen, and had served in the Garde Mobile. He had been shot through the leg; but the principal cause of his lamentation was not his wound; it was that he had not fired a shot the whole day, nor even so much as got a chance of bowling over a

German, though all the while shells and bullets were falling about him like rain, and dealt wholesale destruction on his company. The account which he gave of the fighting outside was terrible; it seemed to have made a deep impression on his imagination, yet did not in the least take from his courage. He told me he had not eaten for twenty-four hours. How, I often said to myself, could soldiers fight, who were habitually suffering from hunger, cold, and fatigue, like these poor fellows?

All this time the ground literally shook from the conflict which was going on outside the town. I think that, as an artillery fight, it was second only to Sedan.

It had been freezing very hard every night, and snow was lying deep on the ground.

If people at home (and there are some who talk much around their comfortable fires about going to war on every paltry provocation) could have seen the waggon-loads of half-frozen wounded which were brought in to us on the night of the 4th, and those again who lay outside the town without assistance, their wounds uncared for, and exposed to the bitterly cold night air, how soon they would change their idle tone! how they would loathe and abominate the very name of war!

I can understand that men find a pleasure in studying the art of fighting, as they do in playing a game of chess: and I have allowed in my own case the fascination which even its horrid reality is capable of exercising over one. But for the man who deems it a pleasure and a glory to use the science of war as a weapon wherewith to annihilate thousands of human beings, for the delusion called "prestige," or in the game of politics, I would have him to know that it is a foul and monstrous thing, full of hideous suffering, cruelty, and injustice, with nothing to redeem it, save the courage whereby such miseries are endured.

However, let me go on with my proper theme. Immediately the darkness set in on the 3rd, the cannonading ceased. This night we snatched but a few hours' sleep; for, at the first dawn of daylight, a repetition of yesterday's performance began with redoubled vigour. From the belfry tower of our church, during the past two days, we had been able to get a fair idea how the battle was going. It commanded a fine view of the country around. But now that the Germans had driven the French back on the outskirts of the town we could see much more of the contest. Early on the 4th we beheld the whole cavalry, numbering about 3000 men, come down the Rue Royale and pass over the bridge on the Quai du Châtelet,—some at a swinging trot, others at a gallop. It was a rare sight, for here were represented men of every regiment in France—Cuirassiers, Lancers, Chasseurs d'Afrique and the rest.   This host of armed men and horses, extending as far as the eye could reach (which was certainly half a mile), formed a *coup d'œil* not easily forgotten ; and the clatter they made on the pavement, during their stampede, was loud enough to have been heard far outside the town.

Towards evening I availed myself of a few minutes' leisure to ascend the church tower and watch the battle, which still continued.   The roar of the fighting, which was now going on in the vineyards and entrenchments at the end of the Faubourg Bannier, baffles description.   The heavy French marine guns were all going simultaneously, while on each side of the town the infantry also were in close conflict.   Quite near us, at the end of our own Faubourg St. Vincent, just where the convent stood in which Miss Pearson and Miss McLoughlin were at work, the fighting seemed heaviest.   On some portion of the ground that was not so thickly covered with vineyards, the dead were strewn in heaps, many being the victims of their own mitrailleuses which the Germans had captured, and were now using with more precision and deadly effect than their original possessors.   But all this time, the French, though retreating, kept up a continuous and well-directed fire upon the advancing Prussians, whose losses, as we afterwards discovered, were quite as great as those of the vanquished.

This they attributed themselves to the great tact and ability which the French marines displayed in the management of their heavy guns. But for these, indeed, as I have heard the French say, it would have been difficult, if not impossible, for them to have covered the retreat of their army.

The sun shone brilliantly that afternoon of the 4th, and the arms and accoutrements of the contending forces were flashing brightly, as they moved about among the vineyards. In the distance we could see in several places the field-artillery galloping along in different directions, wheeling round suddenly, and stopping, when the little puffs of smoke told us their reason for doing so. But these reports were lost in the general tumult of the battle. One or two more repetitions of these little puffs, then a limber-up, and a dash ahead as before in their onward course, only to repeat the same manœuvres further on; such were the tactics which, as from a box at the theatre, we repeatedly noticed, standing in the belfry of Ste. Euverte.

And here I may mention an incident witnessed by Drs. May and Tilghman. There was a hot contest being waged close to the Hospital, among the double rows of trees on the Boulevard St. Vincent, when, in the midst of the confusion, a young lieutenant of the Line was seen stepping out from a house just beside the church. He had gone but a few paces, when a young girl rushed out after him and took a last embrace, after which he moved quickly out of her sight. But evidently he was not yet out of the mind of the young girl; for she stood as if rooted to the spot, gazing after her lover, heedless of the bullets which were whistling past, and of the storm of the battle raging round her. In another moment, May and Tilghman realised her frightful situation. May sprang over the paling which was between them, but arrived only in time to receive her bleeding and senseless into his arms. A spent bullet had struck her between the angle of the eye and the cheek bone, and had stripped back the soft parts of the side of the face as far as the ear, with a portion of the scalp.

The wound, though not so very dangerous,—for the bone of the head was only grazed and not broken,—was, nevertheless, an ugly one. The girl was at once taken into her own house, where May and Tilghman skilfully adjusted the torn portions of the scalp by a neat operation, bestowing on the case every attention in their power. It will doubtless be gratifying to my reader when I tell him that this girl made a splendid recovery. I had the privilege of watching her convalescence in the absence of Dr. May. Nor was she much disfigured; for, in consequence of the prompt treatment, the parts united admirably, leaving an almost imperceptible scar, which was, however, sufficiently well marked to remind her of that romantic, but perilous, moment at Orleans. Love is proverbially blind. In this case, love was blind and deaf too.

I was kept hard at work in the Hospital, and could steal only a moment to observe the stirring scenes which were going on around. Each new-comer brought with him, in addition to his own sad story, a list of harrowing details from the day's battlefield. But things were all going one way. Early in the afternoon, the main body of the French army had fallen back upon the town. The Germans had gained possession of the two principal approaches of the Faubourgs Bannier and St. Vincent, and had already demolished numerous buildings on the outskirts. They did not, however, shell the town itself, as we feared they were on the point of doing; and when night set in, there was a temporary armistice. Both sides, by mutual consent, desisted, on the understanding that the bridges were not to be blown up.

Now it was that the whole French army commenced their hurried march across the Loire, by the pontoon bridge, and the two permanent ones. It was a bright, still, moonlight night, and nothing was to be heard but the trampling of feet, as that mighty host hurried along. I stood at the corner of the Quai du Châtelet and watched them. Some of the regiments, which had happened to lag behind, doubled down the Rue Royale, but they marched over the pontoons at the regulation pace.

Not a word was spoken,—an unusual state of things among Frenchmen,—and all, as they well might, seemed dispirited. Some of the men had no arms; many had lost their képis; and all showed visible signs of having lately seen hard times. Tired, at length, of watching them pass in that unbroken stream, I went to my quarters at No. 64 on the Quai hard by.

I had hardly entered, when my attention was called by the tramp of feet on the pavement outside the open window. On looking out, I beheld what appeared to be the remains of several regiments. Most of them were without arms, and all went limping along, evidently quite foot-sore, while numbers were slightly wounded, to judge from various bandages, which they displayed round their heads, legs, and arms. They looked more like a procession of invalids out for a walk, than soldiers still capable of fighting. The poor fellows were dead beat, and did not so much march as shuffle along, some in a tottering condition, and lagging behind the rest, having evidently done as much as was in their power.

But what was my rage and indignation, when a captain, in the rear, who carried in his hand not a sword, but a thick cane, belaboured with it, again and again, any unfortunate who did not keep up with the rest! One of these poor fellows made a sign to me for something to drink. Swiftly as possible, I seized a large can of water which stood beside the window, and poured it slowly on the footway. Several that were near put their mouths under the little jet, and then began a sort of scramble for what one of them told me he had not tasted during fourteen hours. But their gallant leader, having dealt half a dozen blows at random with his stick among this thirsty crowd, dispersed them, indulging the while in strong language, and gesticulated at me in the most excited manner. However, the frame of mind I was in—to say nothing of my safe position— made me equal to the occasion. I complimented him on the able style in which *Monsieur le Maré-chal* used his *bâton;* and he slunk away, muttering curses, as he did so, at me and his men.

This piece of excitement over, I went to the pontoon bridge, where the stream of soldiers continued to pour across. Although I had been on duty the previous night and all that day, I could not but stay up to watch this historic and interesting spectacle,—the retreat of 200,000 men, composing the whole Army of the Loire, across that river. It was now nearly eleven o'clock, and they had been passing for hours. But the living current flowed on unceasingly during the night, until the last of the troops were over. When this had been accomplished, then the silence of the frosty scene was broken by the sound of hammers, hatchets, and saws; and the air resounded with the hacking and the chopping of the sappers, who were busily engaged cutting the moorings and the cross planks, while others set fire to the bridge in about a dozen places. Just at the same hour, there was a great tramp and rattle of horses and waggons over the permanent bridge to our right, caused by a number of batteries of artillery, which galloped furiously onwards in head-long career. They were the last of the fugitive army. The battle of Patay had been lost and won.

Now the Loire was much flooded, and the blocks of ice borne down in the current were very large, so that when the different sections of the bridge were cut loose,—and, later on, when they became again subdivided, as well as during the process of freeing themselves,—the grating, groaning, creaking, and crashing of one against the other, and also against the great blocks of ice, was unlike any other sound I ever heard. Moreover, every raft of boats and planks formed the base of a pillar of fire, which brilliantly illuminated the snow-covered slopes, the trees, and the ice-bound banks of the river,—reflecting in the water above and below us, as if in a looking-glass, the arches and the battlements of two of the finest bridges in France, which now stood out, in all their architectural beauty, relieved against the pitchy darkness of the night.

As each of these burning sections of the pontoon became disconnected from its fellow, it turned round on its own axis, and staggered about in the river for a short time, until finally, having arrived in mid stream, it swept down with the current,—making a loud grating noise as it struck the ice blocks,—and at last with a tremendous crash was hurled against the mighty granite bulwarks of the bridge. There it either became a total wreck, or, being broken up into fragments, swirled hither and thither till it passed out of view. It was a strange and magnificent spectacle, unequalled by anything I have seen before or since, in the combination of light and dark, the enormous power displayed, and the gigantic ruin upon the waters.

When I was taking a last look at all this before retiring to rest, a number of soldiers came up, intending to cross over; but they found the bridge demolished, and themselves cut off from retreat.

These, I heard afterwards, were some few hundred men, inclusive of the Foreign Legion, who formed the rear guard of the army, and had got lost in the darkness. They neglected to avail themselves of the railway bridge nearest them, which, like that in our neighbourhood, was also, during this night, taken and guarded by the Prussians.

CHAPTER XXIII.

FIGHTING IN THE STREETS.—THE TOWN CARRIED BY
ASSAULT.—NARROW ESCAPES.—THE RED PRINCE
ENTERS WITH HIS WHOLE ARMY.

OVERCOME by fatigue and excitement, I had thrown myself on my bed just as I was, and never stirred until daylight, when Warren awoke me with the news that fighting was going on in the streets. I rubbed my eyes and went to the window, when, to my utter astonishment, I beheld six Prussians confronting about fifteen Frenchmen. They had come upon the latter by surprise round a corner, and the French looked at first as if they were going to fire; but, on seeing a large body of Prussians advancing under cover of the trees, they lowered their rifles, and coolly stacked their arms not twenty paces from my window. The six Germans, meanwhile, quietly stood round them with fixed bayonets. In another minute they were walking off up a by-street as prisoners.

All this came upon a man who had been just awakened rather by surprise; but, when I heard some desultory firing in different parts of the town, I made up my mind that we were to have hot

(268)

work in the streets. Having performed a hasty toilette, I sallied forth, eager not to lose the sight of what was going on. I had not proceeded many yards up the Quai, when I perceived a body of Prussians stationed near the bridge at the end of the Rue Royale. Seeing these drawn up in battle array, and finding myself the only person on the Quai du Châtelet, I paused for a moment or two, and looked down in the other direction towards the railway bridge. There I beheld a goodly number of Frenchmen, ranged over against the church of St. Aignan at the other extremity of the Quai. Thinking that this looked like business I remarked to Dr. Warren that we were in an awkward position, and had better retire. The words were no sooner out of my mouth, and we had only just stepped back into the hall, when a volley of bullets whizzed along by us in the direction of a French officer, who was galloping across the bridge at that moment. Some of the balls must have gone very close to him, for he ducked his head repeatedly behind his horse's neck and redoubled his speed. Shot after shot went after him until he lay quite flat on his saddle. How he rushed the guard on the bridge was a mystery I could never solve; but that he did escape I can certify.

This was the signal for a general fusilade. The Germans at the end of the Rue Royale, advancing on the bridge, knelt down behind the parapets, so that we could see nothing but the spikes of their helmets and the muzzles of their rifles which glittered in the morning sun. The French answered from behind the trees on the Quai, and from the corners of the by-streets. We now perceived that a company of Prussians were advancing in single file down the Quai towards us, and were entering the houses. This was more than we could stand. So slipping out of No. 64 up the nearest lane, we ran out by the rear into our headquarters at No. 66.

Here we found Dr. Parker, who had just been out in another part of the town, but was very nearly seeing and experiencing more than he had bargained for. . In going up a side street off the Rue Bourgogne, he found a sharp cross-fire opened from each end of the street, and as the bullets struck the wall beside him, he had to take refuge in the doorways, in order to escape them. The company of Prussians, to whom I have already referred, were still advancing slowly in our direction ; and a brisk return fire was kept up by a small knot of French at the other end.

The manner of the Prussian advance was peculiar. First went four sappers, who in one second broke through each of the doors which did not happen to be open. These carried hatchets, handsaws, jemmies, and crowbars ; and it was marvellous how short a time they took to enter, and how they made the timber fly like match-wood. Our gate was thrown open, and in due course a number of men filed in one by one from the next house. Three of them went through the form of searching the place, while the remainder, about a dozen in number, were ordered out, two by two, to kneel on the footway and fire at the enemy. When they had done so, they withdrew until their turn came round again. The house was speedily filled with smoke, for the soldiers crouched close into the wall, and remained almost inside the porch.

The necessity of this proceeding was soon apparent. For in another minute bullets came hitting the wall beside the door, and sent the plaster flying into my eyes, while I was craning my neck round the jamb of the open door to see what was going on. Luckily, they glanced off the flags a couple of feet away from where I stood.

The leaden pipe, which ran down beside the entrance, was now riddled in various places; our old English flag, which hung down over the door from a long pole above the window, was likewise torn; but I have it in my possession yet.

We were at the highest pitch of excitement while all this was going on. Prompted by curiosity, I went upstairs, and looking out from one of the windows, saw standing in the middle of the street, exposed to all the fire, a German Captain of the Line, coolly giving, or rather shouting, his orders to the various non-commissioned officers and

soldiers, who lined the walls or manned the doorways above and below us. I expected every
moment to see him fall. Amongst the French,
who were replying persistently from their position
at the end of the Quai, I espied one Zouave in
particular, who fired five or six shots at this
officer. I felt satisfied that it was at him he
aimed, for he singled himself out from his
comrades, and crept on his hands and knees
to the middle of the roadway, taking a deliberate
shot, and we could not perceive that there was any
one else in the direct line of his fire. When the
Zouave had discharged about the sixth shot, a
ball from the Prussians tumbled him over on his
back with his legs in the air ; but for all that, he
was not killed, as he scrambled away with the aid
of a companion. A thud and a splutter of the
plaster on the wall just beside me, suggested the
advisability of curtailing my observations ; so I
shifted my quarters to the hall below, where I
found Dr. Parker giving some of the Prussians
a nip of brandy,—in order, as he jocosely remarked, to put a twist in their powder. I knelt
down behind one of the men at the doorway, as
he was taking aim at the Frenchmen, and looked
over the sight to see where his game lay. He
fired, and, as he did so, a ball struck the pavement
above five yards from where he and I were
kneeling.

It was a regular business of sharp-shooting ;

for a head, or a head and a pair of shoulders, were all we could see of the enemy.

In the midst of the practice great commotion was caused by an old woman appearing on the Quai. For a few seconds firing was suspended; an officer came out into the middle of the street and made signs to her to retire, which the ancient dame speedily did. What she meant by coming out thus, it would be vain to conjecture, unless she was stone deaf. She was clearly no Jeanne d'Arc.

In a short time the French, seeing that they had no hope of making good their retreat across the bridge, ceased firing. A flag of truce went to them from the Mairie, stating that the town had been in possession of the Germans since midnight; and they had better yield. They laid down their arms; and the town of Orleans, as we had all along anticipated, was once more in the hands of the Prussians. It was eight o'clock in the morning of 5th December. An hour passed, and the Prussians came marching in, the bands playing their most lively strains; and we found ourselves among our old acquaintance.

The first step which the invaders took was to get together all their prisoners, numbering 10,000, and shut them up in the Cathedral.

Of course, the minute we were free to do so, we all got off to our work at Ste. Euverte, where we already found many of our old friends awaiting us.

The little Captain Schrenk was there; also the young ecclesiastic of whom I have spoken; and, later on in the day, the giant cuirassier stalked in, gorgeously arrayed in scarlet and gold, and seeking for his hidden cuirass. They shook hands with us over and over again, exhibiting unmistakable satisfaction and pleasure at finding we were still at our posts, and safe and sound. Surgeon-General Von Nussbaum paid us a visit, and complimented us on the manner in which we had stood by their wounded during the French occupation. In fact, congratulations rained down on all sides; and from this time forward the Germans looked upon us as their staunch and trusty friends, giving us notice that in due time our services would be officially remembered. The wounded now began to pour into the town, and our Hospital church was quickly crowded, together with every house in the vicinity.

At eleven A.M. we went to our quarters for breakfast; but hearing that the entry of Prince Frederick Charles's troops had commenced, I snatched a few mouthfuls, and hurried off to witness the scene from a window in M. Proust's house, No. 12 Rue Royale, with which I was to be more intimately acquainted ere I left Orleans.

The troops entered with bayonets set, flags flying, bands playing, and all the pomp and circumstance which are usual on such occasions, and the air resounded with a storm of military music.

It was noteworthy, indeed, to see that host pass by, consisting of 130,000 as fine-looking men as any country in the world could produce; and what was most astonishing about them was the neatness and cleanliness of their dress, the brightness of their arms and accoutrements, and their general well-dressed appearance, reminding me more of our handful of soldiers at home, as they marched past the Lord Lieutenant in the Phœnix Park on a field day, than of an army that had been fighting all the past week, and had endured the privations and hardships of a six months' campaign.

The sun shone through the frosty air, and, as the mist had now cleared off, the helmets and bayonets of that mighty array flashed and glistened everywhere. While these sturdy, well-built and well-fed fellows passed on, I compared them mentally with the regiments I had seen straggling onward to the bridge. The difference spoke eloquently in favour of that elaborate and admirable scheme of military organisation which had brought them to such a degree of perfection. It also elicited from a British officer who was with me at the time, a remark that, unless we ourselves take up some more comprehensive system of organising our forces, we shall be thrashed by this ambitious race of soldiers the first time we come into conflict with them. Nay, more, it is possible that they might invade and overrun England in a short campaign, should they ever become as great adepts in the art of war on the high seas as they are on land.

Many of the German officers whom I have met were of opinion that such an enterprise was not beyond the scope of German ambition and German energy. More than once I heard them anticipating that the result of their victorious career would be to bring all the nations of Europe under the wing of their Imperial eagle. And though willing to allow that England would be the last to come in, since without a mighty fleet they could not get at her, yet she too must share the fate of her neighbours. It amused,—perhaps it angered us,—to find these highly intellectual men of the world holding such views, gravely arguing among themselves and with us, that such would be the inevitable result of a united Germany, and that all she wanted to annex Europe, and carry out the ideas of Alexander the First of Russia, was a little time, and a favourable opportunity.

The army of Prince Frederick Charles, now marching through Orleans, was on its road to Blois, and in pursuit of General Chanzy. Turning from this splendid sight, I went back to St. Euverte ; and there spent the remainder of that day—and a long day it was—in assisting at the operation-table, and dressing and attending to the wounded who were brought to us in crowds. As we had only accommodation for 250, we were obliged to send out into the houses of the Rue de St. Aignan all who were not seriously wounded ; after which we still found it necessary to lay a number of those who were gravely wounded on the floor, with straw under them. These latter were not at all so badly off, when we consider that some half score waggon-loads of men had to remain out in the frost and snow for a whole night and part of the next day, so greatly did the demand exceed the supply of accommodation in Orleans just then. To add to their misfortune—and I am speaking literally of hundreds,—there followed a great scarcity of bread, which was felt chiefly by the civil population, and by those quartered on them. It did not affect the garrison in the least ; for their commissariat never failed.

An army entering thus, devours, like a swarm of locusts, in a few hours everything that is eatable in a town, and leaves the inhabitants nothing but what they can supply from their secret stores—which, however, they always manage to reserve. The condition of chronic hunger, from which the inhabitants of Orleans suffered for several weeks at this period, was truly distressing to witness.

By noon on the 6th of December, all was quiet again, the garrison had been billeted in their quarters, the sentries were at their accustomed posts, and everything in Orleans betokened the return of the old orderly *régime*, to which we had been so long accustomed. There was an entire absence of that wild disorder, and noisy confusion, which had lasted, not for hours but for days, after the French took possession of the town, and which I have endeavoured to describe. but have not adequately depicted in the words at my command. And thus began the second German occupation of Orleans.

CHAPTER XXIV.

DESECRATION OF THE CATHEDRAL.—MY FIRST CAPITAL
OPERATION.—MORE FIGHTING.—WOUNDED BA-
VARIANS.

Soon after the mayor had issued his parlementaire, all the French prisoners, to the number, as
I have said, of 10,000, were marched into the
Cathedral, where they were confined until such
time as preparations could be made for their
transport into Germany.

As the weather was bitterly cold, the prisoners
—it will be remembered that they were French
and Catholic—began at once to break up the
chairs and benches with which to make fires.
These they kindled at the base of the great stone
pillars for which the Cathedral is celebrated.
Towards evening, as I happened to pass that
way, I saw the men and lads warming themselves
at these great blazing fires, that lighted up the
whole edifice, the roof of which, however, could
scarcely be seen through the wreaths of thick smoke
that formed a dense cloud overhead. It was an
ungodly spectacle, the more so that many of the

men sang and joked, while one amused himself at the organ.

I confess the scene was very disagreeable to me. Every now and then one of these fellows would lay hold of a chair, and with one blow shatter it in pieces against the tiles or the nearest pillar, and then cast the fragments into the blaze. There they sat, smoking, eating, and drinking,— what little they could get to eat and drink,—cursing Bismarck and the Emperor, and rehearsing that oft-told preposterous lie, how universal treachery was the cause of their presence there that night. I stood for some time looking on at a display which, if curious, was still more revolting. The stalls of the Sanctuary, which I had seen a few days previously graced by the canons and other dignitaries who surrounded Monseigneur Dupanloup, during the pomp and splendour of the Episcopal ceremonies, and at High Mass, were now filled with the vilest of the French soldiery, some of whom lolled about at their leisure and conversed together, while others, overcome by hunger and fatigue, were lying fast asleep all over the church. On the steps of the High Altar fellows were stretched out in deep slumber, and not one appeared to regard the nature of the place in which they were quartered. The lines of fires down each side of the building, the din and the confusion to which this herd of men gave rise, and the manner in which they seemed to be swarming about all **parts of** the Cathedral, as the light **of** the fires glanced on them, made an extraordinary combination, **and** one might have fancied that **the** age of Gil **Blas had returned in the** nineteenth century.

For **two** days the **Cathedral** was possessed **by this motley** congregation ; **then the** prisoners were sent off in batches **by train** from Orleans, and we were glad to **get rid of them.** Their destination, **as** usual, **was** over the **Rhine.**

I met one of these convoys **on their way** to the station. **They were** marched, **or** rather driven along, before half **a** dozen mounted troopers ; **and** when any straggled or fell behind, **these** put **spurs** to **their** chargers and rode **in** amongst their **captives, in some** instances trampling them under the horses' feet, and lashing them with their riding whips in the most wanton manner. The sight **was** enough **to make** one's blood boil. Had **any** one told me of such a thing, I should have received **his** statement with **caution, if not with** distrust ; **but I** relate that **of which I** was myself an eye-witness. When **I had** cooled down **a** little, I consoled myself with the idea that such **was the** treatment which these **very** Germans received at **the hands** of their **own officers and** under-officers, while going through their training and their drill, as I have already testified from personal observation. **They gave the** French, therefore, only what they **had been** treated to themselves.

During the whole of the 6th and 7th, and the intervening night, we were hard at work in the Hospital, the greater part of our time being taken up at the operation table. I may here mention a fact, which is highly interesting to me, *viz.*, that now, by permission of our chief, I performed my first capital operation, in a case of compound comminuted fracture of the bone of the arm, which I had to amputate below the shoulder. Nor were the circumstances of the place in which I went through my task, of a common sort. It was Sunday morning; and the operation table stood in a side chapel, at the foot of the Lady Altar, not many yards from the Shrine of Ste. Euverte. But although one's first impressions might be that such work, on such a spot, was a profanation, yet on second thoughts it will not appear so. The deed, though sanguinary, was not cruel; and where should the wounded find refuge if not under the sacred roof?

On the evening of the 7th, we received intelligence that the Germans had come up with the French army; that fighting had begun; and that a general engagement was expected. Accordingly, Dr. Tilghman, with May and Mackellar, started with a supply of surgical appliances and waggons for bringing the wounded off the field.

I was set down for work at the Hospital, and did not go with them. But Dr. Tilghman subsequently gave me a full account of the whole affair, and described the carnage as very great. The town of Beaugency and the neighbouring villages were literally crammed with wounded; and they had hardly any one to look after them, and but very little to eat. In fact, so scarce were provisions that many sank from privation alone, aggravated, indeed, by the bitter cold, which just at this time was intense. He mentioned, among other ghastly details, that owing to the hard frost, the bodies of the slain were glued to the ground, while their clothes were so hard and stiff that it was impossible to move the dead from where they lay.

Dr. Tilghman returned on the 10th with his *confrères*, bringing some waggon-loads of wounded. That the fighting about Beaugency had been severe I could discern from the appearance of all that was left of the Bavarian army, which returned to Orleans about the 14th. Jaded and fatigued, spattered with mud, with their uniforms in some instances torn, and their plumes lost, they trudged sulkily and silently into the town. About 8000 of all ranks had survived of the 30,000 men that left Germany. They, too, like the French, were a contrast to their North German brethren in arms. But, as usual, they had been set in the forefront of the hottest battle; they had everywhere borne the brunt against vastly superior forces; and had in the end conquered, though at the expense of half their numbers. From the beginning of the war this had been the inevitable fate of the Bavarians; they were butchered to make the new German Empire.

In return for these heroic services, the Prussians affected to look down on them; they snubbed them openly; and took pains to hinder rather than to cultivate a friendly feeling between themselves and their Southern allies. I have seen quarrels take place in private houses where Prussians and Bavarians were billeted together, simply because my lords of Brandenburg disdained to share their quarters with King Ludwig's men. Such bickerings went from words to blows, in which the hearty ill-will of both branches of the great Teutonic race to one another became only too visible.

In the week which followed the battle of Beaugency, nothing happened worthy of special record; we were always at work from daylight to dark, and fresh convoys of wounded were brought in daily from that neighbourhood. When one has such an absorbing subject of interest as the routine of an Ambulance, from its very nature, and especially after a severe engagement, the days pass like hours. So it was with us; for, except an occasional few minutes which we spent in listening to the splendid military bands that performed every day in the Place Jeanne d'Arc, we had little to divert our minds from our business. There is, however, a matter of interest connected with the battle of Beaugency that I will ask leave to set down here.

The 11th Prussian infantry regiment, serving under the Red Prince, had suffered severely, and were nearly decimated on the 8th December. Six of these men came under my care. One of them gave me the following history of a most dangerous bullet wound, which he had received through the upper arm. His name was Henry Schroeder, under-officer (*Unter-officier*) in that regiment, and he spoke French fluently and English intelligibly. He was advancing with his company along the skirts of a wood, in the face of a most murderous fire from the French, and his men were falling on all sides, when he perceived two of these, whom he knew to be rascals, edging away from the rest into the wood, with the clear intent of shirking their duty, and endeavouring to screen themselves from the fire.

He sent a soldier to them with this message, that he would have them shot forthwith, unless they returned to their places. Not many minutes had elapsed, when, in the confusion and heat of a charge, as they were bursting along in the open, he received a bullet from behind which felled him to the earth. A single glance made him aware that these two miscreants were at his back, but were now hard at work against the enemy.

This poor fellow, of whom we shall hear more later on, eventually succumbed, at home in Hamburg, to his wounds. He died with the firm conviction that it was one of these two villains who had shot him, though, of course, no one could prove it against the man.

Just about this time it happened that I got permission from Dr. May to amputate a thigh midway between the hip and the knee. As I was on the point of making the first incision, who should walk up to the operation table but Professor Langenbeck, of Berlin? This great person had come into the Hospital to glance at our surgical work, and to observe the manner in which we treated his Imperial master's subjects. For a moment, the presence of perhaps the greatest military surgeon living, and the father of German field surgery, made me very uncomfortable. However, I regained my self-possession pretty quickly, and was fortunate enough to get through the operation without a hitch or misadventure, receiving at the end a gracious bow, and a "*Sehr schön, mein Herr,*" from the old veteran, who diligently smoked a cigar all the while. I need hardly add that my *confrères* had a great laugh over the incident, and at my sudden exhibition of panic, which they assured me was quite evident.

In our Hospital we made, as far as possible, an equal division of labour, by allowing to each man so many beds.   Though I was only an assistant surgeon by promotion, I had practically the position of surgeon and not assistant, having the sole charge of my division, which consisted of all the beds between the pillars and the wall down the middle aisle of the Church, and numbered about thirty-three.   It must be remembered that these beds were occupied by none but the gravely wounded, and that we had under our charge numbers of others, placed out in private houses through the town, along with those who were billeted in the houses just outside the Church. These last were under the same management as those in Ste. Euverte itself.

About the 18th December an incident occurred which caused some stir among our circle.   Mr. Frederick Wombwell, who had started the previous day for Versailles to bring back medical stores, arrived with the intelligence that Dr. Pratt and Captain Hozier had been arrested in Étampes.   It seems that they had met Captain Keith Fraser and the correspondent of the *Illustrated London News*, as also the correspondent of the *Pall Mall Gazette*, on their way to Versailles, and that whole party fraternised and dined together at the hotel.   The Prussian Commandant's suspicions were aroused by this convivial meeting of foreigners, and he promptly placed them under arrest.   Captain Hozier and Dr. Pratt, after a day's detention, were allowed to return to Orleans; but Captain Fraser and his two companions were sent on to Versailles under a heavy escort of dragoons, at which place they were liberated without delay.

Just about this time, also, there was much excitement caused by the arrival from Kiel of two hundred sailors to man the gunboats on the Loire, which had been captured from the French. These bearded tars were fine, burly fellows, and to judge by their rollicking spirits seemed to enjoy the prospect of the job before them.

Another week elapsed in the old routine, without any stirring events having come to pass, and we found ourselves on the eve of Christmas, but with nothing to remind us of its approach, save the snow, which lay more than a foot deep on the ground, and the intense cold of the weather. It was freezing so hard, both in and out of doors, that the water in the jug and basin of my bed-room became almost a solid mass.

The manner in which we spent Christmas Day may be described in five words,—it was all hard work. Nevertheless, we contrived in the after-noon to have a good dinner, and a little jollification over a blazing fire in our quarters on the Quai. The custom of Midnight Mass, so impressive in Catholic countries, had been this year abrogated by the Bishop's order. And there was no re-ligious service for our wounded, though all had been arranged with a view to it. I ought not to omit the reason, which was hardly, in my judgment, a sound one. The hour fixed for Mass was 7 A.M. It came to pass, however, that when in the morning the old Curé learned that the Protestant Chaplain had been before him, and had preached a sermon to his Protestant brethren from the pulpit, he straightway refused to begin his own service. I confess I was much scandalised at this unreasonable exhibition of bigotry. Under the circumstances, I hold, the Protestant Chaplain only did what it was perfectly right and proper that he should do. And I expressed that opinion pretty strongly to the Sisters of Charity, and the Curé himself, who was referred to me as the only Roman Catholic on the staff.

However, we dressed the Church with holly and ivy, and had a Christmas tree in the middle decorated with ribbons. We likewise gave each man a flannel shirt and a pair of drawers, which were looked upon by them as most appropriate and acceptable Christmas boxes.

Friends have asked me since how much I saw of that famous Bishop Dupanloup, and what was his line of conduct during the German occupation. I can but reply, that I never saw him in the city. All the while he remained shut up in his palace, the greater part of which had been converted into ambulance wards, despite a vehement protest from the cathedral chapter. But their protest did not avail; and when the very churches had to serve as hospitals for the wounded, and accommodation was everywhere less than sufficient, I do not know that even a Bishop's palace could have been exempted from so plain a duty of love and compassion towards the suffering, whether friends or foes.

CHAPTER XXV.

CHRISTMAS DAY AT STE. EUVERTE.—GOING THE ROUNDS.—YOUNG HEROES.—ARRIVALS DURING THE NIGHT.—A GLIMPSE OF THE DEAD-HOUSE.

I HAVE not, so far, given a description of our new Hospital, nor any particulars in connection with individual cases ; and I cannot do better than submit to my reader a revised copy of some notes I made while on duty that Christmas night. These may furnish a tolerable idea of the nature of our work, and of such reflections as the time and place suggested to me.

The Church of Ste. Euverte at Orleans is a fine old Gothic building, in the style of the twelfth century. Its exterior would present few interesting details, except for the crumbling granite walls, and the ancient carved portals, on which the hand of time may be plainly traced. The interior also is devoid of ornament ; but the rich stained glass in the windows is not likely to be equalled by any attempt of our modern artists in the same line.

The nave is about 300 feet long, and broad in proportion, while the plain vaulted roof springs lightly from the massive pillars which support it.

The High Altar is of granite, as well as those in the chapels, and they in nowise relieve the cold stern appearance of the building. It had now become the third Hospital which we of the Anglo-American Ambulance had set up in this hotly-contested city.

It was late on Christmas Eve that I repaired to the Church, and took my turn of night duty. The night was bitterly cold. It had been freezing for weeks, and the snow lay deep and crisp underfoot. Let me describe what followed in the present tense.

As I approach the long narrow street, at the end of which the gloomy mass of buildings can be seen through the darkness, I hear the steady pace of the Prussian sentinel who keeps guard before the gate. The dim light of a lantern hanging above the door shows my uniform as I pass, and the soldier, checking his half-uttered "Halt!" salutes. The door is opened by a Zouave, who also salutes; but this time in French fashion. He is an old Mexican campaigner, and wears, among other decorations, the war-medal given by his now deposed Sovereign, who is spending Christmas at Wilhelmshöhe, a broken exile. He swings open the heavy, studded oak door, and I enter. I pause for a moment to contemplate a scene, the misery and pain of which none could realise who have not beheld it.

Along the central aisle, to the right and left,

are double rows of beds, each with its suffering occupant. On every pillar hangs a lamp, one to every four beds. Precisely the same arrangement has been made along the side aisles.

Between every fourth and fifth pillar a stove is burning, with the bright and cheery blaze of a wood fire. Thus a dim light is cast over the beds of the patients, but not sufficient to penetrate the gloom of the lofty roof. Impressive as the sight is taken as a whole, the deep interest which it excites is heightened by the thought that every one of those 300 beds bears its wounded sufferer, and that each sufferer could tell his own long history of privation and pain.

Assuredly the saddest congregation that this old Church has ever held! Around the stoves are huddled knots of soldiers, French and German, whose common affliction has changed bitter foes into sympathising friends. These are men whose wounds are comparatively light; and who, poor fellows, for five or six days have not enjoyed the privilege of a bed. They lie in all postures around the fires, trying to sleep,—a difficult task with a broken arm, wrist, or rib, or with severe flesh wounds; and they have no covering of any kind, and only a little straw and the hard flags to rest upon.

Passing along the lines of beds are Sisters of Charity, who administer every comfort they can, arrange the patients' beds, smoothe their pillows, and whisper words of solace and consolation. In the stillness of the Christmas night the tones of agony and suffering echo through the Church, which for centuries has resounded at that hour with the grand and solemn music of the Midnight Mass. What a comment on the words of the "*Gloria in Excelsis*," in which these Christians say they believe! "*Et in terra pax hominibus bonæ voluntatis.*" Man, I cannot but observe to myself, thou art as much a scandal as a mystery to the reflecting mind!

I begin my rounds, visiting first the more urgent cases. To some of the greatest sufferers I give morphia in pills, or else introduce it in solution under the skin, by means of a syringe with a sharp perforated needle affixed. The effect is wonderful. In a few minutes they are out of pain, and fall asleep quietly. In this manner I am compelled to silence those whose groans would disturb the other patients. I now go on in succession, stopping at every bed to satisfy myself as to the condition of its occupant, giving medicines when required, arranging bandages here and there, and soothing with hypnotics those whose wounds prevent their sleeping.

This done, I repair to the sacristy, which serves the purpose of a surgery and a waiting-room, and read before the fire for an hour, when I return to the Church to see that all is right, and that the infirmarians are awake and at their posts.

As I stand in the Sanctuary and listen, I can hear the heavy tread of the watchers pacing to and fro : nothing else, save the heavy breathing of the sleepers. What a change in less than two hours! The cries of pain are silenced, and the restless day of suffering is succeeded by a night of calm repose ;—a pleasant sight for the surgeon, and one which is entirely due to that friend of humanity, so long as rightly administered,—the drug opium. To be prepared, however, for emergencies, I return to my room, and lay out my instruments so as to be ready for an operation if necessary ; secondary hemorrhage, and such-like mishaps, being of frequent occurrence.

Were such an accident to take place, I have but to send for my "sleeping partner," Dr. May, whose quarters are next door ; and who is only bound to be present when sent for by the responsible officer on duty for the night. Thus as the hours advance, and my previous hard day's work begins to tell upon me, I grow sleepier every moment, and am soon nodding in my chair before the fire. But I have scarcely become unconscious when I am roused by an *infirmier*, who tells me that two men are awake and in their intense agony are creating a disturbance. I rub my eyes, shake myself together, and proceed to see them.

The first I come to is a young Prussian artillery volunteer. He is only sixteen, a mere boy, with large blue eyes, fair soft complexion, and fair hair, and, though stoutly built, has very white and delicate hands. His graceful and engaging manner, and his developed mind, show that he is of a good German family. Yet he is but a private soldier. What has induced him to leave his home and country at such an age? Two reasons alone,—hatred of the French, and a thirst for glory. Poor boy! his leg has been shattered by the fragment of a shell. His large tearful eyes turn to me as I approach his bed, and a kind smile comes over his face, so pale and worn with suffering. He takes my hand, and begins his sad story,—of a kind familiar enough by this time. He tells me that the pain from his wounds has become insupportable; that he can neither eat nor sleep; that every day makes him thinner and weaker; and that he thinks he shall not last long. With as favourable a forecast as I can muster up, I try to cheer him, and give the poor fellow hopes which I fear can never be realised. I bid him go to sleep. I give him some morphia to help that consummation, wish him good-night, and leave him.

My next patient is a subject of special interest to me. I received him some weeks ago into my ward, suffering from a comminuted fracture of the leg; in other words, the limb was very badly crushed. He gave me to understand that he came of a respectable and wealthy family in Wiesbaden. He was the only son of his mother, and the last of **his name** ; and in saving his life, I should save his mother's **too**, for he believed that she would **not survive** him.

Never did I see **a man** cling more passionately to life, **and** never had one **stronger** motives for so doing ; but never again did I see a man so ill and yet so incredulous **of his** danger. Now in **the** stillness **of this Christmas** night I come to his bedside to see him die. **For days and** nights I **have** helped him all in my power ; I **have denied him** nothing that **I could give** him ; and he **has** always been so gentle **and** affectionate that every trouble I took for him **was truly a pleasure.** He speaks **French and** English fluently, **is a graduate** of **the University** of Bonn, **and is** young **and** good-looking. All through **his illness** he has had one thought in his mind, and **that was** his mother. He now complains of excessive weariness and **pains in every part of his body.** He **is an** Evangelical, and at my request **the clergyman had** visited **him** late that evening. I speak **to him in** a low voice, and tell him that I **fear he is** not better. It appears that his last **efforts at** speaking have been too much for him ; **he is now too** weak and prostrate **to do more than gasp out** something about his **mother,** home, **and** Fatherland. Now his lips **quiver, now** they cease to move, and **a cold** sweat **stands** out in large beads over his **face.** I smoothe **his** pillow **and** wipe his forehead, as **I had often done** before.

This makes him alive to the fact that I am in my old place at his bedside. He takes my hand, presses it feebly in his, looks earnestly into my face, and becomes again unconscious. By this time several of the Sisters and one or two of the infirmarians have assembled around the bed of the dying man. For some minutes the brave fellow remains motionless ; his breathing becomes shorter and shorter ; when suddenly he starts convulsively forward, and makes an effort as it were to rise ; his eyes, which are now fixed and glassy, stare out with a vacant expression, and he falls back heavily a corpse. As we gaze for a second, the old tower clock strikes the hour, the sentinel on watch cries out in reply to the challenge of his superior officer who is on his rounds, " One o'clock and all's well". Yes—all is well,—only a poor soldier has given up his life into the hands of his Maker, for his country's cause. One more German mother has lost her son,—one more German heart is desolate.

Not many minutes elapse before the fair youth of yesterday is lifted on a *brancard*, or stretcher, and conveyed to the dead-house. Here the bearers tumble the body on the cold shiny floor and leave it until morning, when the mayor's cart will convey it and the other lifeless remains in that ghastly chamber, to the brink of a deep pit at the back of the church, and into that they will be roughly heaved. A little quicklime will be thrown in, then a little earth; and the burial ceremony is over. Thus the scene closes for this brave lad, who was my friend as well as my patient. "*Dulce et decorum est,*" wrote Horace. Here is the reality of that boast.

Having seen that all is quiet again, I return to my fireside in the sacristy. When I am once more in my cosy chair, the details of what I have witnessed,—to such scenes,—alas, I am now accustomed,—pass from my thoughts, and are replaced by others of a different and more agreeable nature. The little bunch of holly which is set above the Tabernacle on the High Altar reminds me that it is Christmas morning; the glow of the burning wood brings before me the recollection of that bright fireside at home across the water; and as my eyelids gradually close, many a well-known and much loved face appears before me as if to cheer me in this solitude.

I have slept thus for nearly two hours, when my pleasant dreams are put to flight for the second time by the infirmarian of the watch, who tells me in an excited manner that a young Bavarian soldier is bleeding profusely from the mouth, and cannot live if I delay many minutes. I despatch a messenger in haste to call Dr. May; and another second takes me to the bedside of the dying man.

This patient, a young Bavarian, has been shot through the open mouth. Curiously enough, the ball had traversed the substance of the tongue from apex to base, and had buried itself in the back of the throat, from which position it has hitherto been impossible to get it removed.

At once I compress the common artery of the neck with my thumbs, and while thus supporting him, kneeling up behind him in bed, I am able for the time being almost to stop the blood completely. But when I look into the basin that is placed beside me on a stool, I perceive to my horror that it is half full of what appears to be pure blood. I now ask the infirmarian why he had not made me aware of the fact, and called me sooner. He answers that some five minutes previously the sick man had sat up in bed, and had been, as he thought, very sick in his stomach. By the extremely faint light he had not perceived that what the sick man was ejecting was blood. Immediately upon discovering the true state of things, he had come for me.

In a few minutes Dr. May arrives; but he and I are both too late. The man becomes ghastly pale, and writhes as if in a fit, then he is still for an instant, and sinks heavily and without life into my arms.

A momentary feeling of sadness comes upon me, while I gaze on the remains of that unhappy young man, the victim of such an awful, such an unnatural death! But I must quickly repress my feelings; I have to see that these sleepy fellows remove the body, change the bedding, and clean the blood from the floor, so as to make way for another, who will at once occupy the place that has been thus left empty.

This done, I pass round to the bedside of the young soldier whom it will be remembered that I visited first. His dreams of glory are now at an end; for he sleeps the sleep that knows no waking. Doubtless his spirit is at peace. What would his mother feel did she know that her son had died this lonely death in a dreary place, with no hand save mine, that of a stranger, to wipe his brow! When he, too, has been consigned to the dead-house, I return as before to the sacristy, where I take another interval of rest.

Between four and five o'clock the infirmarian awakes me for the third time, to say that there is a waggon at the gate with three wounded who are begging earnestly to be admitted. I have only two vacant beds; the third was occupied already by a bad case which had been lifted from the floor. I order two of the arrivals to be brought in. Upon examination I find that both have been badly frost-bitten in the feet. One, indeed, showed me half his foot almost black and simply rotting off. Their tale was a fearful one. They had been wounded,—one in the hip, and the other in the fleshy part of the thigh—in a skirmish about a fortnight before, near Beaugency. Overcome by loss of blood, each had dragged himself into a thicket—for the spot was a lonely one in the open country ; and there they had remained in terrible frost and snow, during the whole night and part of the next morning. Some peasants discovered them, and they were removed to a cottage several miles distant. Here they had remained until now without surgical treatment ; and hence their miserable condition.

Their sufferings are not to be described ; and I administer at once a hypodermic injection of morphia, which gives them speedy relief. Then I go to see the remaining occupant of the cart. By a gleam of the lantern I perceive that his leg is badly fractured ; and the blood which oozes through the bandages, and trickles down the mutilated remains of his trousers, indicates that matters have not been improved by an eighteen miles' journey over rugged country roads. The sight of this famished and half-frozen unfortunate, whose agony is increased by the bitter cold of the winter night, and his pitiful supplication to be let in, determine me at once to make out a place for him. This is the work of a minute ; for I know of a comparatively light-wounded fellow whom I can dislodge from his bed, although he is sound asleep and does not want to be stirred. The garments of the new-comer are, some stripped, some cut off him ; and he is put into the bed which is still warm from its late occupant. A hot bowl of bouillon is swallowed down with avidity ; to the fracture I adjust a temporary splint, for he is much too weak to undergo an operation. A sleeping draught is given, and I leave him to enjoy some hours' repose.

Once more I satisfy myself that all is right, the fires burning up, and the men on duty at their posts ; and as I yawn, and stretch my weary limbs in the arm-chair again, I find it difficult to imagine that it is Christmas Day.

Another walk round the Hospital, and dawn is here at last. Soon after I repair to a neighbouring house, where I address myself to a large bowl of café-au-lait, and a loaf of bread, with some Liebig's extract of meat. This accomplished, I return and find our staff assembled, making ready for the day's work. I give in my report to the chief, and immediately set about attending to my own wounded.

I never felt the long watch in the least irksome, nor did the others. At ten I assist my seniors during two amputations and a resection. One of the amputations is our arrival of the night, who last occupied the waggon : a consultation has just decided the fate of his limb.

The operations being over, I return to my men, and work away, with the assistance of two male nurses and Sœur Berthe. The Sister is a native of Luxemburg, as bright and active as possible, and my great mainstay. At three my work is finished, and in our house on the Quai I get a good substantial dinner.   But I must still go back to Ste. Euverte, and wait the expiration of my term of duty.

On looking into the dead-house to make sure that my poor friends of the night, with their companions, had been committed to the grave by the Mayor's officials, I perceive that one is still unburied, probably because the dead-cart was full. It is the young soldier, on whose sad end I have dwelt, I hope not too insistently. I felt very sorry for him. Our affection in that short space had grown to be that of brothers; for we were, after all, only boys together. I shall miss him even in the stir and excitement of these unruly times. But I can do no more. Dr. Mackellar comes to take my place, and my watch is at an end.

VISITORS.—NEW YEAR IN HOSPITAL.—THE CHURCH
EVACUATED.—I GET FURLOUGH,—AND CATCH A
NIGHT-GLIMPSE OF PARIS.

CHRISTMAS week passed away, and we had anything but a pleasant time of it. The frost and
cold were so intense that it was with much difficulty
we could keep ourselves sufficiently warm to enable
us to do our work. About this time we had
several visitors at our quarters. They were
Captain Brackenbury, of the Royal Artillery,
Prussian Military Attaché; Captain Frazer, also
of the Artillery; and Colonel Reilly, French
Military Attaché,—the last of whom had been
captured in Orleans on the morning of 7th
December, by the Prussians, and kept there ever
since. He was now ordered with an escort of
Uhlans to the frontier. We had a great laugh
when he walked into our place on that unlucky
7th; and related how, on awaking, he found to his
surprise that the town was in the possession of
the Germans. It was certainly not pleasant for
him.

We had also with us Major de Haveland, a

knight of Malta, and, as I was informed, the only English member of that order. It is well known, however, that the knights of St. John are divided in their obedience ; and I do not believe that the Grand-Master, who lives in Rome, would recognise many who in England are spoken of as Maltese Knights. The major, I presume, was of the Roman Obedience. Two members of the press were our guests, Mr. Mejonelle of the *Daily Telegraph* and Mr. Holt White of the *Pall Mall Gazette*. The former, who was an artist, made sketches also for the *Graphic*. He has given a representation of Ste. Euverte, in which several of us figure. The day I was showing him round, there was a dead soldier laid out on the High Altar, wrapped up in his sheet, with nothing but his head and toes to be seen. He had been taken out of one of the beds beside the Altar immediately after his death, so as to make room for a fresh occupant, and merely laid there while the infirmarians were arranging the bed. The sight struck our guest forcibly, as it could not fail to do ; it was most uncanny.

These gentlemen expressed their satisfaction at the way in which everything was carried out at Ste. Euverte, and the clean and decent condition in which we kept the Hospital, despite the presence of almost every circumstance which could militate against cleanliness and order.

Another couple of days, and we found ourselves celebrating the obsequies of the old year, and welcoming, after the fashion of heathens, the advent of the new, by partaking of the unlimited supply of rum punch, which nigger Charlie served up. I have already praised it.

On the evening of New Year we dined together, and toasted not only our noble selves, but our respective countries, homes and friends ; endeavouring to feel as happy as possible in the midst of occupations which demanded good spirits as the best way of keeping up our health and courage. It would be unfair to nigger Charlie if I forgot his most eloquent and humorous oration, delivered in choice Virginian or negro dialect, in reply to the toast of his health which Colonel Hozier proposed. The most remarkable portion of it was, perhaps, that in which Charlie exulted over the former wealth and greatness of Dr. Pratt's family, as large slave-owners ! What could a Declaration of Independence do for such feudal enthusiasm as this ?

The weather continued bitterly cold ; and Henry Schroeder, the sub-lieutenant whom I mentioned as having been shot at Beaugency by one of his own men, asked me as a favour to find quarters for him in some private house in the town. After much trouble I heard, by accident, that at the convent of Notre Dame des Récouvrances, the superior, Mère Pauline, desired much that the cloisters, dormitories and schoolrooms which the convent possessed, should be occupied by our Ambulance. The Sisters were afraid lest the Germans should establish in their house an Ambulance of their own, to which the nuns highly objected.

But the fact that Mère Pauline was an Englishwoman, in great measure accounted for her anxiety to have us. I need hardly say that I did not want much pressing ; at once I had Schroeder, Rüdiger, and four or five others, removed into their new quarters, and took formal possession in the name of the Ambulance.

Here, in good beds and warm rooms, with every care and attention paid to them, and good food to eat, they were very snug and comfortable—a pleasing contrast to the cold, dreary church which they had just left. I appointed one nurse, Sœur Léopoldine, to look after these men, whose number, in a few days, I increased to ten, so that I had quite a hospital there, though on a small scale.

The patient named Rüdiger, a young fellow of seventeen, and a volunteer, whose leg was fractured, became a particular favourite with his nurse and with Mère Pauline. He had not a hair on his face, which was of a ruddy hue, and wore a perpetual smile. He spent his time mostly in learning the French Grammar, a task in which he was helped by Sœur Léopoldine during her spare moments. Most of the others were Bavarians, and, I must say, a sleepy uninteresting lot.

Schroeder was the son of a wealthy tobacco and wine merchant in Hamburg. He had one brother, who was captain in an infantry regiment. Their mother was still living. He told me with pride that he had supplied Bismarck with many a cigar; and promised me a case of them and a barrel of oysters, when he returned. Poor fellow, he little knew what was coming; for at this time he was comparatively strong, and, in the opinion of many, out of danger. But, from my conversations with him, I learned that his family history was very bad; and from the first had grave misgivings about his case, which, however, it was my duty to disguise from him. When, occasionally, without being able to help it, I looked serious, he used only to laugh, and chaff me, singing, in the most comical way possible, the well-known English ditty, "Champagne Charley is my name". I liked Schroeder.

I now put two of my men from Ste. Euverte into No. 44 Rue de Bourdon Blanc. They were Martin Dilger, my old patient—the survivor of the railway-shed—and Jacob Venheiser. There they received the kindest care and attention from their good host and hostess, M. and Madame B——.

By 4th January I had removed all my worst cases into private quarters in the town; leaving only about a dozen in the church, all of which were now on the high road to convalescence, and fit to be removed to Germany by the next ambulance train.   On this happy disposal of my patients I had greatly to congratulate myself; for just now pyæmia and hospital gangrene of the worst type, showed themselves in the church; and we knew from our experiences at Sedan and the railway station how sure they were to be attended by terrible results, where such a number of wounded were kept together.

And so it proved now.   In a few days, blood-poisoning made great havoc among the men, and its victims lay piled one above another in the dead-house,—truly a sorry sight for those who had spent so much care on them! We determined at once to evacuate the church; for even the convalescent were not safe from this dread malady, which some of the savants in our profession tell us is preventable; such, however, is not my experience.   Disinfectants and carbolic-acid dressings were used unsparingly.   Fresh air, as I have said, is of paramount importance in the management of this disease; and it must come to the patient in a continuous current,—moreover, to be effective, it must be dry air, while about the patient it requires to be warm, or at least the patient himself must be warm, and at no time suffer a chill.   Every day the members of our staff eagerly sought new quarters for their wounded in the private houses of the town, which was now not a difficult task, the garrison not being very large, for Orleans had ceased to be that theatre of war which heretofore it had been.

As time rolled on, and fresh arrivals did not come in, we had more leisure. And well for me that it happened so! I had begun to find the work tell upon my health, and now a little relaxation was as necessary as it was agreeable.

During all this time no startling event happened, save an attempt that was made by some demented person at Orleans to assassinate a Prussian soldier. For this offence a fine of 600,000 francs was levied on the town; and to show the amount of trade which was carried on by the French with the invaders, out of this sum imposed, 400,000 francs were paid down in Prussian money. The fine was demanded on the 16th, and paid up fully on the 23rd of December.

Now, as I was daily beginning to feel more and more exhausted, and feared my health was becoming undermined, I determined to seek leave of absence for a few weeks. Dr. Tilghman, who was again *locum tenens* during Dr. Pratt's absence on business for ten days, knew how much I wanted a change, and did not hesitate to give me leave, under condition that I would report myself again before that day month. A matter of urgent private business obliged Dr. Sherwell to start for Hamburg on the next day, and I resolved to get ready that evening, 7th Jan., 1871.

I went with Dr. Fritz to the Commandant of the place and the Head Military Surgeon, from whom I obtained sick passes all through France and Germany, and Railway and Hotel billets free. The Northern parts were still in the hands of the French, so that I had no chance of getting home in that direction. I handed over my cases to the care of Dr. Parker, who, with his usual good nature, promised to give them his best attention in my absence. I made as little as possible of my departure to them, merely saying that I should be back at the end of some days.

At six o'clock next morning Dr. Sherwell and I were at the Railway Station, where we found that a train full of wounded was to be put under our charge as far as Corbeil. Our way of getting on was a novel one, for we were to be drawn by horses the whole distance. After much confusion and waiting we started. The entire train was composed of goods trucks, in which the wounded were laid on straw, using their rugs to cover them. There were many officers among them who took pot luck with the men, for there was no special accommodation. Every three trucks were drawn by four horses, and thus it was that we took the train to Corbeil, —a distance of some fifty miles.

The morning was bitterly cold, and a dense fog hung about, which made it hard for us to keep ourselves warm ; but matters mended when we came to Artenay, where hot soup and bread were awaiting us.

In one of the trucks sat Martin Dilger and one or two other of my patients, all in high spirits at the thought of getting back to the Fatherland, though minus a limb each. In another carriage we had a company of soldiers as an escort to the cavalcade, and these made themselves useful when required.

Thus we went along at a snail's pace; but Sherwell and I got out now and then, and ran ahead of the train to warm ourselves, for the weather did not mend, and many of our charges suffered severely from it. During the journey I fell into conversation with the sergeant of our guard, a mere lad, like so many others, and a volunteer. He spoke English well, with hardly any accent, and had lived and studied in London during the past two years, hence his knowledge of the language. He had been at Gravelotte, of which tremendous affair he gave me a most interesting account.

He was a gentle youth, with a soft musical voice, and plainly of position, as well as education. He said that he had been recommended for the Iron Cross. Here was the third volunteer I had met under the age of twenty, and all three were of good social standing.

There was one old wounded colonel who had a large flask bottle of chartreuse, with which he repeatedly plied Sherwell and me during the journey. I think we neither of us disliked it just then. The next stop we made was at Étampes, where we remained half an hour to have some hot coffee served out. At dusk we had got as far as Juviose, where we changed lines, and in due time arrived at Corbeil about 8 P.M. Our convoy excited notice and wonder among the country people in the districts which we passed, and in many places they came out in crowds to see us go along. When we arrived at Corbeil, we called on the Etappen-commandant, got our passes checked, and went to the major for our billet and rations,—in other words, our requisition for board and lodging, which he gave us on a very snug well-furnished little house in a central part of the town. Having dined off a piece of coarse beef and some bread and beer, we strolled out for a short time. Next morning we were up betimes, and went out to see the town, which is a quaint old place. We stood on the ruins of the bridge, which we had crossed over on piles and planks, in the parts where it had been damaged by the French explosion. It formed a pretty sight when seen at a little distance.

What struck me most about the place was that all the trade of the town seemed to be in the hands of German sutlers, principally Jews, who had followed in the footsteps of the army. Few of the inhabitants kept establishments open for the sale of merchandise. In one of these shops where we turned in to buy some trifles, we met a friendly German civilian, who told us that our best route eastwards was by Lagny, beyond Paris, —a station some forty miles from Corbeil—which was in direct railway communication with the Rhine. He added that a convoy of provision was to leave at noon for that place, and advised us to secure a seat in one of the waggons. Accordingly, we found out the conductor, promised him a couple of thalers for the lift, and secured places in one of the least uncomfortable of these vans. It was, by the way, of very simple construction. The body, made of osier-work and tapering to a point, rested on a heavy beam which ran lengthwise, and which rested, in turn, on the pair of axles, the upper part being supported by stays which went from the main ribs of the boxes of the wheels ; in short, the whole resembled a boat resting on a piece of timber, which again found support on the axles. Then there were twists of osiers overhead, covered with canvas which made the thing like a gipsy's tent.

In this queer turn-out we started from Corbeil, drawn by two Dutch ponies ; but, though our horses were fresh and spirited, our progress was very slow, the ground being as slippery as ice. Just before nightfall it began to snow hard, and when we came to the hamlet of Brie, our conductor would go no further. The roughing on

his horses' shoes was worn, and it would be too
dangerous for us to travel at night on such un-
endurable roads.

We got down, therefore, rather unwillingly,
with our traps in our hands ; and going about in
quest of lodgings for the night, as fortune would
have it, we espied at the further end of the village
a line of waggons similar to that which we had
just left.   Upon hailing the conductor, we found
that they also were for Lagny, and starting at
once ; so that again we took our seats, this time in
a waggon load of hay, which helped to keep us
warm, or, at all events, prevented us from being
thoroughly frozen.   It was snowing fast, and by
now was quite dark.   We thought the cold fearful.
As we went along the horses seemed to take it
in turns to fall ; but sometimes our ponies would
be down together : happily, they were not en-
cumbered with harness, and soon righted themselves.   Yet, once or twice it took the united
ingenuity of us all to extricate them from the rope-
traces, in which their legs had become entangled.

We had a lantern hung out over the front of
our waggon, by the dim light of which we were
barely able to see the road before us.   In time,
to our great relief, the snow-storm, which had
lasted for hours, cleared up.   We had been afraid
that our steeds would either miss the road, or
tumble us into a ditch.   At one place I got out,
and trudged through the snow for a couple of

miles. There was a part of this road turning round the crest of a hill, from which we could see the flashes from the forts round Paris, and hear the booming of the cannon distinctly. Several times I saw the little thin streak of sparks rising into the sky, which the fuse of the bomb-shells threw out on their journey, while sudden flashes in the air, followed by a loud report, signified that a shell had prematurely burst.

It was a splendid sight, and resolving to get the best view possible, I climbed into an apple tree by the way side, where, kneeling on a huge bunch of mistletoe, I could see every few minutes a shot directed from the forts and one in reply, each leaving its comet-like train of fire behind it. Though the besiegers and the besieged were many miles distant, I could hardly realise that they were not close at hand. So little, at the time, did I comprehend the magnitude of the siege guns, and the remoteness at which they could be heard. Much as I should have liked to linger on the scene, I could not tarry; I had to come down from my apple tree, and trot along until I had rejoined my waggon. Such was my second glimpse, and that at night, of the siege of Paris. My first, if the reader has not forgotten it, showed me the assault which ended in the burning of St. Cloud.

CHAPTER XXVII.

TRAVELLING IN FROST. — AMMUNITION TRAIN IN DIFFICULTIES. — FERRIÈRES. — THE CAMP OF CHÂLONS.—HOW GERMAN OFFICERS TREAT JEWS.

THE snow-storm had given over, but it was freezing hard, and the road was now almost impassable. Our horses were constantly falling, and we were getting on very slowly indeed. At last we came to the hamlet of Chivry,—it does not deserve the name of a village. We could see no inn ; it was stark midnight ; and, except a lonely candle in one small cottage, there was not a light in the place. At the cottage, therefore, we knocked. A regular parley ensued ; and after much explanation and fair promises, the door was opened by an old woman, who admitted us into a warm room, as clean and neat as any room could be, though everything testified that the owners were in humble circumstances. The only other inmate of the house, an old man, was in bed. All we asked was a cup of coffee, and a mattress to lie upon, both of which our hostess readily provided. As to eatables, we had brought a loaf of bread with us, which we finished without delay, then took a pull at our flasks, and so made a meal which for my part I relished as much as any I had ever eaten.

Next, divesting ourselves of our outer clothing, we threw ourselves on our mattresses, and slept a deep and refreshing sleep until seven next morning, when we made the acquaintance of a well in the yard, at which we performed our ablutions, after the manner of professional tramps. This done, we notified to the old lady that we were still hungry, and asked her to get us some bread and meat. She replied civilly that she had neither the one nor the other;—an unpleasant piece of news, for we were famished. I enlarged to her on our inward sufferings, and at the same time slipped four francs into her hand, bidding her get as good a meal as she could, and as soon as possible.

This douceur had its effect. Madame, or "la bourgeoise," as country-folks say, disappeared, only to return with a loaf of fresh bread, though a few minutes before I had been assured by a peasant that none was to be had for love or money. The truth was, that we were taken for Prussians, and treated accordingly. After a while, the dame announced that breakfast was ready, mentioning that she had a pot of stewed rabbit for us, which we set about demolishing with the loaf of new bread. As we sat devouring, neither of us spoke; but morsel after morsel of the rabbit disappeared, and we eyed one another significantly, for the same horrid suspicion was passing through our minds, that this white, insipid stuff was not rabbit at all, though what it might be we could not guess. Our natural history declared it to be cat, but we could not tell, nor did we much care. However, I inquired afterwards whether rabbits existed in the neighbourhood, and was assured that never a one dwelt within ten miles of it.

Just as we were wishing ourselves at Lagny, who should pass through with his waggon, but the driver of the convoy with whom we had started from Corbeil? An accident to his waggon had delayed him on the road, which was a great piece of luck for us; and we thanked our hostess at once for her equivocal, but nourishing breakfast, put our traps in the buggy, and drove off. It was the 10th of January. We found it still very difficult to travel, but lest our driver should pull up as he did before, we plied him with brandy and liqueur out of a stone jar, that I had bought at Orleans. In consequence, he was in the best of humour all through the journey, and not in the least disconcerted when the horses fell or stumbled about.

Some miles of our route lay through the Forest of Champigny; but here the road was impassable, for it had thawed during the small hours and frozen again, making the causeway one

solid sheet of ice.   Wherever we could we
travelled along the edges ; but it was dreadfully
slow work, and the horses themselves, poor
beasts, were afraid.   While we were loitering at
this funeral pace, I witnessed a sight that I never
shall forget.   We fell in with an ammunition train,
about half a mile in length, conveying war
material of all kinds to the positions before Paris.
Our own waggon we had to draw in among the
trees for safety, as the horses were falling every
minute ; and now when we looked along the line,
we could see as many as ten horses on the ground
at once.   Sometimes two of the animals would
slip down side by side, and fall again and again
whenever they attempted to pull on their traces.
Nay, more, I saw a team of four horses all come
down simultaneously, not once, but twice.   No
description, indeed, could exaggerate the confusion
of the scene,—drivers shouting, waggons slipping,
and horses falling in all directions ; while the
more their guides interfered the more they fell,
until the poor brutes became so terrified, that
they trembled all over from fright.

   The ground was amazingly hard.   In one
place I saw a heavy ammunition waggon drawn
by four horses, when coming down a slight incline,
slip five or six yards along the road, and then
glide off into the ditch, without a single wheel
having turned on its axle.   As it was now evident that they could not proceed through the

Forest without inflicting grave and perhaps fatal injuries on their cattle, the men began to pick out the middle of the road where the horses trod, and strewed along it coal dust, which they carried with them on purpose. This made the road sufficiently passable to allow of the train to advance. But, meanwhile, it was about two hours before we of the convoy could move, though when we did we rattled on at a spanking pace. From time to time we met numbers of newly organised cavalry,—with droves of horses led by halters; and of these steeds I was ready to lay any odds that some were Irish bred. Men and horses were on their way to the front to replace the maimed, killed, and wounded, and to contribute themselves to a similar contingent.

Early in the afternoon we came to Ferrières, where having dined, so to call it, we paid a visit to the splendid château of M. de Rothschild. Unheeded and unhindered, we roamed through this lovely demesne, marvelling at the beauty of house and grounds which, as all the world knows, would not disgrace the abode of royalty. The mansion of cut stone, the terraces with their marble statues, the flower-gardens, shrubberies, stables,—these last, a wonder in themselves,—all were in perfect preservation. Not a stick or a stone in the whole place had been touched by the Prussians, nor did a soldier set foot in it. Such was the good pleasure of William I.

who had taken up his quarters here, such the
reverence paid to the kings of finance by the
House of Hohenzollern !

We started again on our journey, but had
proceeded only half a mile, when we fell in with
a train of siege guns, some of them drawn by six
horses. They were on the road to Paris, and
would do service there. I remarked that some
of the smaller guns were of brass, and shone in
the sun like gold.

The country we passed through was
charmingly wooded, and looked pretty enough
in its garment of snow. It was night when we
arrived at Lagny. On demanding our billet, we
were directed to the sick officers' quarters, in the
upper portion of the station house, where we
should find plenty of room. There we came upon
two of our friends who had been quartered at
Orleans. They, also, were on their way out of
France, and we engaged to make a party of it.
At four o'clock next morning a couple of soldiers
called us, and at five we started. There were
several officers in the carriage, from whom
Sherwell and I received every civility. Passing
Meaux we arrived at Epernay, and later on
traversed the great camp at Châlons, which now
presented a vast and beaten plain of enormous
extent. By way of Vitry and Chaumont we came
on to Toul and Nancy, of the fortifications round
both of which we got an excellent view, in par-

ticular at Nancy, where we halted for some time, and were able to look about us.

None of these places, however, was of so much interest to me as the little town of Lunéville. I knew nothing of the famous treaty concluded there by the First Consul, and had never heard of the Court of King Stanislaus, or of Voltaire and Madame la Marquise du Châtelet, in connection with it ; I simply admired the view. Lunéville is situated on a hill, with some of its fortifications overlooking a steep precipice which serves as a natural protection for perhaps a third of its extent. From the railway which runs along the flat country, below the town, it appeared to be an impregnable stronghold ; for where nature's protecting barriers were wanting, there were huge embankments, deep fosses, and steep artificial declivities. A picturesque place too. The face of the cliff and the old turreted walls were covered with ivy, a broad stream ran beneath the hill, which on the lowest slope was well wooded all round,—and now imagine all this clad in new-fallen snow, and you will have as lovely a scene as I remember.

Close to the town we passed a bridge which had been blown up, but was now reconstructed on timber piles. It had been destroyed, not by the regular army, but by a band of Francs-Tireurs. This I learned from one of the officers who knew all about the place.

I had seen Ferrières, the palace of a Frank-
fort Jew, with admiration, all the more that it had
been respected as a sanctuary by orders from the
Prussians. Yet it was during this same journey
that I witnessed an incident in which a Jew was
the hero or the victim, that filled me with astonishment, as it may do my readers who happen
not to be acquainted with the ways of the
Fatherland. I had frequently heard the Jews
spoken of by my German friends in language of
supreme contempt; but never did I realise the
depth of that feeling until now.

In the railway compartment in which I
travelled, all were German officers except myself and one civilian. The latter had got in
at a wayside station, and sat at the furthest
corner opposite me. My companions began
without delay to banter and tease him unmerci-
fully, all the while addressing him as Lemann.
He was a small stunted person, in make and
features an Israelite, and not more than twenty-
five. The behaviour of his fellow-travellers
seemed to give him no concern; as they fired off
at him their sneering jests, he scanned them with
his sharp eyes, but did not move a muscle.

I inquired of the officer next me, who spoke
English well, how it came to pass that they knew
this stranger's name. He explained that Lemann
was the common term for a Jew in their language,
going on to describe how much the sons of Jacob

were detested throughout Germany ; and for his part he thought they were a vile horde, who laid hands on everything they could seize, in a way which we English were incapable of fancying. The officers, he added, were all getting down to have some beer at the next station, and by way of illustration he would show me what manner of men these Jews were ; and as he said the words, he took off his hairy fur-lined gloves, and threw them across the carriage to our man in the corner, remarking, "There, Lemann! it is a cold day".

The Jew picked up the gloves eagerly, which he had missed on the catch, and pulled them on. When we were nearing the station, the officer who had thrown the gloves at him, took off his fur rug, and flung that also to the Jew. Once more he accepted the insulting present, and quickly rolled the rug about him. Finally, a third threw off his military cloak, and slung it on the Jew's back as he was passing out. This, again, the wretched creature put on ; and their absence at the buffet left him for the next ten minutes in peace.

Presently the horn sounded, and our Germans came back. One seized his rug, another his cloak, and finally, my first acquaintance recovered his gloves by one unceremonious tug from Lemann's meekly outstretched fingers. My own face, I think, must have flushed with indignation ; but the others only laughed at my superfluous display of feeling ; and Lemann, shrugging his shoulders, — but only because of the sudden change of temperature when his wraps were pulled away,—took out of his pocket a little book with red print, which he began to read backwards, and, turning up the sleeve of his coat, began to unwind a long cord which was coiled round his wrist and forearm as far as the elbow. Every now and then he would stop the unwinding, and pray with a fervour quite remarkable, then unwind his cord again, and so on till the whole was undone. For a time the officers resumed their jeering ; but, seeing that it was like so much water on a stone, they turned the conversation, and allowed the unhappy Jew to continue his devotions unmolested till he got out at Strasburg.

What would these officers have done, had they travelled in the same railway carriage with M. de Rothschild ?

CHAPTER XXVIII.

AT half-past nine we arrived at Strasburg, and were all billeted together in the most central part of the town, at a grand hotel, where we had the best of living and accommodation. There were about thirty officers quartered there, with whom we messed. I strolled out in the evening through some of the busiest streets. They were brilliantly lighted up ; the shops were open, and as much bustle and business seemed to be going on, as if we were in the heart of a peaceable country, and no siege of Strasburg had just taken place.

However, before long I learned that a large section of the inhabitants looked upon the Germans with anything but friendly feelings.

Next morning, 12th January, we went out, six in number, to see the town. We visited the fine old Cathedral, and hung about it for an hour, examining every detail so far as time permitted. One of the chief attractions was its famous clock, which I was quite ready to admire ; but the complicated details, and curious performances of this wonderful timepiece are too well known to need description. When Sherwell and I parted from our companions, we went to visit the ruins of the great Library and the Theatre, both of which were burned to the ground during the siege.

Our dinner in the evening was splendidly served, in the French style, and with abundance of wines.

Next morning Sherwell, myself, and two of our old travelling companions chartered a spacious waggonette, in which we set out, determined to see all that we could in and around Strasburg. We first drove through that part of the town which was destroyed by the besiegers,—a dreary but most interesting excursion. So far as I could judge, about one fifth of the suburbs had been ruined. When I say ruined, I don't mean simply made roofless and windowless,—that might have happened in a huge conflagration ; but that whole streets were reduced to long heaps of stones, with a few yards' interval between, which marked where the roadway had formerly passed. Nothing could have given a more vivid idea of the effects of a bombardment now-a-days. Even where the demolition was not so complete, and where portions only of the house had been carried away, the sight was appalling. Some of the furniture still remained in its place on the half-shattered floors, being too high to reach easily, or not worth the trouble and danger of removing it.

Here was a second edition of Bazeilles, on a far more extensive scale. I believe one of the best accounts of what took place during the siege is to be read in Auerbach's novel on the subject, called *Waldfried*.

Having wandered for a couple of hours through the ruins, we drove outside the town. Then we alighted, and one of our party, a captain of artillery who had been through the siege, acted as our guide, and made all the particulars clear to us. Walking along the fortifications, we arrived at the immense breach in the parapet which sealed the fate of Strasburg. It was of great extent, and already hundreds of men were at work repairing it;—but in the interests of Germany, not of France, from whose dominion the city had passed, for who knows how many years? Further on we saw a second breach, not so wide as the other. We now proceeded a considerable distance along the parallels and rifle pits, and visited the captured French lunettes, which seemed to be matters of intense interest to my military friends. A curious fact I learned about this siege was, that of the garrison in the town a comparatively smaller number were killed than of civilians, who met their death in the streets by the bursting of shells. This I was told by several who had been present, **and** who were likely **to** be well-informed.

When we **had explored** the various evidences **of** the mining operations during this memorable blockade, it was almost evening. **We** returned to our hotel, overcome with admiration at the skill of those who had not only devised, but successfully carried through, these **intricate** plans for approaching, storming, and capturing **a** stronghold with such mighty defences. Assuredly, the campaigns of 1870, in **the open**, and about the historic fortresses **of** France, afford examples **of science,** courage, and endurance which it **will not be easy** to **match**, and may **be** impossible **to surpass, in** the future.

On the 14th, I was up early, **went** out to make **some** purchases, came home, packed up, and set off from the station. **We** crossed the Rhine on the beautiful bridge to **Kehl, took our** seats in a fresh train, and started northwards. **We went by** Karlsruhe and Heidelberg, at the latter of which places we halted twenty minutes; **and** soon after **leaving it we** found ourselves **in a** hop-growing district, where there was **nothing to** be seen but hop-stacks; **we passed, also, through** extensive **vineyards:** but, as yet, **had only an** occasional glimpse of the Rhine in the distance.

During part **of our** journey, we skirted round **steep mountain** barriers, **which, at** times, towered above **us with their impenetrable** masses of fir-trees, at others, being thickly sprinkled with snow and tipped with hoar-frost, shone resplendent in the sunlight, as if silver dust had been shaken all over them, while here and there peeped out the snow-capped towers of some old castle or baronial hall. I do not pretend that these hills would have looked anything wonderful, had they not been covered with snow, and had not the pellicles of ice, formed on the fir trees by a thick fog the night before, first run into tears, and then been frozen hard, covering the trees with brilliants which sparkled in the sun. These decorations, indeed, gave them an air of fairyland.

On arriving at Darmstadt I took leave of Sherwell and my fellow-travellers, who were going on to Hamburg, and took the train to Mayence. It was very late when I got there, and I stayed the night at the Railway Hotel; for, having a sick officer's pass, I could break my journey where I pleased, which was a great convenience, besides being a cheap mode of travelling. I had practically nothing to pay; my sufficient warrant was the pass, stamped with the royal seal, which I exhibited to inquiring officials.

Mayence is not interesting. I went on next morning as early as I could, had to wait at Coblentz and Bonn to allow some special military trains to pass, and did not get into Cologne till the afternoon. The Rhine scenery, which one gets at times from the train, is very fine; but somehow this was the grand disappointment of my journey. It did not come up to my expectations; and I felt far more delight on viewing the unrivalled beauties of our own Killarney, and of the river Blackwater. But I had not yet gone up the Rhine in a steamboat, which is quite another expedition than the one I was taking just then.

From Cologne, which I explored in a few hours, I travelled by Aix la Chapelle to Liège. At the Hôtel de l'Europe my quarters seemed comfortable; but I had no longer a free billet, and might consider myself to be now in the enemy's country.

It was the 16th, and I went off to call on my friend Vercourt, with whom I spent the forenoon. Then by Ostend, London, and Holyhead, I prosecuted my journey, and arrived in Dublin on the morning of the 19th, and at home at Scarteen on the 22nd.

My furlough was made out for a month: but eight days after my arrival, a telegram came from Dr. Pratt, saying :—

" I return to-morrow ; go to Versailles as soon as possible, find out Ambulance, and join it ".

I had no alternative but to pack up and start next day, which I did by the morning train on Jan. 31st. On reaching London, I called at the English Society's rooms in Trafalgar Square, and reported myself to Colonel Lloyd Lindsay. Mr. Pearce, the secretary, made me known to Captain

Burgess; and I met there my *confrère*, Dr. Frank, who greeted me cordially, and sent many affectionate messages to his former colleagues. It will be remembered that Dr. Frank was chief of that section of our Ambulance which had a hospital at Balan and Bazeilles, and which afterwards established itself at Épernay, where it worked for some months before disbanding.

Having got all requisite papers and certificates of identification, I started from London Bridge for Newhaven. As I was taking my ticket I met Captain Brackenbury, who told me that he also was going to Versailles to rejoin the headquarters of the Crown Prince, that he had a private carriage at Dieppe, was going to drive all the way, and would willingly give me a seat. This kind offer I gladly accepted, and was delighted to have so entertaining and accomplished a host on my journey. At Newhaven, as we were crossing by night, we turned at once into our berths, and slept until called by the steward in sight of Dieppe.

Going up on deck I found it was a lovely morning, warm and genial, and very unlike the weather we had been enduring of late. As we approached Dieppe in the morning sun, we could see the glistening bayonets of the ubiquitous Prussian sentries. They were pacing to and fro on the pier, in what appeared to us an aggressive, not to say, menacing fashion. I confess the sight startled me : we had the vision of England still in our eyes, and these ambitious warriors seemed too dangerously near. I felt that I should have liked to take them by the collar, and pitch them into the sea. I could not help saying to Capt. Brackenbury that I felt inclined to ask them what they were peering at across the Channel.

But, as he dryly remarked, their answer might be that they were peering at a little island fortress on the high seas :—a mere speck in creation when compared to the great German Empire which had just been proclaimed at Versailles. He was in the right of it ; and we had already held conversations on this subject at Orleans, which I should like to set down, were not my space fast running out.

The carriage in which we travelled from Dieppe was a large and comfortable sort of landau, from which we could view the country at our ease.

The weather was now mild and bright, the snow had disappeared, and our journey became a pleasure. But when travelling between Mantes and St. Germain, as I was getting out of the carriage to walk up a steep hill, I had the mis-fortune to lose out of my overcoat pocket all my passes, letters of identification and the other documents I carried with me. At the gates of the Forest of St. Germain, a Prussian non-commissioned officer stepped out, and demanded our papers. I was minus every document which would have accounted satisfactorily for my being there; and I should certainly have been arrested and sent off to the Commandant of Versailles under an escort, had not Capt. Brackenbury assured the officer on duty that he had seen the papers in question. I had, as it happened, shown them to him that very morning. This satisfied the guard, and I was allowed to pass; but I need hardly say that I was supremely uncomfortable at the case I was in, and thought my journeys along the valley of the Seine were always doomed to misfortune. Last time the Francs-Tireurs had arrested me; now it was the turn of the Prussians.

When we reached St. Germain, we dined, in spite of my lost papers, and visited the Palace and the Bois, from the terrace of which there is such a glorious view, away to Mont Valérien and one or two other of the forts. As we were looking about us, there was quite a stir, bordering on excitement among the soldiers. King William, now the Emperor of Germany, and the Crown Prince, were expected every moment from Versailles, and the road was lined with infantry and cavalry to receive them. But we waited an hour, and his Imperial Majesty did not arrive, so we resumed our journey to Versailles.

There I left Capt. Brackenbury at a private house, where he and Dr. Russell, the *Times* correspondent, put up; and thanking him for his

great kindness I bade him good-bye.   This
was the last time I saw him.   It would be
difficult to do justice to the character of this noble
soldier ; a more generous heart or more gracious
disposition, I never had the privilege of knowing.

My business now was to search for lodgings,
I could no longer requisition one at the Mayor's,
since I had lost all my papers.   Having secured a
niche, I resolved to call at the Hôtel des Réservoirs, where I knew I should find Prince Pless,
or some one who would recognise me, and get me
these important testimonials.   By way of introduction I looked in at the office of the Military
Ambulance stores, and inquired whether all those
belonging to the Anglo-American Corps had
been taken to Orleans or not.   This was a happy
thought ; for they informed me that all the particulars I required would be given by Major de
Haveland in the Rue des Réservoirs,—the Maltese
knight to whom I have referred as visiting us at
Ste. Euverte.   This was what I wanted.   I called
at once on the Major, and he undertook to see the
commandant of the place, and explain the whole
matter.   Thus, thanks to his kind attention, I
was given the necessary papers next day, and
that evening I chartered a car to Étampes, from
which place I could get to Orleans by train.

CHAPTER XXIX.

IN ORLEANS ONCE MORE.—PEACE IS SIGNED.—AN
EASY TIME.—SENDING AWAY THE CONVALES-
CENTS.—THE AMBULANCE BROKEN UP.

I HAD to bribe the driver whom I thus engaged
with an extra napoleon, so afraid was he that his
trap and horse would be seized ; but when I
showed him my German papers he knew that he
was safe. Accordingly, I started before daylight,
and after a pleasant journey arrived at Étampes in
the evening, soon enough to escape an awful
downpour of rain, and to catch the night train to
Orleans.

The train was crowded with peasants, some of
whom had no tickets, and it was amusing to watch
the stratagems which they adopted in order to
hide themselves from the German guard. This
fellow was much too good-humoured and indifferent
to pretend to see them, though all the while
knowing their whereabouts, as I could tell by the
twinkle in his eye when their crouching forms
betrayed them. It was nothing to him, and he
left them under the delusion that they had got
to the blind side of their Prussian,—a parable

which might serve to describe the whole French
tactics during the war!

When I arrived at Orleans it was nearly midnight, and as there were no vehicles at the
terminus, I had to tramp across the town to the
Quai du Châtelet, where the door was opened to
me by our faithful Turco Jean. This barbarian,
becoming excited at seeing an old friend, shrieked
with delight, and gave utterance to much unintel-
ligible jargon, accompanied by low bows, rever-
ences, or salaams, all which, I believe, is the
orthodox method of greeting adopted by Moham-
medans.

As I entered our general sitting-room, I heard
a ringing cheer from my *confrères*, who, in this
most cordial manner, welcomed me back. I
confess that I felt pleased and proud at this
spontaneous outburst of kindly feeling.

Nigger Charlie, who had been grinning from
ear to ear for the past ten minutes, now disappeared, and after the lapse of a quarter of an hour,
came back, bearing in his hands the historic bowl
of punch. That was his salaam,—not unkindly
meant either.

Next morning I went to see my patients in
the Convent of Notre Dame des Récouvrances.
Mère Pauline, Sœur Léopoldine, and the other
sisters welcomed me into the wards, and Henry
Schroeder cried so heartily that I had to put it
down to the weakness from which he was suffering.

Young Rüdiger cheered, Kirkhof clapped his hands, and all my patients looked pleased,—which things I mention as giving me a real gratification in themselves, and showing what rewards a doctor who tries to do his duty may expect.

I went on to see other patients, among whom were two in the Rue de Bourdon Blanc. One of these had had his knee joint resected, an operation in which both ends of the bones of the leg and thigh, which enter into the formation of the knee joint, were removed, the limb remaining otherwise intact. It was at this period rather a rare operation, and was performed by Dr. Nussbaum of Munich, who then handed the invalid into my care. The limb was swung in an anterior suspension-splint, which was Dr. May's improvement on the American splint by Smyth. This was a case in which Dr. Nussbaum felt deeply interested, and he inquired of me repeatedly as to its progress.

After one or two days I fell again into the routine, and was running along smoothly in the old groove, which I had left for so short but eventful a period. Several weeks now passed away without anything worthy to chronicle, if I may judge from the blank in my notes. The work had become easier, and my patients, though scattered about the town, had become fewer and less troublesome to manage as they approached convalescence.

We had now much time to ourselves. The armistice continued, and no fresh supplies of wounded came in. Yet, we did not feel sure that hostilities would not recommence, until on the afternoon of the 26th of February, news reached us that peace was signed. Yes, peace was signed! The joyful tidings spread quickly through the town, and exclamations and prayers of joy and gratitude were on every tongue ; nor was it easy to discern whether the townsfolk or the garrison were filled with greater gladness at the news. Indeed, the change that came over the face of the town in an hour was marvellous. Civilians rushed about the streets shaking hands in the most frantic style with those German soldiers who had hitherto been their deadly enemies, while the soldiers cordially returned these friendly advances on the part of their vanquished foes. As the evening drew near, the cheering and confusion increased, and the streets became crowded with a mixed assembly of soldiers and inhabitants. Nor did the authorities appear to object ; nay, all the military bands in the town turned out, and marched up and down the principal streets, play-ing popular French airs, and even the " Marseil-laise ".

It was amusing as well as touching to see these mighty processions, the bands in front, and long lines of French and Prussians linked arm in arm, marching some fourteen abreast, and keeping time with the music. Thus in one hour did the memory of yesterday seem quite obliterated. While I was following one of the bands, and listening to the stirring airs which they were playing, I descried a white figure among the crowd, and what was my astonishment to find that this was Nigger Charlie! Still in his white kitchen-suit, with white sleeves and a paper cap, he was carrying on all kinds of antics, and grinning for the amusement of the juveniles who crowded after the procession.

Our duties now became so light that I was able to do all my work in a couple of hours, and generally had the rest of the day to myself. This time I employed in making excursions on horseback and on foot, to all the places of interest in the adjoining country. I could always get a mount from the ambulance equerry when I wished for one. As March came on, the weather grew fine, and I rode out to Gien, Chevilly, Patay, and Coulmiers; but Olivet and its neighbourhood, and the picturesque Source du Loiret, were especially my attraction. Dr. Warren, who, like me, preferred walking to riding, often accompanied me on these excursions.

But time rolled on, and we found ourselves in March, with March weather accompanying it. I now met Miss Pearson and Miss McLoughlin, who gave me a stirring account of themselves and their doings during the battles outside Orleans;

for the convent, full of wounded, of which they were in charge, was situated in the suburbs. The adventures undergone and the work accomplished by these energetic English ladies have been admirably described in the volume which relates their experiences during the Campaigns of 1870 and 1871. Too much praise cannot be given for the untiring zeal and heroic self-sacrifice which they always displayed in the discharge of their mission, under circumstances which were constantly most trying.

On the 3rd, Dr. Pratt, who had some time back returned from headquarters at Versailles, announced to us that our mission was over, and he must now disband us. We agreed, however, not to separate until we got to Paris, for which place we were to start in a few days. There we should meet Dr. Duplessy, and the heads of the French Ambulance, into whose hands we could deliver the horses, waggons, and *infirmiers* that we had originally received from them in the Palais de l'Industrie. We wished, also, in the presence of the above-named gentleman, to give an account of our stewardship, so far as the care of the French wounded in our charge was concerned. Accordingly, every preparation was made to start. I sent away the wounded that were on my hands, including poor Henry Schroeder, who said, that since I must leave, he would leave too. I had the poor fellow conveyed through town to his railway carriage in a sedan chair. When we parted he shed bitter tears.

I had grave misgivings for the ultimate success of his case, for his arm was suppurating profusely ; and he had that delusive hectic freshness of appearance, which I had now learnt was so untoward a symptom. Afterwards I had the pain of hearing from his brother that my forebodings were verified, and that Henry died soon after his return home.

On the 4th of March, we had finished nearly all our preparations ; and our kind host Proust seemed inconsolable at losing Warren and myself, towards both of whom he had evinced a parental affection. But my time to leave Orleans was not yet come.

CHAPTER XXX.

ONE bright evening, as I was out walking on the
bank of the Loire, I had felt a dead dull pain at
the back of my head and in my back. On my
return the pain became so intense that I was
obliged to go straight to bed. All night and
next day I felt very unwell, and Dr. Bouglet
was sent for. He pronounced me to be in fever,
of what kind he could not exactly tell; but as
small-pox was prevalent in Orleans, he feared it
might be that. Subsequently he came to the
conclusion that it was low fever of a typhoid sort.

On the 6th, I felt very ill indeed, and beyond
a dim recollection of saying good-bye to my
confrères, and the consciousness that my old
friends Warren and Hayden were continually at
my bedside, I can recall but little of what passed
around me for the next fortnight.

In a few days all the members of the Anglo-
American Ambulance, who had been my friends
and companions throughout this adventurous

campaign, were off to Paris. So there was I in No. 12 Rue Royale, away from home, and prostrated by a dangerous illness. To those who read this, it may appear that I was alone and friendless. But it was not so. For no father's care could have been more tender, no mother's solicitude more lavish, than that bestowed upon me by M. and Madame Proust, on the one hand, and, on the other, by my guardian angel and nurse, Sœur Berthe, from Notre Dame des Récouvrances.

During five long weeks, this indefatigable woman never left my bedside day or night, save for an interval of an hour or so. She had been working under me in the Hospitals, attending the wounded for many months ; and to her valuable and skilful aid I owe any success which may have attended my efforts on behalf of the patients in those wards. Now this good sister saw me, a stranger, but a fellow-labourer in the same cause, struck down at the end of the campaign ; and she bestowed upon me, as she was wont to bestow upon them, with that grace of manner and beaming kindness which characterised all she undertook, the same devoted attentions. It was a privilege to be ill in her hands. I learned much from her ; and I should be ungrateful indeed, were I to forget the lessons which her refinement, self-sacrifice, and unwearied good temper printed on my mind and heart during those weeks.

Dr. Bouglet came and went, sometimes making a second visit the same day. Evidently he thought my case a serious one. At the end of about ten days from the beginning of my illness, I became so stupid and lethargic that I remembered nothing for the next fortnight, save that during one of my lucid intervals I saw Hayden, Parker, and Warren at my bedside, the first two having come from Paris for the express purpose of seeing me. Warren stayed until I was getting better, and wrote home for me. He finished his letter, but almost failed in getting the address from me, so weak was my mind at the time. Hayden, on being questioned by one of the townspeople as to the chances of my recovery, answered, that it was all up with me. Sœur Berthe, likewise, wrote to Scarteen in my name ; but I could do nothing of the kind myself.

About the fourth week I had completely regained consciousness, and was daily getting stronger ; but that was not saying much, for I could neither turn in bed, nor lift an arm. I was simply skin and bone, and used to wonder how my knuckles did not come through the skin. When I looked at my limbs, I began to cry like a child, and this loss of control over my feelings was particularly distressing to me. They never let me see myself in the mirror until I was far advanced on the road to recovery ; and then I beheld what looked more like a corpse than my living self, and was much taken aback. When allowed to speak, many hours were spent in pleasant conversation with Madame and M. Proust, and with Sœur Berthe, who was always an interesting and lively companion. She used to pray with me, read to me, both serious and amusing books, and instruct me in the secrets of the science of which she was mistress. She would bring me flowers and fruit according to my fancy. And so the weeks passed by, and, with the assistance of such good friends, they were pleasant enough.

Before my brain got quite clear, I used to imagine that I saw numbers of my friends at home, and was talking with them. Nor were the persons phantoms. For I spoke to those who happened to be paying me a visit to see how I was going on. Upon discovering my mistake, I felt it bitterly, but was soon put into good humour again by Sœur Berthe. I have not yet said much of my hostess Madame Proust ; not because she was wanting in any way,—far from it, indeed. That kind lady put her house and all therein at my disposal, and was a most agreeable and sympathetic friend. Occasionally, after returning from her walk in the town, she would tell me of the people who were inquiring for me, which was an equal pleasure and help to a convalescent.

Just about this stage of my illness the Germans evacuated Orleans. I can remember well hearing the last **of their bands** playing in one direction ; while the French were advancing in the other. This was succeeded after **a** while **by** frantic cheering, by the din of music, and the tramp of soldiery,—a tramp which I knew to be very different from the measured tread that I had heard **an** hour previously. And so **had** come and gone the second German occupation of Orleans,— an epoch in the life of **those** who **took** any share **in** it which is indelibly stamped on their memories.

As time wore **on I was** removed **to the arm-**chair by the open window, **where I used** to remain for several hours every day, **when the** weather permitted, propped up with pillows and covered against the cold. Many of the passers-by seemed **to** think me worth looking at, for quite a number stopped in very French fashion to stare up at me. This was only curiosity, and by no means rudeness. At last I was able to go out, or rather to hobble out ; and for the first few days had enough to do to keep on my legs while shaking hands with the many kind and friendly townspeople who **came** forward to greet me. I would go into one **shop** and rest there for **a** few **minutes, and** then move a few doors further **on.** Thus **I** spent some hours every day. Many of **our old** Ambulance friends and acquaintances **came also to** pay **me a visit.** There was no end, I may truly say, to **the** kindness I met with **on all sides.**

One day I went to the Church of St. Aignan, which is at the end of the Quai du Châtelet, to hear a grand High Mass, offered up for the regeneration of France, which was attended by the *élite* of Orleans.   I settled myself in a chair at the end of the church, and presently the ceremonies began by a procession.   As it passed me a priest stepped out of the ranks, and, taking me by the arm, led me up the church, and, to my great confusion, showed me into one of the stalls in the Sanctuary.   I never saw the priest before or since.

When I look back on those days of trial and sickness, and how I lay on that bed unable to stir hand or foot, I remember what a longing came over me for the sight of one familiar face, though but for a few minutes.   One was still in one's youth ; and I fancied, whilst my head was buried in the pillow, that if I could but speak just a few words to my mother, or to some one at home, it would be enough to cure me.   Until then, I never knew how much I loved my native land, or realised my heart's deep devotion to that little spot called home, and to all those dear friends about it.

Little by little I came round.   I used to drive out with M. Proust to his lovely little country house near Olivet, and visited the camellia houses and orange groves, all of which were under glass, at the great château there.   But during my convalescence, the event of the day was the morning post, which brought my letters and newspapers, every line of which I read and re-read with the greatest avidity, until I knew them by heart. One letter in particular, from a great friend of mine, was so amusing, and had such a reviving effect on me, that I read it certainly a score of times, and I laughed as much the last time as the first.

I was strictly prohibited by the doctor from writing ; but in spite of his orders I coaxed Sœur Berthe to let me have pen and ink. Her consternation was great when she saw me fainting from the exertion. One letter I wrote to my mother while my hand was held on the paper, placed on a desk before me ; so that I had only, as it were, to form the characters. I used to write a sentence or two every day, and so put them together bit by bit. I compiled several commonplace and uninteresting productions, and sent them home in great glee at the success of my performance. I could not guess how startled they would be at receiving these curious epistles, some of which afterwards came back into my hands. They resolved to send my brother Arthur to fetch me home ; and he travelled immediately to Orleans, where he received a hearty welcome from M. and Madame Proust and my other friends.

I insert as an Appendix, from the journal

which my brother kept, the impressions made on us both by a visit we paid to the field of Coulmiers.

It was my last view of the scenes in which I had taken part.

My brother arrived on 8th April, and on the 21st we bade farewell to our home in the Rue Royale, and the friends who had made it such, and set out on our journey to Ireland.

CHAPTER XXXI.

AN APPENDIX.—M. AND MADAME COLOMBIER.—VISIT TO THE BATTLEFIELD OF COULMIERS.—THE SOLE FRENCH VICTORY.—CONCLUSION.

(From Arthur Ryan's Diary, Wednesday, 19th April.)

OUR déjeûner had not long been over when a carriage drove up, and Charlie bade me prepare for a drive with some friends into the country. We wished M. and Madame Proust good-bye for the day, and stepped into the carriage, where our new host and hostess were awaiting us. M. and Madame Colombier welcomed me cordially as the brother of their friend, and I was not long in their company before I knew how truly they had been such to him. M. Colombier had been a Papal Zouave, but, on the outbreak of the Franco-Prussian war, had joined the ranks of his countrymen. A middle-aged man with a frank warm manner, and evidently very proud of his wife,—as well he might be. I have seen but little of men or women; but I fancy that many years of experience may fail to remove Madame Colombier from the place she gained that day in my

23   (353)

estimation. She was a heroine, and, what is still rarer, a humble heroine. Being a Canadian she spoke English very fairly ; and as we drove along she told us many stories of her war experiences, and with so much gaiety that I felt it hard to believe those experiences had been so often bitter ones to her and her husband. Privations, loss of property, personal danger, all were related as if she were inventing and not recording ; all were jested about whenever they affected only herself. But when she spoke of the sufferings of others, of her husband's danger, of the poor soldiers whom she had lodged and tended to the last, then her woman's heart revealed itself, and showed that though gay it was tender, though buoyant it was thoroughly unselfish ; and, through all, she seemed so perfectly unconscious of any merit on her part, that one would have thought that her services had been remunerative or a part of her ordinary duty, instead of absorbing as they did the great part of what the war had left them.

A shower came on, and to my surprise Madame Colombier unpinned her warm shawl, and insisted in wrapping Charlie up in it, lest in his weak state he should take cold. "This is my campaigning dress," said she, as I expressed my fears as to the insufficiency of her black silk dress in the teeth of the driving rain ; but little she seemed to care, her only anxiety being to shield the "poor invalid" from the storm.

After what seemed a short drive, we were so pleasant together, we came to the battlefield of Coulmiers. On each side of the road the ground was littered with the débris of camp fires, and with the straw that had served to keep some of the soldiers off the frosty ground, as they slept after their fight. Deep ruts—ploughed by the wheels of the guns, cut up the roads and fields; but beyond these marks, and the general bare, down-trodden look of the ground, nothing remained to speak of the terrible battle that had so lately covered these fields with the dead and dying. But as we drove into the Château Renardier, M. Colombier's country place, the sad remembrances of war were multiplied tenfold. The great trees on each side of the drive were riven in all directions, by the shot and shells; and I remarked several thick firs cut clean in two by what was evidently a single shot.

But here we are at the Château. It was a large house, in the regular French style, prettily situated in the midst of a well-planted lawn. It was not, however, at the architecture of the house, nor at the beauties of the lawn, that I looked, as I drove up. No: what riveted my gaze was the number of round holes that perforated the front in every direction. The shells had done their work well; shattered windows and pierced walls were sorry sights for M. Colombier to show his guests; and little more could be seen of the

Château Renardier on the front side. As we entered, and passed from room to room, we began to realise the full extent of the damage. Deep stains of blood were on the dark oak floors, which in many places had been splintered by the bursting shells. Madame Colombier took us to her boudoir. Panelled in gold and white, it must have been a lovely room—but now it was a wreck. Right through the mirrors had the splintered shells crashed; in one corner of the rich ceiling the sky was visible through a large shot hole,— "and here," said our hostess, "here they used to skin their sheep"; and she pointed to the chandelier, which had sadly suffered from its unwonted use, and beneath which the floor was stained, this time not with human gore. "This is my room," said M. Colombier, as he showed us into the billiard room. The slate table was cracked in two, and on the tattered green cloth lay the remains of the oats which had fed the horses; for that room had served as a stable.

We passed into the garden. It had been the scene of a French bayonet charge; and little shape remained, or sign of garden beauty, save that in one trampled bed, we found some plants of the lily of the valley sprouting to the early spring sunshine. Deep in the gravel walks, and through the once well-trimmed turf, had the wheels of the guns sunk, as the Prussians made their hasty retreat before the victorious French;

and it must have been some consolation to the
fair owner of this desolated garden, to think that
it was the scene of the solitary French victory
in that disastrous war.

In the front garden every vine was dead, cut
from the wall. For the wall had served as a
shelter for the German soldiers, and was pierced
all along for rifle rests, and by every hole was
a heap of empty cartridge cases. The green-
house and conservatories,—who shall tell their
ruin? Glass is a poor protection against artillery,
and the fierce frost had completed the work.
There were the plants all arranged on their
stands; there stood the orange trees—all were
dead and brown—not a twig was alive. I
thought of my mother and her flowers, as Madame
Colombier turned with a sigh from her ruined
conservatory, and walked back through the
melancholy garden. But she was gay enough,
though her husband seemed to feel deeply the
destruction of his lovely home. He had been
married but five years, and had spent much
money in making this a happy spot for his wife
and children—and now, the wreck! But even
M. Colombier laughed with us when we came to
the piles of empty bottles that lay in the yard;
they were all that was left of two well-filled cellars.
The French soldiers had celebrated their victory
at the expense of the master of the Château
Renardier.

In the coach-house were Madame Colombier's two broughams; they had been used in the battle as temporary fortifications, and were literally riddled with bullets. We walked to the fish pond—a piece of ornamental water in the lawn. It had been netted, and not a fish was left. I stumbled on something under the trees by its brink. It was a Prussian cavalry saddle, not a comfortable-looking thing, thought I, as I surveyed the angular hide-covered wood,—but certainly economical when it is so easily lost. But evening was coming on; so having had lunch in the Château (the strangest ruin I ever picnicked in), we bade adieu to Renardier, and drove back to Orleans.

M. Colombier's house there had, like his country château, been used during the war as a little hospital; and Charlie told me, as he waited in the drawing-room before dinner, how many wounded and dying inmates that room lately had.

Dinner was served in an ante-room, for which Madame Colombier made her apologies, as her dining-room was occupied—by whom we presently saw. Having dined heartily, and been highly amused by the penalties with which the children threatened the Prussians,— such as feeding them on poisonous mushrooms, wood, and such like, I was surprised by Madame Colombier taking out a cigar case, handing it round, and helping herself. "Necessity has made me a smoker," she laughingly observed, as she saw my ill-concealed wonder ; and if any lady would condemn my hostess for her cigar, let her follow Madame Colombier as she slips quietly out ; and see for herself how false is that delicacy which would place a difficulty in the way of true and heroic Christian charity. We were not long before we followed our hostess. We found her in her dining-room, which had been fitted up as a temporary hospital. There she was tending the wound of her last patient, with a skill which was the result of long and hard-earned experience. And here we will leave Madame Colombier, with the firm trust that her unselfish charity and un-ostentatious heroism will not go unrewarded before Him, who has promised to repay a cup of cold water given for His sake.

EPILOGUE.

A QUARTER of a century has elapsed since the occurrence of the events which I have described. When I view the scenes of those eventful days through this long vista, and when sometimes for a moment one particular picture of hospital or camp life presents itself before my mind, I start as if awakened from a troubled dream, to find there still the shape and form of fact.

The years have come and gone, and with them have passed away many of the principal actors in that great drama.

Wilhelm, Napoleon, Moltke, the Crown Prince, the Red Prince, Gambetta, d'Aureille de Paladine, Bazaine, MacMahon, have disappeared from the stage.

Modern surgery and medicine have lost some of their ablest pioneers in Langenbeck, Nussbaum, Esmark and Marion Sims ; and I personally have to mourn for many who were kindly and helpful to me in those days, amongst them M. and Madame Proust and General Charles Bracken-bury.

(360)

I have often wished to revisit Sedan and Orleans; but the desire to make the most of a somewhat limited holiday-time, and to gain fresh experiences, has always led me to new districts and countries previously unknown to me, and I have never had my wish fulfilled. I am glad to say, however, that I never quite lost sight of my old friends M. and Madame Proust, and a visit from their nephew revived all the old associations and remembrances afresh.

It may interest my readers to hear something of our ambulance surgeons. Sir William Mac-Cormac, who succeeded Marion Sims at Sedan, is now one of the greatest living authorities on military surgery and gunshot wounds. His colleague Dr. Mackellar is distinguished on the staff of St. Thomas's Hospital, and Dr. Parker is an eminent London specialist. The others, scattered over the face of the globe, I have lost sight of, but would fain hope one day to meet some of them again.

One object I have had in view in publishing these notes may be worthy of mention.

As I have tried to write down exactly what I witnessed, they may help to afford some idea of what war really means,—war as a hard practical fact—stripped of all the glamour, and poetry, and pride of conquest, that are so attractive when seen in history.

Even from my own observations I could

gather that all is not victory to the victors themselves.

When the German soldiery learnt that Louis Napoleon was present in the trap at Sedan, there broke out among them the wildest exhibition of delight ; for they believed—wrongly as it came to pass—that his capture would end the war and enable them to go back to their homes. And when peace was finally proclaimed, the Germans in Orleans were no less demonstrative and enthusiastic than the French, whose cup of suffering had been filled to overflowing.

Now-a-days there is perhaps a tendency to undervalue this aspect of the case. People talk very lightly of the great European war that is said to be inevitable. It can do no harm to measure as far as possible what such a war may mean.

Those who count the cost in advance are far more likely to be able to meet it, should the necessity arise, and to bear themselves resolutely and bravely to the end, whatever the event, than those who rush blindly forward, depending mainly on enthusiasm for organisation, and on the reputation of the past to achieve victories in the future. That seems to be the great lesson taught by the war of 1870 and 1871.

There never was, perhaps, a more flagrant instance of disregard for that wise Shakesperian saying familiar to us all :—

> " Beware
> Of entrance to a quarrel : but, being in,
> Bear it that the opposed may beware of thee ".

However, my readers will probably be disposed to form their own opinions on these subjects, and will have far more attractive material elsewhere on which to found them.

Before concluding, I think I am not out of order in mentioning a notable occurrence which took place during the year 1895, and which to my mind affords a favourable augury for the future of France. I mean the celebration at Orleans, with all the pomp and ceremony due to the occasion, of the festival of Jeanne d'Arc. From the general enthusiasm then displayed by the French people, I cannot help thinking that greater things and brighter hopes are in store for that beautiful country, the fortunes of which have ever been as dramatic in their circumstances as they are interesting in themselves.

Finally, I wish here to record, if I may, my own admiration, sympathy and delight in the bright and genial character of the French, and to bear witness that as this feeling was at first so it is now ; nor do I think it will ever change.

My task is finished. Though the re-writing of these notes has been a source of great pleasure to me, bringing back as it does old memories and picturesque scenes so vividly, yet I lay aside the unaccustomed pen with—perhaps not unnaturally —some little sense of relief, trusting to the indulgence of my readers that they will overlook the blemishes incidental to a first literary performance. And thus I bid them farewell.

THE END.

Essoyes
Mussy
Montiers
Châtillon
Airey
Montbard
Ser
Bibl. Street

INDEX.

www.ingramcontent.com/pod-product-compliance
Lightning Source LLC
Chambersburg PA
CBHW032015120726
47902CB00013B/928